"A wonderful voice, great storytelling, and a completely unique character."

—First Clue

"Sharp and fun to read."

—Esther Schnaidman,
Association of Jewish Libraries

"Down in L.A., Andy Weinberger's detective Amos Parisman is a Talmudic gumshoe—he's ethically motivated, and often in his investigations, life is really more about asking the right questions than assuming you will actually find the right answers.... Weinberger is an astonishingly gifted and big-hearted storyteller."

—Howard Norman,
author of *Next Life Might Be Kinder*

"If you wish someone still wrote classic, hard-boiled detective novels, Andy Weinberger does! Every installment in this series is a pure pleasure to read.... Any fan of authentic detective fiction will adore this novel."

—Amy Stewart,
bestselling author of the Kopp Sisters Series

"The Amos Parisman series is equal parts suspenseful and soulful, witty and worldly wise, entertaining and heart-breaking. And he's Jewish, too! What's not to like?"

—Elliott Kalan,
co-host of *The Flop House* podcast

REASON TO KILL (BOOK 2)

"Amos Parisman is one of the most unique PIs in literary history...a superb character study.... Amos Parisman serves as a guide, leading readers from one crime scene to another while reflecting on mankind's moral decay. His reflections on life are witty and insightful (and sometimes depressing). He provided me with many reasons for wanting to read future installments in the Amos Parisman Mystery series."

—*Gumshoe Magazine*

AN OLD MAN'S GAME (BOOK 1)

"Delightful... Mr. Weinberger writes as his hero detects, at a measured and thoughtful pace."

—Tom Nolan,
Wall Street Journal

"Pure entertainment... As characters go, Parisman is as no-nonsense as Philip Marlowe or Sam Spade, but unlike those classic detectives, there's a bit more heart and nuance to our central character."

—*San Francisco Chronicle*

"As with most good detective stories, the real pleasure here is in watching the gumshoe at work.... This is sheer fun."

—*Booklist*

"Parisman is a kind of 'Paris Man' in the sense that he is urbane, witty, and charming in a Jewish, tough-guy L.A. way."

—*New York Journal of Books*

"Add [Weinberger] to Michael Connelly, Walter Mosley, and Joe Ide, writers who embrace the underrepresented people of LA, articulate the distortions of power, and cast a light on the darknesses we humans carry within us."

—John Evans,
owner, Diesel Bookstore

"The writing here, to quote Sam Shepard, is 'full of crazy and comical pathos,' and the story itself brings the L.A. Jewish community fabulously and vividly alive. This is a ribald private-eye tale full of genius and originality."

—Howard Norman,
Whiting Award–winning author of *My Darling Detective*

"While the mystery is intriguing, the thoughtful, retired Jewish PI is the draw for this…mystery. As he and his wife age, he deals with her onset of dementia with love and patience, that patience being a part of his nature as an inquisitive PI."

—*Library Journal*

"Andy Weinberger has created an absolutely charming private investigator that readers will follow from book to book. L.A.'s Fairfax District—get ready for your close-up!"

—Naomi Hirahara,
author of the Edgar Award–winning Mas Arai mystery series

"Not only does Weinberger (and his aging, retired detective Amos Parisman) have a great sense of humor, but his take on Los Angeles makes this a joy to read for all of us locals…. I loved every minute and look forward to the next installment."

—Bookseller Terry Gilman,
owner of Mysterious Galaxy and Creating Conversations

THE GONIF

More Amos Parisman Mysteries
by Andy Weinberger

An Old Man's Game
Reason to Kill
The Kindness of Strangers
Die Laughing

THE GONIF

An Amos Parisman Mystery

ANDY WEINBERGER

PROSPECT
·PARK·
BOOKS

PROSPECT PARK BOOKS
AN IMPRINT OF TURNER PUBLISHING COMPANY
Nashville, Tennessee
www.turnerpublishing.com

PROSPECT
·PARK·
BOOKS

The Gonif: An Amos Parisman Mystery

Cover art by Ben Perini
Cover design by William Ruoto
Book design by Ashlyn Inman

Library of Congress Cataloging-in-Publication Data
Names: Weinberger, Andy, author.
Title: The gonif / by Andy Weinberger.
Description: Nashville, Tennessee : Prospect Park Books, an imprint of Turner Publishing Company, 2024. | Series: Amos Parisman mysteries
Identifiers: LCCN 2024002724 (print) | LCCN 2024002725 (ebook) | ISBN 9781684421305 (paperback) | ISBN 9781684421329 (hardcover) | ISBN 9781684421435 (e-pub)
Subjects: LCGFT: Detective and mystery fiction. | Novels.
Classification: LCC PS3623.E4324234 G66 2024 (print) | LCC PS3623.E4324234 (ebook) | DDC 813/.6—dc23/eng/20240202
LC record available at https://lccn.loc.gov/2024002724
LC ebook record available at https://lccn.loc.gov/2024002725

Printed in the United States of America
1 2 3 4 5 6 7 8 9 10

For Beth Hanson

THE GONIF

PROLOGUE

I had to be what—nine years old? No taller than a pogo stick, any-way, the first time I heard the word gonif. We were sitting around our kitchen table with Uncle Al. That was when we lived in that ratty upstairs apartment on Normandie, and Al would come by to visit, angling for a free meal. To tell you the truth, he was my great uncle, my Baba's kid brother, but we didn't make those distinctions back then. To us, he was just Uncle Al. It was Al who taught me how to play poker. He liked kids, dogs, and pretty women—but not necessarily in that order. He liked to laugh. More than anything, he loved to gamble. It dawned on me later in life that he was addicted to gambling. He bet on basketball games, boxing matches, dog races. Whatever moved, really. He spent a week in Vegas every year. He'd go to Hollywood Park and Santa Anita, and when he won big—which he did every now and then—he'd take us all out to eat Chinese. Noth-ing fancy, but since my parents never had much money and never took us anywhere, well, it stood out. When the bill arrived, it was thrilling to watch my uncle pull out a thick wad of green from his pocket and peel off a couple of twenties. Made me feel, I dunno, like royalty.

Al always said he immigrated from Canada. That was a lie. He came from Russia. The whole family did. Only, for some reason I never understood, he wasn't allowed in, so he went to Toronto instead. Then, one night, when the border guards were looking the other way, he hiked a mile through the woods and found himself in Vermont. Welcome to

1

America, huh? When he got to LA, he started working at a hot dog stand near Union Station. A few years later, he won the hot dog stand in an all-night card game. Then he sold it and bought a pawn shop in Reseda. In the end, he was an old man who owned three pawn shops in the Valley.

We were playing poker that afternoon, the three of us: me, my dad, and Al. I'd brought my jar full of coins to the table, which was all I had in the world. It was just a nickel-and-dime affair, and if there was two dollars in the whole pot I'd be surprised. That's when my dad grabbed Al by the wrist and yelled at him: "You fucking gonif," he said. "You're dealing off the bottom of the deck!" Al's face turned red. My dad stood up and told him, "Nobody cheats my little boy. Get the hell out. Go on."

That was the last time I ever saw Al. A year or so after that, he got colon cancer and died. We went to the funeral in Reseda. The rabbi talked about what a free spirit Al had been. How he thought rules were made to be broken. How he joked his way through life—what a great laugh Al had.

Afterwards in the reception hall, there was an open bar and a huge buffet with roast chicken, chop suey, hot pastrami, kreplach, and little Swedish meatballs—all the foods Al adored. My mom said that as soon as Al found out he was going to die, he'd set a chunk of money aside. That's how he wanted to be honored, with a big party. His treat. We lined up with our plates and shuffled along. I noticed my dad was piling his high. Are you really gonna eat all that? *He winked at me.* Come on, boychik! He owes us.

CHAPTER 1

You live here long enough, you get to know the neighborhood. That's just how it is. Nothing magical about it. My particular neighborhood is about ten blocks square, maybe a little more, depending on how far I end up walking every day.

The doctor tells me I have to walk if I want to stay alive. Dr. Flynn is in his early fifties, neat and trim. Loretta chose him for me because she said he was efficient. Board-certified. A serious fellow. You don't want a comedian for a doctor, right? I've never seen him without a tie and a white lab coat. If I had to guess, I'd say he probably sleeps that way.

"How long do you want to live, Amos?" That's what he asks. He's holding a clipboard containing the results of the latest battery of tests he's run on me. The look on his face suggests I've come up short again.

"I have a choice in the matter?"

"You do. Pick a number."

His office looks out over Beverly Hills. Every time I come to see him, the sun is shining. It seems like a pleasant, upbeat place to work. He has charts and beautifully illustrated drawings of the human anatomy. There's a detailed one of the lungs, and the kidneys, and, of course, the human heart. He also has plastic models lying about, exact replicas, like the plastic sushi you sometimes see in the window of Japanese restaurants.

"You want to live to be a hundred?" he asks, exasperated that I haven't replied.

"A hundred's an awful long time," I say. "I'm not sure I'd want to stick around that long. Could get lonely, you know."

"How about another year or two?"

"Sure, I'd like another year."

"Yeah, well, unless you start moving your tuchus every day, you can kiss that goodbye."

He scared me with that kind of tough talk; so now I'm out on the street, rain or shine. Usually I go west on Third, past Whole Foods and the Farmers Market, until I get to Fairfax. Then up Fairfax to Beverly, then right on Beverly to La Brea, then down and back. Sometimes I cheat—I take a little detour and stop at the La Brea Bakery on Sixth for a cup of coffee and a nosh. This is wrong, I know. And I don't tell Loretta, even though she probably can guess. A week ago, she found some leftover bits of croissant on my bomber jacket and put two and two together. It's not that big a deal, I figure, not as long as I keep the weight off.

And anyway, Loretta has her own issues, which, in my humble opinion, are much worse than what I've got to deal with. I'm still on the job as a gumshoe. She had to retire from the Iron Workers' union last May when her thinking clouded over and she couldn't remember things. You can't run an office if you can't recall where you put the bills. Things fall apart. I have to admit they were decent about it, the iron workers: she walked away with a pension. But now she doesn't dare drive, so I have to schlep her back and forth to her doctors. I don't mind. It's what married people do for each other, right? But our life has narrowed from what it once was, let me tell you. I prowl the neighborhood; she sits in Apartment 9J at Park La Brea, gazing out the window all day or watching TV with Carmen, our housekeeper.

Doc Flynn lectures me. He wants to know just how long I want to live. And I want to say to him, *You call this living?*

*   *   *

I'm standing with a young, well-dressed Korean couple in the art deco lobby outside our elevator, waiting for it to open. It's the beginning of May. The elevators are lovely to look at, but they've been running much slower than usual lately and residents have been complaining. The woman is muttering quietly to her husband, and every once in a while he says something monosyllabic or nods his head in silent agreement. I have no idea what they're talking about, of course, but I have to think that, like everyone else, they're bad-mouthing the elevators. Personally, I figure, it's a minor miracle that you can step into one of these tin boxes, press a button, and within a minute or two you're a quarter-mile up on the ninth floor. I tried climbing the interior stairs last week to get my heart going, just to see what it's like. It took nearly twenty minutes, and I was exhausted.

"These elevators," I say, "they predate the dinosaurs, you know."

The man studiously ignores me. The woman regards me as if I've lost my mind.

"That's why they don't work so good," I explain. "They're old. Look at me, I'm old, too."

Now both of them are ignoring me. Just then, the phone rings in my coat pocket. I walk outside the building, where the reception is clearer.

"Mr. Parisman?" A lilting woman's voice. I don't recognize the number—but I haven't had a case in over a month, so if it rings I answer.

"That's me, all right. Hello. What can I do for you?"

"This is Harriet Reines. I was given your name by a man named Malloy, Lieutenant William Malloy of the LAPD. He said he's good friends with you. He trusts you. In fact, he thought you might be just what I need."

"He did, huh? Well, that was very generous. That doesn't happen every day. You tell him the check's in the mail."

The minute I say that, I want to take it back. I'm being too informal. There's something stilted in her voice. She goes silent for a moment, as if reconsidering. "I'm looking for help here, Mr. Parisman. I have a serious proposal, but if you're not interested—"

"Whoa, whoa! Hold on. I'm interested. Just tell me what it is."

"I don't think we should discuss this on the phone. I'd like to meet with you first, if you don't mind. Lieutenant Malloy spoke so highly of you. I want to see for myself."

"That's fine," I say. "Give me a time and a place. I'll be there."

She suggests we meet in the lobby of the Biltmore Hotel at ten o'clock the next day. "Do you know where that is?"

"I grew up here, Mrs. Reines."

"Good," she says. "Then ten o'clock it is."

"Wait!" I say. "The lobby can be a crowded place. How will I know you?"

"Don't worry, I'll wear something black and elegant," she says. "You put on a hat. We'll find each other."

*   *   *

That evening, I see to it that Loretta dines on a nice broiled lamb chop and some broccoli and settle her down on the couch in front of *Jeopardy!* These days, Loretta loves game shows. Which, trust me, wasn't always the case. She used to love to read, but that was before she had what they believed was a stroke, and the good doctors at Cedars Sinai started monkeying with her prescriptions. Blue pills, yellow pills. Two of these, three of those. After six months of scans and blood tests, all you wanna do is watch TV, right? At the first commercial break, I go into my office and call Bill Malloy. Harriet Reines is right about one thing: we *are* old friends.

I haven't spoken with him for weeks. In January, he took charge of the homicide unit in Hollywood, which is a big promotion, but keeps him busier than a barrel of monkeys. As a result, I'm trying not to bother him. Bill would be my brother, I think, if I had been raised a Jesuit instead of a Jew. At some level we're sorta brothers anyway. He'd probably take issue with that, argue the notion until it turns into a fine dust, but that's also what makes us alike, the arguing.

"So who is this Reines woman, Lieutenant? And why did you

give her my number?"

"Reines?" He sounds momentarily perplexed. The name means nothing to him. Or maybe I interrupted his dinner. Malloy cherishes the nightly dinners with his wife.

"Harriet Reines," I continue. "She called me with some kind of job offer this afternoon. I don't get many of those at my age."

"Oh, right," he says. "Her. She called, very insistent. The dispatcher gave it to Remo, who passed it on to me. She's a do-gooder. Worried about this Jewish temple over on Beverly, as I recall. Said someone's going to get hurt unless we step in."

"Which temple?"

"Hell, I don't know, Amos. They all sound the same."

"No, they don't."

"Excuse me, I don't speak Hebrew like you."

"I don't speak Hebrew either, Bill. I went to Hebrew school, but it didn't take. I blame my parents. They should have been more ruthless. I coulda been a rabbi by now."

"Anyway," he says, ignoring everything I just said, "she's worried. They've had a few minor break-ins the last month or so. Maybe it's kids out on the street making mischief, maybe it's more than that. But she's willing to spend some cash to find out, and, as far as I could determine, there's no call for the police to get involved."

"Not yet."

"Right. Not yet. And so I suggested you."

"Huh."

"That's all you're gonna say? 'Huh'? Aren't you gonna thank me, at least? When was the last time you saw a paycheck?"

"I don't like taking chances, Bill. When I was a kid, I thought I was immortal. All kids do."

"And now?"

"Now it's different," I tell him. "Now I've got Loretta to take care of. You could be sending me out to die."

There's a pause on the other end. Malloy's a thinker, but he's more reserved, he doesn't wear his feelings all over his sleeve like I sometimes do. I'm sure I make him nervous. "Look, friend," he says as calmly as he can, "I've had a very long day. She and I had a very short conversation. And on behalf of the LAPD, I took some initiative and bowed out. Why don't you ask her yourself?"

*　*　*

Carmen comes in a little after nine the next morning. She had to take two buses to get here from El Sereno because her car is in the shop again, waiting for a new transmission. I tell her I'll give her a ride home. I'm grateful she's on the job, because Loretta no longer does anything around the house and my skills in that department are primitive at best. I mean, we could probably get by without someone like Carmen—I have done my share of cooking and dusting and vacuuming, after all—but why? Carmen is a natural at this, she's sweet and caring, and, best of all, she and Loretta have kinda fallen in love with each other. For the seven hours when Carmen's here, they're best friends, anyway. They giggle like little girls and whisper secrets I'm not allowed to hear. They play dominos and gin rummy together, though they're both pretty vague about the rules. When her car is running, she takes Loretta out on field trips. This usually involves simple pleasures—ice cream or See's candy. Carmen also has a thing about window-shopping, so they wander around Ross Dress for Less, or cross the street to Nordstrom, looking at overpriced shoes and lingerie. They rarely buy anything. Even though she still has a credit card, Loretta's a pretty cheap date. She can't get enough of the escalator at Nordstrom.

As soon as Carmen puts her sweater and purse away, I tell her I have to go out, I have a job interview.

"A job?" she says with alarm. "I hope it's not like the last time, señor. When you followed that nasty man around? ¿Recuerda?"

I remember all too well. The man I was following was named Robbie Barner. He used to be a professional wrestler, then he worked as a bouncer in a high-class bar. Trouble was, he liked to drink too much. The years went by; he grew paunchy, bald, and ornery, and they let him go. I guess that's when he figured he needed a new career. He was bringing girls in from Thailand and Vietnam, setting them up in massage parlors and gradually grooming them for a life of prostitution. I finally caught up to him in an alley off Gower one rainy night where he was "teaching one of his girls a lesson," as he put it. I didn't see him hit her, but I could tell he had. She was hunched over with her knees on the pavement, touching the side of her face. She was barefoot, wearing a thin dress, and she was soaked to the bone. If she was seventeen, I'd be surprised. I ordered him to back away.

"You gonna make me?" he asked casually.

That's when I drew my gun on him and pointed it a few inches from his forehead. "No," I said, "but this will."

Just like that, his expression changed. He raised his hands and sheepishly backed away in the direction of Gower. *Let him go*, was my thought. I bent down and tried to help the girl to her feet. That's when he opened fire. Two shots whizzed by my ear. I lifted my gun and fired into the rain. Later, the cops asked me where I'd learned to shoot like that.

"Vietnam," I said. "Marines."

"Well, you must have been a marksman. You nailed him in the chest."

"I got lucky," I said.

Now I look at Carmen. "I'll be back as soon as I can. Don't you worry."

* * *

To say that the Biltmore Hotel is a grand old edifice is like saying Itzhak Perlman is an okay fiddle player. It doesn't do it justice. Built in the twenties, when Hollywood was coming into its own, there's probably no place in town more storied, more extravagant, more over the top than the Biltmore. I can't tell you all the things that went on there. Most of them happened before I was born; and the others, well, I never had the price of admission. Charlie Chaplin, Clark Gable, Spencer Tracy, Doug Fairbanks, Ginger Rogers—they

all took a whirl on the ballroom floor back then. Among its many
famous guests, the Biltmore could brag about hosting US presidents
and corporate high rollers, also low-lifes like Al Capone and Bugsy
Siegel. Even the Beatles stayed there briefly, though they couldn't
check in at the counter like everyone else—the crowds were too
dense—so they landed on the roof in a helicopter.

The Biltmore faces Pershing Square, which used to be a favorite
hangout for labor organizers and protest rallies. A lot of speechifying
took place there, back in the day. It's also right across the street from
the Diamond Mart. I've never set foot in there, but my impression is
it's full of Orthodox Jews in black suits and hats and ties. They're the
only folks you'd ever see going in or out; they walked fast, with their
heads down, and they often carried leather briefcases handcuffed to
their wrists. Which of course raises eyebrows. And if jewelry didn't
interest you, there were other diversions: the Pussycat Theater was
half a block away, and around the corner the Grand Central Market
sold shrimp tacos and pupusas. Pershing Square was always alive,
raucous, unpredictable.

Then Ronald Reagan got elected governor. In his infinite wisdom, he decided it cost too much taxpayers' money to care for the
thousands of mentally ill in California, so overnight he turned them
loose. But where's a poor lunatic supposed to hang his hat, I ask you?
I've pondered this for years, and I still don't have an answer. Maybe
Reagan thought they'd come to their senses once they were released.
Go out, get a job, become fine upstanding citizens. Maybe that was
his dream. But the truth is, a lot of them settled in places like Pershing Square. They wandered around, smelly and barefoot, wrapped
in plastic garbage bags, talking to themselves, peeing and brushing
their teeth in public. It wasn't pretty then, and it's only gotten worse.

Harriet Reines isn't hard to locate. She is sitting in a dark padded leather chair beneath an enormous skylight with gold mold-
ing around each pane of glass. Her legs are crossed and there's a
cup of tea or coffee on the end table beside her. She's wearing black
pants and some kind of silky black top, along with a double string of
pearls. Her hair is short and colored, reminiscent of Liza Minnelli in

Cabaret. She's what I would call fashionable, especially for her age, which must be around eighty. She points to a chair opposite her to indicate where I am to sit.

"Mr. Parisman? You're very punctual."

I glance down at my watch, which says five minutes to ten. "Actually," I say, "the way I look at it, I'm late. I like to show up twenty minutes ahead of time."

"Do you?"

"Yeah. It gives me a chance to check things out, you know, see what's what. Just in case I'm walking into a trap."

"Well, let me assure you, this is not a trap." She smiles genially. Her pale blue eyes take me in. For an older lady, she has an engaging way about her. I don't know what she's done in her life, but it's clear to me that she feels she's still got a lot of tread left on her tires before it's over. "We do have a problem, however."

I nod. "Okay. So, let's hear about it."

She swallows and leans forward. Her voice drops. "First, I think you ought to know who you're dealing with. My married name is Reines. Before he died of cancer eight years ago, that's really all I was: Mrs. Phillip Reines. The wife of a very rich man."

"How long were you married?" I have no idea where she's headed, but when someone leads off with a dead spouse in the first ten seconds, well, this seems like a fair question. She looks wistful, like she wants to talk about the relationship.

"Fifty-six years," she says. "A long time. We had quite an adventure, Phil and I. He made a lot of money buying up companies that were bloated and poorly run, then firing half the employees."

"And just how do you make money doing that?"

She looks at me like I was born yesterday. "You make money because very few investors walk around a factory floor to see what it's really like. They trust their own instinct. They look at numbers—overhead, projections, profit-and-loss statements. They sit in their nice comfortable living rooms in Connecticut or New Jersey and they think—they imagine—you've turned things around. They think that because that's what they read in the reports. They pour their money in. That's when you get out. Phil always knew when it was time."

"I see."

"However, it's not him I want to discuss. He wasn't the most ethical man in the world, but I've ended up with a very tidy sum of money, far more than I'll ever need." She pauses a moment or two to let that fact sink in. "His evil made me rich. And now I'm free to take a different path."

"And just what path do you want to take, Mrs. Reines?"

"Philanthropy, I guess you'd call it. I have a nice room on the fourth floor here. We used to have a big house in Benedict Canyon, but that was just because Phillip needed it to entertain his clients. Now that he's gone"—she waves her hand in the air—"well, this is more than enough."

"Lieutenant Malloy mentioned a temple on Beverly."

"Yes," she says, "that's become a little cause of mine. It's called Anshe Amunim. Does that ring a bell?"

"I know of a few synagogues around there. Not that one, though."

"I'm not surprised," she says. "They're poor Sephardic Jews, not Ashkenazim. And it's nothing to write home about architecturally; it used to be a private home. It's old, and they don't have much money for the upkeep. I don't even understand how they can support a rabbi."

I study her more closely. Reines isn't a Jewish name, but the way she's talking makes me think she didn't always go by that. She may live at the Biltmore and have a bank account the size of Henry Ford's; but once upon a time, in some Russian shtetl long ago, our ancestors crossed paths. We're *mishpucha*, family. "So what's the problem, exactly? How can I help?"

She takes a sip of coffee and dabs her lips with a napkin. "Last week there were a couple of attempted intrusions. Someone tried to jimmy the back door with a crowbar, but he didn't get very far. The next night that same someone smashed the window in the men's room. He stood on a trash can, tried to worm his way in. Evidently the space he created was too narrow."

"Okay," I say. "A couple of failed attempts. And I assume someone at the *shul* notified the police?"

"Yes, of course. The police came out, walked around. Said it was probably kids with too much time on their hands. That was it."

"Well," I say, raising my palms, "are you surprised? What do you expect?"

"I expect them to do their job, track these people down!" she says, testily. "I don't think it was just kids. Whoever did this had a darker purpose."

I give a shrug. "People—kids for the most part—do that pretty regularly. I'm just saying. . ."

"You're wrong," she says defiantly.

"Okay, let's say, for argument's sake, you're right and I'm wrong. So, what's going on here, then? Antisemitism? Antisemites break into synagogues now and then, it's true. But they usually let you know who they are. Your average antisemite—he'll take out a can of spray paint and leave a swastika on the wall. Something like that."

"That's just it. It wasn't antisemitism."

"You've ruled that out, too, have you? Not kids? Not antisemites?"

She nods, leans back, and clears her throat. "I'm sorry, I guess I've been dancing around the edges, Mr. Parisman. It could well have been a teenager who did this. And he was probably no friend of the Jewish people. But this is not your everyday crime."

"I can see you're invested in this case," I say. "But I've been in this business going on thirty years, and I have to tell you—"

"No, please," she says, "let me tell you. It's a short story: In May of 1940, the Germans conquered France in just six weeks."

"A tragedy," I say.

"And for reasons of their own, they let Marshal Pétain and his Vichy government run things in the south."

"I know."

"Then I presume you also know that Vichy control extended beyond France, and included their possessions in North Africa."

"Yes, yes," I say, "I'm familiar." Actually, I'm not all that familiar; now we're drifting into deeper historical water, and I'm ashamed to admit that most of what I know stems from watching a dozen reruns

of *Casablanca* with Humphrey Bogart and Lauren Bacall. Still, I
get the gist of what she's saying. The Vichy French were sleeping
with the Nazis. They probably thought they had no choice, and they
probably weren't as mean or as competent as the Nazis. They could
be bought off now and then, or persuaded to look the other way.
That's what I took from watching Bogart. And who knows? Maybe
some of them, in their heart of hearts, felt like patriotic Frenchmen,
but it was one of those open questions.

"What you may not be familiar with," she continues, "is that
there were a good many Jews living in North Africa then. Sep-
hardim. They were an ancient community. They traced their ori-
gins back to the very beginning of the Diaspora, when the Romans
threw us out of Israel."

"That's two thousand years."

"Yes. And until then, basically, they'd gotten along with their
Muslim and Berber neighbors. It wasn't a perfect arrangement, of
course. Things weren't always equal, but they managed. They spoke
French and Arabic, and they had temples and schools in big cities.
Oran, Fez, Tangier."

Her face seems to get more animated the more she speaks.

"This doesn't sound like a short story, Mrs. Reines. You said it
was. I'm still waiting for the punch line."

She stops. I seem to have confused her. "Punch line?" The word
seems rude, abhorrent, juvenile to her. "This isn't a joke."

"I get that," I say. "But maybe if you could, you know, just skip
ahead to the present? I mean, we're sitting here in the Biltmore.
It's a nice sunny day. And I don't think you brought me all the way
down here to talk about North Africa, did you? So, what is this
really about?"

CHAPTER 2

Just as she is about to answer, her cell phone rings. She stares at the number. "I'm sorry," she says, "I have to take this."

I nod. It sounds like she's talking to someone at a hospital, and they're asking for authorization for something. She does a lot of nodding. *Yes, yes, sure, go ahead. I'll pay for it, certainly.* Ten minutes later she's still on the phone. She glances up at me, makes a face like she's caught in the middle of a protracted dilemma. Then at one point she tells them to hold and says, "We'll have to continue this another day, Mr. Parisman. I apologize for bringing you all the way down here. We'll be in touch. All right?"

I stand. "Oh, sure," I say, "sure, no problem." And just like that, I'm out the door. The sun is already heating things up in Pershing Square. After I retrieve my Honda from the twenty-four-hour parking lot and head for home, a slightly queasy sensation comes over me. It's like my stomach's depressed. I'm feeling both frustrated and relieved at the same time. Lately, this happens to me more often than I'd care to admit. I chalk it up to my age. Carmen will be pleased I didn't land the job, I think, but then me not landing the job is pretty much par for the course these days.

The next morning, I set Loretta up with her coffee and oatmeal. She's in a buoyant mood because she and Carmen are going to the art museum. They're going to see the Marc Chagall exhibit again. It's the third time in two weeks. Carmen's a practical sort. She never set foot inside an art museum when she was a little girl in Cuba, and she probably doesn't know one end of a paint brush from another, but she knows this: *Loretta loves Chagall.* That's all that matters. I bend over, put my arm around Loretta, kiss her on the cheek.

Just then, my phone rings. It's Mrs. Reines. "Come downstairs," she commands. "We can talk in my car."

"What are you driving?" I ask.

"I'm not driving anything," she says. There's a dismissiveness in her tone, as if I'll never understand the ways of the rich. "Geoffrey is driving. Just come down, we're outside, you'll see us."

"Finish your oatmeal," I instruct Loretta. "I'll be right back."

A shiny black Lincoln with tinted windows is parked in the visitors' section directly in front of the glass doors of our Park La Brea building. As soon as I walk outside, its headlights flash hello to me. I give a little wave and climb inside. It is nice and roomy. Not presidential, but I look around at the black leather and the television set and all the amenities and I think *Yeah, this isn't half bad, I could get used to this.*

Mrs. Reines greets me brusquely, as though the interruption of yesterday was just a minor hiccup. She's a busy woman, after all. There's so much good that needs doing.

"Anshe Amunim is a small, poor congregation," she says. "They don't advertise, and they don't have a building fund. You say you've never heard of them, and you'd probably walk right past their place on Beverly. It's nothing to write home about. Rabbi Josef tells me they often have trouble cobbling together a *minyan* for services these days. But sometimes God favors the meek. Isn't that so?"

"Sometimes. Maybe," I say. "I dunno."

"Well, I do know, Mr. Parisman." Then she launches into a *leinga meisa,* a long saga about another little synagogue, this one in Algeria. Oran, to be exact. How, in 1941, things were getting very tense. Especially for Jews. Everyone was scared. There were roadblocks, dusk-to-dawn curfews. It was dangerous to have a radio in your house, and Arabs they had known all their lives suddenly no longer felt free to speak to their Jewish neighbors. Rumors were flying—they were being watched; they'd soon be rounded up, thrown into prison. They'd read accounts of how their fellow *landsmen* in Europe had been beaten and murdered; they'd heard about the bonfires fueled with prayer books and the broken glass and the camps, but no one had a full picture. No one imagined it would touch them here in this remote corner of the world. It was inconceivable. Then one night a traveling merchant from Fez, a fellow named Michel Farber, came to dinner. He told the rabbi what he'd just learned through his grapevine of informants: that the Germans intended to build a railroad across the Sahara, and they planned on using Jewish slave labor to do it. That was the last straw.

"The Oran *shul* had only one prized possession," she says: "a Torah they thought might be two or three hundred years old. It came from Alexandria in Egypt, and amazingly it was still in good condition. They didn't use it much—it was so delicate, after all—but nobody wanted to see it burned. So, before he left for home that night, the rabbi walked Farber around the corner to the temple, opened the ark, and entrusted him with the Torah."

"This Farber guy," I say, "he was a stranger, right?"

"They'd met before, I imagine, but I don't think they were close, no. There wasn't time."

"A stranger, then, basically."

"Yeah."

"And the rabbi just hands him this two- or three-hundred-year-old Torah. Out of the blue. And what did he do with it? I mean, they must have had some agreement, some shared expectation, something?"

She gives me another dismissive look that suggests I'm really not the cleverest man she has ever encountered. "Farber recognized what he had. I gather he was a responsible man; he kept it safe in his wine cellar for a few weeks, then passed it on to a friend of his, another merchant named Georges Hassan, in Casablanca. Hassan was in the import/export trade. He smuggled it to one of his underlings in Lisbon. That man wrapped it up and put it on a freighter to Rio de Janeiro, and somehow—you'll excuse me, but the trail gets a little murky—it found its way here to Los Angeles."

My head starts itching. It always does when things become con-voluted. I'd done my share of reading about the Holocaust. I knew what lengths Jews in Europe went to, trying to hide their valuables, hide their children, hide themselves. Sometimes it worked; often it ended badly. "And now you're telling me this grand old Torah is sitting in that dilapidated *shul* on Beverly. Am I right?"

"In a word, yes."

"Can I ask you a simple question, Mrs. Reines?"

"Certainly."

"Who told you this?"

"Who told me what?"

"About the Torah, where it came from. The merchant from Fez. The boat ride to Rio. It all sounds very romantic."

"You think I'm making this up, Mr. Parisman?" Now her look is far colder and more critical. She thinks she's made a mistake, and she's turned her fury on me. Harriet Reines doesn't allow for mistakes in her life. But even more, she's angry with herself for con-tacting me in the first place. "The rabbi told me," she says. "I was skeptical in the beginning, but after we sat down and he explained the history, well, it made sense."

"All right," I tell her. "Fine. So maybe I'm naïve, but last I heard, the Second World War's over. The good news is, we won. We don't have to worry about the Germans. You say you want to help, and you have the cash to do it. Why not just ship the Torah back to the temple in Oran?"

She frowns. "Well, first of all, for the simple reason that the temple no longer exists. Someone—the Nazis, or their Vichy friends, or maybe the Arabs—burned it to the ground. Whatever happened, it's gone. The Jewish community there has been erased. The remnants that survived the war were expelled. Some went to France. Some left for Israel. As Gertrude Stein used to say, 'There's no there there.' Not anymore."

"Okay. So, what is it you want me to do?"

She glances at Geoffrey, who is sitting rigidly in the front seat with his eyes fixed straight ahead like a well-trained soldier. It is difficult to surmise whether he is listening or not. Maybe he's listening and doesn't care. Or he's driven her around long enough that she doesn't worry about his loyalty. Hard to tell, just staring at the back of his head. Then she turns to me. "Some thug has set his sights on that Torah," she says quietly. "He may not be sophisticated, but he probably realizes there's a market for rare Judaica. The right person would pay a lot of money for it. Our young man might even have been hired by a private collector somewhere, for all I know."

"Again, Mrs. Reines, I need to hear what you want me to do about this."

"Well, if you could catch the would-be *gonif*, that'd be a great start. As I told you, the police in this town are hopeless. They're just sitting on their hands."

"I can give it a try," I tell her, "but I'm only one man. In the meantime, you might want to beef up security around the *shul*. Maybe you can pay for surveillance cameras. Put in some motion detectors. Install a few extra locks on the doors."

"I'll do that," she says, brightening. "Those are excellent ideas."

"Until you get that together, you should hire a night watchman. That's not a permanent fix, you understand, but it's not nothing, either."

"I've already done that. Ace Patrol has a man walking the perimeter."

"Is this Ace fellow armed? Do the cops know he's there?"

"Good questions. I have no idea. But why tell the police?"

"Because if they come back and see him poking around in the dark, they might shoot him, that's why. Didn't you say the police were hopeless?"

She nods.

"And here's another thought: you might also want to persuade Rabbi Josef to move the Torah out of the sanctuary, at least for the time being. It doesn't *have* to be at the temple, does it? Does he own a wine cellar like Farber?"

My feeble attempt at humor seems to sail right past her. "I think they're attached to it right where it is at Anshe Amunim," she insists. "The rabbi and his people—they don't much like to be told what to do—you know how stubborn Jews are—and besides, it's given them a sense of continuity. Not many congregations can boast that they own a Torah with such a glorious provenance."

"I would hope they aren't boasting at all," I say. "Maybe that's how the thief found out in the first place."

I lean my head back into the recesses of the luxurious dark leather. She's wearing some sort of fancy perfume, not a lot, but you don't need much in the backseat of a limousine to be effective. She's regarding me intently, as though she's made her case to her own satisfaction.

Now the ball is in my court. "I don't come cheap," I say, by way of a reminder. "I hope Lieutenant Malloy mentioned that when he told you about me."

"We didn't discuss fees," she says dryly, "but that won't be a problem." She bends down, picks up her delicate purse, unsnaps the gold clasp, and draws out a red leather checkbook. "How much do you need, Mr. Parisman?"

*   *   *

As I watch Geoffrey and Mrs. Reines roll silently past the guard at the gatehouse and onto Hauser Boulevard, I take a closer look at the pale blue check tucked in my shirt pocket. I'm still slightly in shock. The check is drawn on the Bank of America, and it's gotta be the most generous one I've ever seen. Which is bizarre, because I told her exactly how much I needed, and what did she do? She doubled it—then added a zero. Part of me, of course, thinks this is marvelous (what a lucky sonofabitch you are, Parisman!); but another part of me, well, that part can see right through her high-handed charade. That part resents it.

I'm not as old as she is, but I've been around long enough to see how things work. I've learned that no one enjoys being bought—but no one enjoys starving, either. I fold her check in half and slide it into my wallet.

Ten minutes later, I phone up my friend Omar Villaseñor, and ask him if he'd like to meet me in front of the *shul* on Beverly at noon. "I have a job for you, amigo. A good-paying job for both of us."

Omar used to be a wrestler when he was a kid in Oaxaca. He's strong and dark and nimble. He doesn't just think with his brain, he thinks with every muscle in his body. If Omar were an animal, he'd be a panther. If he were a vegetable—well, scratch that. If anyone's a vegetable, it's me; that's why I need Omar.

He had his share of trouble with the cops when he first landed here in Los Angeles—the boys down at the Rampart Station seemed to have it in for him. It's a long story, but the gist of it is that he didn't rape anyone. With the help of the public defender, I managed to prove he was innocent. It kept him out of prison, and for that, he's never forgotten me. He's a high school graduate now, still trying to figure things out, living with his sister and mom in Boyle Heights. Whenever I get work, I try to spread the wealth.

For tax purposes, Omar prefers to be paid in cash. I like to have something in my wallet as well, so after I explain to Carmen and Loretta where I'm headed, I stop off at the Union Bank on Wilshire, deposit the check, and draw out a small, crisp bundle of green.

We arrive at almost the same moment in front of Anshe Amunim. I tell Omar we've been hired to stop a burglary at a Jewish temple. I don't tell him about the Torah and its long trip across the sea. That's a critical part, and he'll hear about it soon enough, but Omar has little interest in organized religion. He stopped going to mass years ago, and if I tried to explain the significance of the Torah to him—how it's the tree of life to Jews—his eyes would glaze over.

Harriet Reines was accurate when she described Anshe Amunim as nothing to write home about. We stand around in the shade of a pepper tree across the street and take it all in. It's a tan, squat building with an aging shingle roof, and if I were putting a date on it, I'd guess it was built in the thirties or early forties. It's now sandwiched between a thrift store called Oldies but Goodies, and a Vietnamese

nail salon with a purple neon sign. I say sandwiched, but it's really
forgotten. Before Beverly Boulevard went commercial, this temple
was most likely someone's private residence. It's set back from the
sidewalk and you can see where, once upon a time, there were the
makings of a front lawn. Now there's just a broad swath of baked-in
dirt and gravel that leads up to a dry, two-foot-tall boxwood hedge.
A gardener appears to have trimmed the hedge recently; a few clip-
pings remain on the ground. What leaps out at me is how modest
the *shul* is—there's no sign over the double doors, no bronze plaque
on the wall, nothing obvious to indicate that this is a house of worship. And no windows, either, at least facing the street. Anything
that was charming, that might have invited you in, has long since
been plastered over.

"Looks like somebody's tomb," is Omar's first response.

"Kinda does," I say. We approach the front door, where I notice a
small tin *mezuzah* nailed vertically at eye level.

"I guess that's all the sign they need," I say, pointing to it. "You
know what a *mezuzah* is, Omar?"

He looks at it, shakes his head. "Not a clue, man."

"It's a symbol that we're about to enter a holy space. There's a
little verse from the Bible rolled up tight inside. My people, the Ashkenazim, we hang our *mezuzahs* at an angle. That's the tradition.
These guys are Sephardic. They put theirs in straight up and down.
Go figure."

"I don't know what the hell you're talking about, man. Let's go
inside. Check it out."

We knock, then try the door, which is unlocked. Immediately,
we find ourselves in a cloakroom, two long wooden closets opposite each other with coat hangers and sliding panels. A small round
table sits in the middle, with open cardboard boxes of blue and
white yarmulkes and tallit, just in case the worshippers come unpre-
pared. There's a built-in shelf with prayer books stacked up. We pass
through another door. This is the sanctuary; it's a large, plain room
with a parquet floor from a bygone era. A vestigial calm comes over
me as I enter. All four walls are concealed by beige curtains, and a

couple of dozen metal folding chairs are arranged in a semicircle, facing a wooden ark. That's the focus, the ark and the Torah inside. An older, gray-haired gentleman is bent over before it, fiddling around and shaking his head. He's frustrated. Something seems to be stuck. What can it be? I wonder; there aren't many moving parts in an ark. Our footsteps on the hollow floor alert him. He wheels around.

"Can I help you?"

"Rabbi Josef?" I smile.

The sound of his own name seems to relieve his anxiety. He nods, gestures toward the folding chairs near him. "Please," he says, "please sit. To whom do I owe the pleasure?"

Benjamin Josef is a short, cheerful, wizened man in his sixties or seventies. A wispy beard. His forehead is permanently wrinkled. He's got thick wire-rim glasses, sallow cheeks, and a maroon jacket with patches sewn at the elbows like a college professor. No yarmulke or tie, much less polished shoes, but I'm thinking this is just the middle of the week. His audience hasn't arrived; there's still prep that needs to happen. He pulls up a folding chair.

"I'm Amos Parisman," I say, taking his hand. "And this is Omar Villaseñor. We're here about the break-ins. Mrs. Reines thought we could help."

"Ah," he says, "she's an angel, no question about that. Last night, for the first time, we had an armed guard here to protect us."

"Right, she told me that was in the works. That's good, but don't be surprised if we make a few other adjustments to your situation." My thumb points to the ark. "You've got a very valuable item in there, Rabbi."

"It's not valuable, Mr. Parisman."

"No?"

"No. It's priceless."

"Exactly. And as much as possible, we aim for you to keep it."

Rabbi Josef chews on his lower lip and wags his head pensively from side to side. I can't read his mind, but I've spent more time than I care to remember in the company of rabbis. The truth is, they are given to arguing. They'll argue with you just to make sure you've got all your marbles—and if you're not up to the task, they'll argue with themselves. It may not be genetic, but it comes with the job description. "The Torah," he says, using his own thumb as a pointer—"*this* Torah—is important historically, I suppose, and we're blessed to have it. But we also have two other scrolls. They're perfectly acceptable. What matters are the words. The words, and the wisdom they contain. *Etz chaim*, huh? A tree of life. I'm sure you'd agree."

"Of course," I say. "Judaism continues; it won't be snuffed out, no matter what happens. But whoever smashed up your back door the other night and broke your window the next, that man didn't come here with a burning desire to study Torah. He's dangerous. And he's still on the loose."

"Granted," the rabbi says. "Evil exists in the world."

"Yes. And so, to ward it off, you'll need security cameras, maybe motion detectors. Mrs. Reines will be taking care of it."

"If," he says, "if we allow it. This is a question. I have to discuss it with everyone first. She has a lot of ideas, and don't get me wrong, she's very magnanimous, but—" he holds his palms up in a gesture that says stop—"you'll forgive me, but it sounds like she's planning to turn this synagogue into a bank. That's not who we are. I don't want to go overboard."

I give a quick glance at Omar. He's frowning. His arms are folded in front of him. He hasn't said a word, but he's not impressed with this genial old man who reads too much and clearly doesn't understand what's at stake.

"Well, that's between you and your congregation," I say.

"We appreciate that."

"All these improvements, you know, the security guard and the cameras, they're all fine and good. And you can decide what you need. But we're here to track down the intruder himself. That's okay with you, right?"

"Sure, sure."

I pull out my pencil and notepad. "I just have a few questions."

"Excuse me," he asks, "but aren't we mixing apples and oranges? Aren't the police supposed to do that? Track down the intruder?"

"The police are supposed to do a lot of things," Omar chimes in, derisively. "But in a town this size, you need to make it easy for them. Or worth their time. This is neither."

"I see," the rabbi says.

"So let's start with the basics," I say. "When did you first receive this Torah?"

"Oh, it's been years. Four or five years at least."

"And who gave it to you?"

A mystified look. "It's come a long way, Mr. Parisman."

"Yeah, I heard it ended up in Rio during the war."

"And it's been several places since then." He ticks them off on his fingers. "Rio. Buenos Aires. Mexico City. The person who delivered it here was from San Gabriel, believe it or not. It was his mother's. How it fell into her possession, I couldn't tell you. She was a widow, I remember, but not a religious woman."

"Jewish?"

"I think so, but don't ask me for a name. She'd been keeping it at home in her bedroom. It might have been a gift from her husband for all I know."

"So how did it come to you?"

"She'd been diagnosed with cancer. Pancreatic cancer? Uterine? Something. The bottom line was, she didn't have long to live. She knew this Torah was precious, she'd been told the history, that it came out of North Africa, from a Sephardic community, and before she died she wanted it to go back to a Sephardic community. Simple as that. Her son brought it."

"But why you? There must be other temples around."

"A few," he says. "Tefereth Israel in Westwood, that's the big one. They have all the glitz and glamour. And Beit Avraham in Woodland Hills. You won't find many Sephardic Jews in Los Angeles. My guess is she chose us *because* we're small and poor, and because we're unlikely to draw attention to ourselves, just like the temple in Oran."

"Okay, it winds up on your doorstep. But something like this doesn't happen every day. You must have been in shock."

"You know something? I trust in God," he says evenly, without blinking an eye. "He's never let me down."

"That's terrific," I say. "God's great, no doubt about it. But this is gigantic news, Rabbi. A stranger hands you a Torah. I'm sure you didn't keep that a secret. Not for long, anyway. So my question is, who'd you leak it to? And how many people in the temple are in on this now?"

"Why, everyone," he says. "I told them all."

"Everyone?" Omar asks. "Everyone? The whole fucking church?"

"Tone it down, Omar," I say. I turn back to the rabbi. "My friend here is upset. I apologize for his language, but you can understand, I'm sure."

"I've heard worse," he says.

Now I feel like I'm walking into a brick wall. "Everyone—that's a lot of potential suspects. Makes it difficult, if you see what I mean. When you say *everyone*, just what number might we be talking about?"

He sighs, scratches his chin. "There are twenty-five families in our congregation now. I don't recall how many we had then, but something like that. Twenty-seven, twenty-five. It hasn't changed that much."

"And those people, they're all aware that you've got a treasure in there?"

The rabbi stares at me like I'm from another planet. "They've known for years, Mr. Parisman. Ever since it arrived. We're friends. We don't keep secrets from each other. And they aren't the issue. None of them are thieves, I promise you."

I nod. "Okay. I'll take you at your word. But before we check out the back door and the broken window, there's one more tiny wrinkle: Anshe Amunim isn't . . . well, it isn't what I'd call a destination in this town. So how did someone like Mrs. Reines ever get involved?"

"Oh, that's an easy one," he smiles. "My neighbor Lottie, two doors down on Formosa Avenue, she told me about her. My wife and I were sitting in Lottie's kitchen, having coffee and rugelach from Canter's. I was complaining. I try not to, but sometimes I can't help myself. I was telling her how this building could stand a fresh coat of paint. And maybe a new roof. It hasn't had any work done on it since I took over, really, and she said Harriet Reines had all these projects going on. Reines? I said. I was skeptical. Doesn't sound Jewish. And Lottie told me Reines was her late husband's name. Doesn't matter. Now that he's gone, she's doling money out to Jewish entrepreneurs, little start-ups here and there, all kinds of folks. Lottie said there was a new yarn shop going in on Melrose soon thanks to her. So I talked to them, and three days later I was talking to her. Then these break-ins happened. I'm still waiting for a grant to cover the paint and the new roof, but hey, do you see me complaining? No, you don't. Like I told you, she's an angel from God."

He says this last bit as he walks over to and opens the ark, showing us the Torah, which is truly a thing to behold. Unlike all the Torahs I grew up with, this one is different: it's housed in a single silver cylinder, not cloth. Lots of filigree and Hebrew lettering all over it. The rabbi undoes the clasp, pulls it out lovingly, and unfurls it so we can have a better look.

"You see here?" He points at where the scroll is nimbly sewn together. "That's not parchment, it's deerskin. That's one reason it's lasted so long."

Even Omar is impressed, and he wouldn't know a Torah from a roll of paper towels.

Rabbi Josef grins. "Not what you call a kosher Torah," he admits, "but still." Then he puts it back where it belongs and leads us outside, through an alley to the rear of the building. Someone has tried hard to pry the back door open: you can see the marks of the crowbar or whatever they used; but beneath its wood veneer there's an inch of solid steel, so they failed. And you'd have to be a contortionist to climb through the broken window above the men's room. Nothing's been done to the door, but a carpenter has screwed a piece of quarter-inch plywood over the window until it can be replaced.

I tell Rabbi Josef we'll be in touch. I hand him my business card, ask him to give me a call if anything comes up, or if he thinks of anything that might be useful. He nods, places the card graciously in his shirt pocket, next to his heart. We shake hands again and smile, and he returns to the sanctuary as we make our exit.

"Well, what do you think?" I ask Omar.

"About the rabbi? I think he's an idiot. I think he's stuck inside his head. He deserves to be robbed, you ask me."

"No, not about the rabbi."

"About the case? What case? We're never going to find out who did this, Amos. Not unless we can get some cameras in there maybe, and he tries again. And now that there's a night watchman on the job, hey, why would he? I mean, would you?"

"Probably not right away, no. But I think Mrs. Reines is right on one level. This can't be just simple vandalism. Whoever he is, he's tried twice. He wants in, and you've seen the inside of the temple. There's nothing worth stealing there except that Torah. The question is, how does he know about it?"

"Twenty-seven families know about it, for Christ's sake!" Omar's face is turning red. "I don't care if they're all friends of his, I don't care if they're cousins. That many people can't be counted on to keep a secret."

"They kept it for years, apparently."

"Right. Until they didn't."

We wander around to the front. Cars are zipping past on Beverly. The sun is shining. White-haired ladies in the Vietnamese nail salon are sitting back and chatting while they soak their hands.

"Somebody should probably ask the rabbi for a list of all the people in his congregation. We can start there, see if there's someone who just joined in the last few months, somebody he doesn't know that well. It's not much of a net to toss out, but who knows?"

Omar nods. "Yeah, maybe. Doesn't sound like they've been pulling in many new people lately, but it's worth a try."

"And you could talk to the other shops here. See if they've had any break-ins, or noticed any suspicious characters in the neighborhood.

Anything out of place. Retailers always have their ear to the ground."

"Okay, will do."

I take a couple of Benjamins out of my wallet and hand them to him. "Here, buddy. That'll get you started. We'll talk in a day or two."

As Omar walks away, I sit in my Honda for a few minutes and ponder my plight. On the one hand, he's absolutely correct: we have nothing to go on. This case is ice-cold, even before it starts. A broken window, big deal. On the other hand, Harriet Reines has given me a great deal of money to find a thief. But there hasn't been a theft yet, so what is she hocking my chinik about? I mean, don't I have enough headaches as it is? Maybe I'm wrong, maybe this isn't about the Torah at all. The rabbi says it's priceless. It won't shake his faith in God one iota if it gets ripped off. Mazel tov, I say. Fine. On the other hand, who can say what a thing like that is worth on the open market these days?

Then all at once it hits me. Pete Zaslow.

CHAPTER 3

Next morning, bright and early, I take the freeway out to Pasadena to visit him. Pete lives on El Molino, but way south of Colorado Boulevard. It's a green, leafy neighborhood he inhabits. Beautiful people everywhere. What do I mean by that? Well, for starters, no schmutz on the sidewalk. None. Also, you can see your reflection in the vehicles parked in the driveways. The lawns and gardens are impeccable; they belong in a travel magazine. They've been pruned and watered and manicured on a daily basis; you wonder how anyone could possibly afford to pay for them. And that's not to mention the maids and cooks, the butlers, the nannies—all the no-nonsense folks who run these mansions with their huge picture windows looking out on the street.

Of course, when you grow up poor or working-class, that's always the first thing you think about, right? The money. You can't help but compare. Beautiful people don't ever worry about money. Not in the least. It's about posture, your stance, how you carry yourself in life. A very rich man explained this to me once. So maybe that's my problem.

I ease my little blue Honda Civic, the one with the Earl Scheib paint job and the slightly dented fender—the fender I once paid a poor man from Budapest twenty bucks to fix with a rubber hammer and some Bondo—I plant that tired carcass of an automobile right in front of Zaslow's house. I turn off the engine and yank up the hand brake. Even just sitting quietly by the side of the road, I realize I'm lowering his property values. *But why the hell can't I have this*, I wonder. *It would be heaven to live here.*

Pete greets me at the door with a big bear hug. He doesn't care how rich or poor I am. "It's been too long, Amos. Come in, come in."

We go into his study, which is lined with newspapers and random books everywhere—new and used—books on the shelves, on the table, books from floor to ceiling. This is a great space; it smells like sweet-cherry pipe tobacco, a habit Pete still can't seem to kick. He used to be an academic before the Feds recruited him. He loved to immerse himself in art history. And somewhere along the line, he started getting fascinated by copycats and forgers— people good enough to paint pretty convincing replicas of Gaugin or Manet or Picasso, and unscrupulous enough to palm them off on the unwitting public. He doesn't talk about what he does for the government, and if you ask him, he'll tell you he's officially retired. But he helped me out a few years back when a gallery in Beverly Hills bought what they thought at first was a Richard Diebenkorn. Turned out it was done by a guy named Mel Seeger, who was clever and talented in his own right. He was also, unfortunately, strung out on heroin. He'd come to the point where he'd paint anything just to get through the day.

Forged art is still Pete's main schtick, but lately he has branched out. Suckers keep being born, and now there's a booming market in pre-Columbian pottery, it turns out. Who cares if it comes from a factory in Shanghai?

For a few minutes we sit around and shoot the breeze. Pete's wearing chinos, flip-flops, and a tattered maroon Harvard T-shirt. He knows how to dress like a grown-up, but at home he often acts like the sixties never ended. I tell him how Loretta is getting on; he tells me about the miracles Muriel has been baking in the oven.

Then I come to the point. "What do you know about old Torahs, Pete?"

His eyes light up. "You have one?"

"No, but there's a synagogue in my neighborhood that does. They say it came from Algeria. It's supposed to be two hundred years old."

"Wow. A Torah that old, do they even exist?"

"That's what they tell me. I'm guessing it's true. They seem like honest folks."

"I'm sure," he says, "but there can't be many left with that kind of mileage on them. They get damaged, eventually. It's inevitable. And then you can't read from them anymore. In fact, if you're Orthodox, I believe you're commanded to bury them."

"The rabbi says it's in good shape. Good enough, anyway."

"So, what's the problem?"

"The lady that hired me is worried that somebody's trying to steal it. I'm wondering what something like that would be worth."

"Gee, that's hard to say. To the right person, a serious collector, someone who values historical relics, it could be a hundred grand. Maybe more."

"Really? Are there people like that?"

His tongue glides over his lower lip. "There's always a market. One man's meat, you know. But this isn't like the art world. This is very particular."

"Come on, Pete, who are we talking about?"

"Well, there are evangelicals out there, born-again folks who have this affinity for all things Jewish. I don't get them, mind you, but I read not too long ago how they've been buying up *mezuzahs* and kiddush cups, as well as Torahs."

"But why?"

"You're asking me? I don't know. Some sort of historical reenactment? Maybe it's a lead-up to the Rapture. Maybe this is how they plan to get closer to the original Jesus. By owning the stuff he used to use."

"I don't picture born-again Christians being that rich," I say, scratching my head. "Just conservative and Republican. And, you know, slightly meshuga."

He looks at me quizzically. "Yeah, I know. It's crazy. But they're out there. Also, I'd bet you'd find some buyers in Israel. They've got a thriving black market in religious relics. I'd look at Israel. And possibly Russia."

"Russia?"

"Jewish oligarchs. Not that they're so Jewish. It's more about economics. They have the cash, and it's a better investment for them to own things that are light and disposable like a rare Torah than, say, a software company that's really Putin's."

"Makes sense." I lean forward then. "You don't have any Russian names you can cough up, do you, Pete?"

He shrugs. "It'd just be speculation at this point. And didn't you tell me nothing's been stolen yet?"

At that moment, Muriel, his wife of forty-four years, comes in, bearing a lacquered tray with a pot of tea and two slices of olive-oil cake. "I know it's early for this kind of decadence, gentlemen, but this is fresh out of the oven and I need a couple of guinea pigs."

We dig in. Muriel has always been one of my favorites; she and Loretta used to poke fun at their husbands and swap recipes whenever we got together. Now, time has passed, and our social lives have diverged; she's become a creature of her book club and her weekly bridge game, and since Loretta doesn't travel to distant places like Pasadena anymore, and can't hold her own with a conversation—certainly not over the phone, at least—that link is gone.

I give Pete the rundown on Harriet Reines. "She's a good-hearted soul with too much time and money on her hands, I think. Lives at the Biltmore. Anyway, I told her what I'd recommend. Put in some state-of-the-art cameras, motion detectors. Better locks. Make it tight, you know. She doesn't need to spring for a detective, the way I look at it."

Beyond the windows in the study, his back yard is beckoning. There's a giant oak tree among all the greenery, and hanging from the tree is a tire tethered to a heavy rope. Pete and Muriel have no children of their own, so I imagine he must wander out there whenever the mood strikes him and he needs to be a kid again.

"On the other hand," Pete says, wiping the cake crumbs away from his mouth, "you're not going to turn down a job offer, right?"

"Not at my stage of the game, no."

*   *   *

That evening, around seven, I give Carmen a lift back to her home in El Sereno. Loretta usually eats at five, but instead she surprised everyone by nodding off at the dinner table. She barely touched her tapioca pudding, which isn't like her. So, we got her up and slow-walked her gently to bed.

"She had a busy day," Carmen says. "I think it was my fault, I don't know. We went to Ross and she tried on three or four blouses, just for fun. None of them fit. Too tight, too loose, what can you do? Then I took her to Whole Foods because she said she was starving and wanted a roast beef sandwich for lunch. Had to have roast beef on sourdough bread, Dijon mustard, mayonnaise. Only those things would do. But when I got her back to the apartment and I made it for her, you know something? She only ate half."

I don't always get a complete report of Loretta's daily activities, such as they are. And Carmen has an issue with people who leave food on their plate, which probably stems from her childhood. She's a lovely person, but she's not a trained social worker or a psychologist, and I'm sure she tried to pressure my wife to eat it all. I'm also sure Loretta said she wouldn't, and this didn't go over well.

She asks me about the job I'm on. I mention that there's been some trouble at a Jewish temple on Beverly, someone maybe trying to steal a Torah.

She nods. I doubt that she really understands what a Torah is, but I tell her it's the Old Testament, the Bible, and that gets another approving nod. Carmen has a tiny gold crucifix she wears under her sweater, and I've seen a larger velvet one dangling from the mirror in her car; she is a serious believer in God, unlike yours truly.

"But why would anyone want to steal la Biblia?" she asks. "That's crazy. I have a Bible in my home, in Spanish, por supuesto. Many people have Bibles. They're everywhere. My best friend, Alma, she works down at the Marriott. They put free Bibles next to the bed."

"Right."

We pull up to the curb in front of Carmen's home and I watch her climb the old uneven stone steps up to her house. She and Antonio bought it a long time ago. They've made a few improvements here and there, but, apart from the new red tile roof, it's basically unchanged from twenty years ago. Now, though, at least it doesn't leak. When she gets to the door, she fishes around in her purse for her keys. And she doesn't turn back to see if I'm still waiting at the curb. She's never once invited me in, I don't know why. I'm sure it's neat as a pin inside, but no matter how outwardly friendly we are toward one another, I can't shake the feeling that she still regards me as her boss. At the end of the day, I'm just the man who's paying her, and that puts a sad cap on things. As I turn the corner and head back through the twilight toward Huntington Boulevard, I wonder what the world she lives in looks like. Whether it's everything she hoped for. Whether she has regrets. My grandparents were immigrants; they were always telling me stories. What they had to overcome to survive. The stark choices on their plate: good or evil, rich or poor, dos or don'ts, dreams or obligations. If they turned right, if they turned left, it took a little piece out of them. How different can it be for Carmen? It must be unforgiving. I'm sure she worries all the time. I'm sure she sees nothing but traps and potholes she has to dodge here. This wilderness she's in, this pulsating box of noise that is America.

Omar calls me to say he's interviewed the merchants on either side of the temple, and across the street, and none report having encountered difficulties. No vandals, no shoplifting; no strangers anyone can remember, either. "But you'll be happy to hear that I've met the new security guard."

"Oh, yeah?"

"Yeah, a nice older guy," Omar says. "Luke Chandler. Says he has trouble sleeping at night, so this job is right up his alley."

"Just out of curiosity, Omar, was he carrying a weapon?"

"I believe he was, yes."

"And what do you think? Does he know how to use it? Will he

use it if he has to? Or is this all just for show?"

"You ask too many questions," Omar says. "I didn't find out what his background was. Oh, wait, he might have been in the Army way back when. I think he said so. But he's around your age, Amos. He can't sleep at night."

"That's no reason to hire him."

"Maybe not. Still, it's not like hundreds of men are applying to work the night shift, are they?"

"No," I agree. "They probably take whatever walks through the door."

"Which is a dumb way to protect things, if you want my opinion. Me, I'd still vote for cameras and sensors."

"We don't have a vote, Omar. Mrs. Reines does what she wants. I'll bring it up again, though, next time I see her. She'd probably have all that stuff there in a heartbeat if the rabbi okayed it."

"So, for now there's Luke," Omar says. "And his trusty pistola."

*   *   *

Loretta is still fast asleep, making light, wispy, lady-like snoring noises when I get back to Park La Brea. Carmen must have really worn her out, I think. I pull the covers over her bare shoulder and kiss her on the forehead. Then I go into our spare bedroom (which also doubles as my office), turn on the lamp, and spend an hour or two poking around on the internet.

I prefer to know who I'm working for, and Harriet Reines is easy to find. There are several entries, particularly after her husband, Phillip, died. She's been giving away money steadily, almost like she couldn't do it fast enough, but it's targeted: usually in small donations and to small local shopkeepers and homegrown causes in Hollywood and downtown LA. The Rescue Mission on San Pedro, as well as a non-profit group that pays the homeless and displaced veterans to recycle tin cans and plastic bottles, they both got a healthy donation right after her husband died. A few new businesses that were run by people with Jewish-sounding names earned checks in undisclosed amounts, and one puff piece in the *Wall Street Journal* referred to thirty students she'd helped to graduate, kids who were living in their cars while attending UCLA and Cal State. As far as I can tell, though, Anshe Amunim is the first synagogue she's devoted any time or money to.

There's more about her late husband, but since he died over eight years ago, I don't see how it's relevant. Besides, most of the bits on him have to do with lawsuits. A number of folks felt wronged by Phillip Reines. Some were investors in the companies he talked up and then dumped; others were the workers he fired to make the balance sheet look good beforehand. He was a smart man, I decide. Not a nice man, but smart. And Harriet Reines was married to him all along. She knew what he was up to. So, what's that tell you? That she made a mistake? Had bad taste in men? That deep down, she approved of his shenanigans? Who knows how the female heart works?

After a while, I give up on her and set out on another safari for Rabbi Josef. He's not nearly so famous in cyberspace. There's a three-line mention of him teaching a course at Yeshiva University in New York, but otherwise nothing. Yeshiva has a big program for Sephardic Studies—they have a big program for all kinds of things—but I don't know if that's where you go to become a rabbi. I also find that he's married to someone named Shayna and they live on Formosa Avenue.

I'm about to turn off the lamp and call it quits when the phone rings.

"Amos?" A gruff voice I recognize. "It's Bill Malloy."

"Lieutenant," I say. "What's the occasion?"

"Hey, I'm sorry to call you so late, but something's come up. You remember how we talked the other day? There was this crazy woman all hot and bothered about a Torah? And I sent her to you?"

"I do, yes."

"You ever follow up on that?"

"That crazy woman is now my client, Bill. And I wouldn't call her crazy. I mean, I'm working for her, and she's certainly rich."

"Well, we didn't keep any record of the call. What I'm looking for is, what was the name of the temple where the Torah was?"

"Anshe Amunim. On Beverly."

There is a long, uncomfortable silence. Any silence that lasts more than a couple of seconds is uncomfortable, but when you're talking to a cop, it's particularly so. "That's what I was afraid of. I'm standing in their vestibule. We've got a man down on the floor. Security guard. The paramedics are working on him right now, but he's lost a lot of blood." He pauses again. I'm not a licensed mind reader, but I know Bill. What's left unspoken is, he's not sure he's gonna make it. "Maybe you could come by?" he asks earnestly. "I'd appreciate it."

"I'm on my way," I say.

I look in on Loretta before I grab my jacket and head out the door. She's still sleeping soundly. But even if she wakes up, which she seldom does, she just pulls the covers over and goes back to sleep. The elevator isn't far, and three minutes later I'm warming up the car.

Bill and I have worked all kinds of cases over the years. Mainly what we do is consult each other. He's got his team of professionals, he's got the law, he's got the whole goddamn LAPD at his disposal—and me, well, I've got my own idiosyncratic way of doing things. He looks at the facts, I ask a lot of questions. He's a builder, I'm more of a *luft-mensch*, a dreamer. I don't have anything *against* facts, naturally. Facts will lead you to the right answer most of the time, or *a* right answer—like, for instance, who did it. That's important. But *why* do people do things? Now that's another jar of gefilte fish.

It's only a short drive over to Beverly. I go straight up Martel and hang a right. I consider calling Omar, but it would take him half an hour from Boyle Heights and there wouldn't be much he could add. He could identify Luke Chandler, the security guard, but the cops probably already know who he is.

When I pull up to the curb in front of the thrift store, there are three cruisers badly parked at various angles, their red and blue lights flashing, and an ambulance from the local fire station. They haven't yet formed a perimeter with crime-scene tape around the area, so maybe that's a good sign. Four women from the Vietnamese hair salon are gossiping and pointing from the sidewalk nearby. One uniform has planted himself in the middle of the street, waving his arms and redirecting traffic; a team of officers on foot is plodding west toward Fairfax with flashlights; another pair is still sitting in their vehicle. I have no idea what that last pair is up to; maybe they just arrived. And the lieutenant is standing right in the center of it all, talking to the rabbi, who's pretty distraught. I see Malloy's assistants, Jason and Remo, working their way cautiously toward the rear of the building. They've got their flashlights out like almost everyone else around here, hoping to get lucky. Their eyes comb the ground. They're on the hunt for shell casings, cigarette butts, chewing-gum wrappers, anything that might qualify later as a clue.

Malloy looks up as I approach.

"What's going on, Bill?"

"Someone tried to break in this evening. Ran into the security guard, who opened fire."

"He do any damage?"

A shrug. "We're on it, but so far nothing. The intruder brought a gun as well. That's where things went seriously south. He was also a better shot."

"How bad is he?"

"Dunno." Malloy wags his head. Then all at once he peers up at the night sky, like he's searching frantically for Mars or Venus or the Big Dipper, like if he just locates one of those, then it really doesn't matter, everything will be in its place, everything will be all right, and he can relax down here on Earth. He takes a deep breath, and when he turns to me again he is his old self: it's business as usual. "The shooter ran off, so whatever he came for—the Torah, or whatever—is still safe, I guess. Rabbi here was in his office working late. Heard the commotion. Called it in."

Benjamin Josef exchanges anguished looks with me and then Malloy. "I need to go back inside. I need to see the guard, Lieutenant, if that's possible. I . . . I can comfort him."

Malloy frowns. "He's unconscious. I know you're upset. But you

just have to stand back. Let the paramedics do their thing. They'll
be bringing him out any second."

The old man nods, bows his head. He understands. Still, it's a difficult moment for him. This is his synagogue, he should rightfully
be in charge here, but they're treating him now like he's irrelevant,
a barely interesting bystander. He's been thrust into another world,
their world, and he stares helplessly down at his feet.

Malloy peppers him with harsh questions, none of which he can
answer. *How many shots did you hear? How long did it last? Did you
get a glimpse at the assailant? Do you think you could identify him if
you saw him again? Which way did he go?*

The paramedics, two strong Asian men in blue track suits, shove
a gurney through the open door just then; there's a body strapped
to it. They're very sober and efficient, these guys, and I only manage
a quick peek of the victim under the blanket. Heavyset, older. A
face like chalk. They load him dispassionately into the back of the
ambulance. One climbs in the back and starts immediately to work
on an IV drip. His partner runs around to the front. Just like that,
the siren begins, and they're gone.

The rabbi watches the blinking lights recede down the street.
His lips part, his frail body sways. Slowly, ever so slowly, I hear
him half-mumbling, half-chanting kaddish—*Yitkadal v'yitka-
dash*—the ancient Jewish prayer of mourning. It's a familiar tune.
It's also the only thing I still remember from my days in Hebrew
school, and, midway through, I find myself joining in, mumbling
along with him.

* * *

Later, after the doctor at Cedars-Sinai informs the lieutenant that
Luke Chandler is still in critical condition, after the forensics team
has slipped off their disposable shoe covers because they're done
checking for fingerprints and DNA, after they've finished photo-
graphing everything from every possible angle, the rabbi, who is
exhausted, leads us back into the sanctuary. It's set up as it was when

I last visited—the metal folding chairs still in a semicircle, the plain wooden ark.

"This is what he wanted," Benjamin Josef says, as he opens it for Malloy to see. "This is what that brave man put his life on the line to protect."

The lieutenant nods. He's read the Old Testament—the King James version, anyway—and he gives it a reverential minute before he speaks. "I'm sure the shooter won't be back tonight. We'll put an extra detail on the block for a day or so, as a precaution, but if I were you I'd find another place for this."

"Another place?" A puzzled look.

"Somewhere less public. That's my advice. At least temporarily. Why don't you just take it home with you, Rabbi?"

"I'd rather not," he says. "As you know, we're commanded by almighty God to share the teachings." He lifts a finger in the air. "*You shall teach them diligently to your children, and shall talk of them when you sit in your house, and when you walk by the way, when you lie down, and—*"

Malloy frowns. I can tell he isn't keen on any of this woolly philosophizing. His patience, probably thin to begin with, is at an end. "Hey, aren't you also supposed to treat all human life as sacred?" he replies. "I seem to remember that from my days with the Jesuits. What about Luke Chandler? He didn't plan on being a hero this evening. He thought he'd be home in bed. He was gonna be fast asleep when the sun came up."

Rabbi Josef stares at him, blinks, sighs. He's equally worn out. "Okay, Lieutenant. Okay, you win. No more dead heroes, I agree. I'll take it home with me, for now."

"But then you're going to bring it back?"

"I don't know," he says. "Another guard may not be the answer. I'll have to talk to my congregation and—"

"You wanna talk to someone, you should talk to Harriet Reines," I say, jumping in. I'm also getting tired of this argument. "Harriet Reines will make you install a real security system. Stop pussyfooting around. Cameras. Motion detectors. Locks. Sensors. That's what you need, if you want to keep it here."

"Maybe so," he says. "But it's a difficult decision. I'd need to consider it all. I want to be responsible." He rubs his cheek. Another thought has occurred to him. "There was a Jewish poet I read about once. From Minsk? Odessa? I can't remember anymore. Doesn't matter. A Jew who survived the Russian Revolution. It was a wild time. Old walls were crumbling. Arrows were pointing in new directions; and this poet, he thought he saw the light. He renounced his faith, this fellow, became an ardent communist, declared himself a modern man. Science would lead the way. The Party could do no wrong. A portrait of Stalin hung in his living room, that's how much he believed. Then, one night, comes a knock at the door. The secret police."

"What are you trying to say, Rabbi?"

"We don't want to get ahead of ourselves, Mr. Parisman. That's my point. I'm saying it's a mistake to assume we know what God has in mind. I've been at this a long time. If I had to, I could conduct the whole Shabbat service in my sleep. But you know what still troubles me the most?" He doesn't wait for me to respond. "Arrogance. I worry about arrogance. Perhaps, when all's said and done, we're simply not meant to be the custodians for such a Torah."

"So, what do you think?" Bill asks me, after Rabbi Benjamin Josef gathers his coat and briefcase and systematically locks up the building for the night. We watch while he gives the front doorknob an extra twist, just to be sure, then turns and trudges off into the summer darkness. Two police officers, who don't know what to make of him, are standing nearby with their thumbs jammed in their duty belts. And despite all the horror of the evening, the Torah is still inside where it was before, though the rabbi has promised he'll retrieve it tomorrow morning when he brings his car along.

"Somebody really wants what's in there," I said. "Somebody's got his heart set on it."

"And somebody's going to succeed," Malloy says, "unless that jackass wakes up and changes his tune."

"I wouldn't call him a jackass," I say. "It's obvious to you and me, maybe. But he's juggling all kinds of questions right now."

"Yeah, well, the only question I want to know is, who shot Luke Chandler?"

"Which is wrapped inside the enigma of a two-hundred-year-old Torah, and who wants it and why. You can't separate this stuff, Bill."

"I guess not," he concedes. "Still, it would help if he'd act a little more appreciative. I mean, we're on his side, for Christ's sake."

"Oh, he appreciates us, Lieutenant. He's just lost somewhere inside his skull. I know these people. But I bet he'll come around sooner or later. And if I can't persuade him, well, maybe he should hear it from Mrs. Reines. She's writing the checks. God knows, she'll give him an earful."

CHAPTER 4

The next morning, after Carmen arrives and puts her purse away, I wander over to Canter's Deli for breakfast. The sun is out. It's a good way to start the day, I've found. I get to stretch my legs in accordance with the doctor's orders. Walking should take me just half an hour, if I don't stop to catch my breath by the Screen Actors Guild at Fairfax and Third—which I do—so, in truth, it's forty-five minutes before I get there. And of course I do half an hour or so on the backside. That's double what Dr. Flynn requires. At that rate, I figure I'll live forever.

Canter's may be the *oldest* delicatessen in Los Angeles, but which one is the *best* is purely subjective. My cousin Shelly, for example, swears by Nate 'n Al's in Beverly Hills. He says it has a certain clientele, which automatically, ipso facto, positively makes it classier. I tell him he's full of soup and not to be an idiot, they just charge a dollar more for the same hot pastrami. Actually, I never tell him "Don't be an idiot." I'd like to, but that's the way fights get started. Shelly's the only blood relative I've got left. He's also diabetic and overweight, and he has a heart condition. Loretta says I'd feel terrible if he suddenly got apoplectic and keeled over in front of me, and she's right. I love Shelly. So I let him stick it to me about Nate 'n Al's. He also favors Langer's in MacArthur Park, though he admits he doesn't go there much anymore because that part of town has gotten a little rough around the edges, and Shelly would worry about leaving his Bentley there, even in broad daylight with a parking attendant on duty.

I'm sitting in a padded booth at Canter's, staring at their menu. I don't need to. I've been here so many times, I've got it memorized. Besides, I already know what I want. But I look at the menu anyway for form's sake—because I'm polite and I'm waiting for Omar to show up—but mainly because if I put it down, Rhonda will reappear with her pad, hovering over me and tapping her foot, wanting me to order. So, instead, ten minutes go by, still no Omar, here comes Rhonda.

"Tell you what," I say. "Why don't you give me a big plate of matzo brei, and a side of applesauce."

"It comes with applesauce. Read the menu. You don't have to ask."

"Fine. And some more coffee." I hoist up my cup to show her it's empty. "But I'm waiting for a friend, so could you just hold everything for another ten minutes?"

She frowns. "Everything?"

"Well, the matzo brei."

"It comes when it comes. Do I look like I run this joint? You tell me."

I've known Rhonda, heck, it must be going on twenty years. She is who she is, which is to say she's like a pair of old shoes. Maybe you can't wear them in public anymore, but you can't throw them out either, can you? Nothing ruffles her. She's part of Canter's. She loves her customers to death and she's always been this annoying little ray of sunshine.

"No, of course not. I just don't want to finish my meal before he gets here."

She puts her order pad in her pocket, taps her foot, and sighs. "I'll try, Parisman. No promises, understand?"

"Try. Hey, that'd be great, thanks. See what you can do."

She shuffles off. Out of the corner of my eye, I catch her conferring with Saul, the cook. They don't bother with fancy titles around here, he's not a chef—nobody would ever accuse him of that. Five minutes later, my matzo brei is on the table.

"I thought you were going to hold the order."

"I tried. You said wait ten minutes. We split the difference. Go on, eat it while it's hot," she says.

Omar finally shows up. He slides in across from me.

"Have you had breakfast yet? I'm buying."

"No, thanks, man. My mom made me try one of her tamales before she'd let me out the door. I'm stuffed. I could use some coffee, though."

I raise my mug hopefully again to Rhonda and point at Omar. She nods.

"It didn't make the news," I say, "but last night someone tried again to grab the Torah at Anshe Amunim."

"Oh, yeah? Well, at least they had a guard on duty this time."

"Yeah, there was a guard." I leave it hanging there. I want to be exact, or at least don't want to get too far ahead of myself, be the bearer of misinformation. A guard was there: that, in itself, was a plus—it altered the outcome. And they did exchange fire, which means Chandler must have had enough time to draw his gun. And who knows? Maybe it's not nearly as bad as Malloy made it sound. Maybe he took a slug in the shoulder, or maybe his wound was even more superficial, in and out, just a spectacular amount of blood. That happens sometimes.

Omar's not buying it, though; somewhere in his ancient Indigenous heart he hears my hesitation. He gives me a puzzled look. "And how did it go?"

"I dunno. Not too well. The Torah's safe and sound, but Chandler's in the hospital now. Lost a fair amount of blood. I'm waiting to hear back from Malloy."

"Why didn't you call me?"

"I thought about it, Omar. But you're a half-hour away. What's the point? It was all over even before I arrived."

We sip our coffee. I push the rest of my matzo brei around on the plate; I've suddenly lost my appetite.

"On the bright side," I tell him, "this is no longer a simple break-and-enter. Now that there's a man all shot up, we've got the whole LAPD involved."

"That's good *and* bad," he mutters.

"You don't have to be so predictable, amigo."

"Am I?"

I nod. Omar's got about the same relationship with the law as I do with colonoscopies. There are some cops in this world he cares for, but when you've grown up on the street as he has, they are few and far between. I've tried to explain to him how the police have a difficult job to do. That they're trained to be wary, to view the public in a certain way. That the good cops continue to evolve, they keep thinking and hoping. But bad cops? Bad cops get crippled by their own experience. If you ask them, they'll tell you: they bust the same people over and over for the same crimes. They send them off to prison, they see them come out again. It gets old.

In that case, Omar always says, they ought to quit. Walk away. Find a new job.

Which makes me smile. He's still a young man. Still thinks he's immortal. He wakes up fresh every morning and chases his dreams. He doesn't realize what it's like to be trapped in a job you maybe hate, because you have a wife and children to support, or because there's a mortgage that comes around the first of every month. At his age, there are no consequences, whatever you do.

My phone rings. It's Malloy.

"I just got off the line with Remo," he says. "Luke Chandler died this morning."

"Hey, I'm sorry."

"Yeah, me too. I just came from visiting with his daughter, Evelyn, in Studio City. Lovely woman. Elementary school teacher. Apparently she's the only relative he has in California. His wife passed away a long time ago. And his daughter hadn't heard about this gig at the synagogue. She thought her dad had retired. The only good news is he regained consciousness for a few minutes at the end."

"Really! Was he talking? Was it useful?"

"Useful? You tell me," Malloy says. "He started babbling to

the ICU nurse. She brought in Remo; he was waiting out in the hall. Chandler mentioned something about the shooter, that he had a beard, a little guy with a beard, is what he said. He said it a couple times."

"That was it?"

"No," Malloy says. "He thrashed around. Then his eyes rolled up inside his head, and he flatlined. *That* was it."

"Little guy with a beard," I mumble. "Narrows the field, I guess. If he even knew what he was talking about."

"Exactly."

I've seen my fair share of death. More than my share, in fact, if you count the tour in Vietnam. And my memory is that in the moments before they died, when they were on the brink and it was imminent, the men I saw were lucid. If they could still talk, they didn't make things up, they didn't exaggerate, and they certainly didn't fantasize. What they said at the end was almost always on the money. Chandler could be wrong about the beard, though. Maybe it was too dark to see. Maybe the shooter forgot to shave. "How about the bullet that killed him?"

"Bullets," Malloy corrects me. "He was shot three times—once in the chest, once in the neck, and once around the groin. Nine-millimeter slugs."

"But he fired back, right?"

"We found two holes that belonged to him. He was stationed in the foyer, where the Bibles and the prayer shawls were. One shell splintered the closet, the other was embedded in the ceiling. We think he was down on the floor when the second one went off. Probably just a reflex."

"Still, enough to scare the shooter."

"Yeah," Malloy says, "he did his job, I guess."

After I hang up, Omar and I look at each other. He hadn't heard what the lieutenant had to say, but he'd heard enough from my end to understand.

"We need to view this as an inside job," he says.

"I agree, Omar."

"They had that Torah all to themselves for years, nobody breathed a word, and it was fine. Now, somebody's willing to kill to get it. What does that tell you?"

"A leak. We'll have to check out the congregants one by one. They may not be at fault. But maybe they have some unsavory friends or relatives."

"Sounds like a job for you," Omar says. "What can I do?"

"I've been thinking about that. Rabbi Josef is coming by this morning to pick up the Torah and take it to his house for safekeeping."

"Permanently?"

"No, just until Mrs. Reines gets some serious security rigged up at the temple. Which could take four or five days."

"But until then," Omar says, "if the little guy with a beard—the one Chandler was raving about—knows where it's headed, well, then, we're looking at another burglary."

"Or worse," I say.

"Or worse, yeah."

Nobody talks for a minute, but I've known Omar long enough. We're both thinking the same thing. One of us—maybe both of us—are going to have to take turns watching over the rabbi's house on Formosa Avenue. At least until he can deposit the Torah back in its rightful place.

"I'll keep an eye on things," Omar says at last with a frown. "But you owe me, man."

*   *   *

After Omar slides out of the booth, I punch in Harriet Reines's number to tell her what happened with Luke Chandler. Her personal assistant answers the phone, someone named Anna. Very officious, full of herself. Talks fast, like picking up the phone is something she has to do but would really rather not. When I tell her who I am and why I'm calling, there's a pause. Then a couple of clicks, like someone's snapping their fingers, and Harriet's voice comes on. She's understandably upset, feels awful—or responsible at the very least—and wants to do whatever she can to assist the family.

"There's just a daughter in Studio City," I tell her. "I don't have her address, but Lieutenant Malloy dropped by to pay his condolences. You might ask him. Meantime, you should really try to amp up the security at the temple. We're running out of time. I spoke to Rabbi Josef, and after what happened with the guard, well, let's just say he's on board with that idea now."

"I should hope so," she says.

"But I wouldn't sit on this," I tell her. "We're playing with fire here. The rabbi took the Torah home with him today. That's not a solution, in my opinion."

"Well," she says, "you're the expert."

Harriet Reines is a smart cookie, and her heart's in the right place, but she responds with her checkbook. If she sees a hole, the first thing she does is stuff some money in it. She doesn't go crawling out on a limb looking for trouble like I do. "Let's put it this way," I say. "That Torah sat happily in that ark for years. All that time, who knew it was there? Everybody. Which means the rabbi, and the members of his congregation. All twenty-five families. And they're decent, God-fearing people, so it didn't matter: nothing happened. Then one day, maybe one of them had a slip of the tongue. Happens. Maybe he mentioned it to his cousin who was visiting from San Diego or Las Vegas. And maybe that cousin ran into a friend of his in a bar, and after a few drinks they got to talking. And maybe that friend of his was down on his luck, or he knew a rich guy who collected weird things like—I dunno—a two-hundred-year-old Torah. Do you see where I'm going with this, Mrs. Reines?"

"I think I do, yes."

"Bottom line, the rabbi shouldn't be hiding that scroll in his house. He and his wife could be in grave danger."

"Understood, Mr. Parisman. I'll get to work on that today."

Rhonda comes back to look in on me one more time. Did I need more coffee? I shake my head no, and she leaves the check on the table. As I pay the tab at the cash register, I consider calling Lieutenant Malloy. Perhaps he'd like to send someone out to watch the rabbi's house. Isn't that what the LAPD is supposed to do? Protect and serve? For three seconds I think it over, then I shelve this idea. He'll tell me he doesn't have the manpower to spare. He'll tell me surveillance costs an arm and a leg and it's the taxpayers' money. He'll come up with a thousand excuses, and he'll be right. But all that means is that in the end it's up to me and Omar to protect the rabbi.

At the Diamond Bakery I buy a half dozen Linzer tarts and a loaf of fresh raisin pumpernickel bread to bring home. Canter's has pastries, but nobody does raisin pumpernickel like the Diamond Bakery. I love to toast it up with butter and share it with Loretta. Always brings a smile to her face.

As for mine, it is red and I'm sweating by the time I turn my key in the side gate at Park La Brea. I take off my Dodgers cap and wipe my brow. A good sign, I figure; Dr. Flynn would approve. That's when my phone starts to jingle. I lay the paper sack with the cookies and the raisin pumpernickel on the bottom step, just before the lobby. I sit down, cross my legs, take a breath, punch the green button, and listen.

"Amos, it's Pete Zaslow. Is this a good time to talk?"

"Sure, Pete. What you got for me?"

"Well, I was on a conference call yesterday with people I know in Washington, D.C., about some long-lost paintings, and I brought up this Torah business you're involved in."

"When you say 'people in D.C.,' you mean FBI? CIA? What?"

"I'm afraid I can't go there, my friend. They're very smart. And they prefer to remain anonymous."

"Okay, fine, don't tell me. But you told them about the Torah."

"I mentioned it, yeah. We were talking about a cold case, a triptych that disappeared from a church outside of Naples seven years ago."

"And?"

"Well, we originally thought the Mafia was behind it. *I* did, anyway. I mean, that's the kind of stunt they'd pull now and again in those days. They'd usually return it, mind you, once they'd squeezed

a little ransom out of the Vatican. They're all good Catholics, right?
But this time, they didn't. It just vanished."

"So maybe it wasn't the Mafia."

"Right. Probably not. But you also wouldn't keep it. It's not the
kind of *objet d'art* you'd tuck away in a palazzo somewhere, not in
Italy. It'd be too well known."

"So nu?"

"So the reason it came up at all is because one of their informants
was in Rublevka last week."

"Where?"

"A fancy neighborhood, just outside of Moscow. She was visiting
with the wife of a wealthy businessman, at his new dacha, and after
lunch she got a tour of the house."

"Nice house, I bet."

"I hear they're a little over the top. Kinda makes you wonder
what happened to all that proletarian stuff, huh?"

"Lenin's spinning in his grave," I say. It strikes me that Pete has
always had an egghead's view of history. His people came from
Poland in the 1880s, and maybe they struggled a bit when they got
off the boat, but the Russian Revolution? That wasn't in his bones; it
was more like he read about it at Yale. For me, it was different. My
grandmother grew up near Kiev. She was in the 1905 Revolution,
the one that failed. She used to sit me on her lap, tell me romantic
stories. How, when she was a teenager, she used to hide illegal lit-
erature in haylofts. How groups of her friends would meet secretly
in the woods to read Karl Marx. How there were always lookouts
posted in the trees. How worried they were, even as they kept their
eyes peeled for the Cheka, the secret police. That was long ago, and,
of course, she ended up here in Los Angeles, an old lady, my Baba.
As far as she was concerned, the Revolution had turned to ashes.
Russia, she said, was a great place to be *from*. But I liked the stories,
and I loved my Baba. Funny, the things that linger.

"Yeah. Well, anyway, the informant was going around from one
golden room to the next with her friend, Anastasia, and the two of
them walked into this study, and there it was—the triptych."

"You sure? How'd she know what it was?"

"She didn't. All she knew was, it was quite old and religious, and it reminded her of something she'd seen in her art history class back in college years ago. She wasn't familiar with the piece, but Anastasia and her husband were devout atheists. They couldn't have cared less about anything to do with religion. So, if it was here, it had to be because the husband thought it was a good investment. If push ever came to shove, he could sell it down the line and make a small fortune."

"Maybe so, Pete. But still, where's your proof?"

"How do I know it's the stolen triptych? Is that your question? Because she snapped a picture and sent it to us, that's how."

"Anastasia let her do that?"

"Actually, it was Anastasia's idea. When our friend said she had an acquaintance in America who collected religious art, a guy who might be interested in this, she said 'Go ahead, send him a photo.'"

"But she must realize it's stolen merchandise."

"Who knows what she knows?" Pete replies. "Or yeah, maybe she knows and doesn't give a damn. They're in Russia, after all. It's not like Interpol is gonna bust down the door."

"No, I guess not. But what's this have to do with the Torah? I mean, it's still here in Hollywood, as far as I know."

"I thought you'd never ask, Amos. My folks in D.C. gave me more background on Anastasia's husband. His name is Dmitri Kuznetsov. He and Putin were classmates in the KGB once upon a time. I suppose they're still good friends, or at least as friendly as the boss gets with anyone. Dmitri owns a company that supplies heat to places like St. Petersburg and Murmansk. He has another one that furnishes the government with stationery products. Now you'd think in a frozen country like Russia—everyone's trying to stay warm, right? But you'd be surprised: paper and forms and envelopes—that's where the real money is. Anyway, Kuznetsov has more rubles than he needs. That's how he got into art collecting. And you'll be interested to know he has help all over the world. In LA, he uses a man named Francis Crocker. Crocker's a salesman; at least that's what he claims to be when you ask the IRS."

"I'm guessing they've looked into him?"

"Oh, you better believe it. And so far, nothing. He does sell things. Homeopathic medicines. Herbal secrets he learned from Natives in the Amazon jungle. There's a catalog he sends around to doctors and health-food outlets. Mostly, what he seems to do is traffic stuff through the U.S. mail. Powders and potions. He's got an office in Thousand Oaks. Of course, the people I talk to in Washington think it's all a cover for what he really does."

"Collecting?"

"Collecting, stealing. They don't have enough to move in on him yet, but when you follow the money, it doesn't compute. You might want to check him out."

He gives me the address. Then he tells me he's got another call coming through and we hang up. I pick up the bag of goodies from the Diamond Bakery, go through the lobby where I peek inside my box looking for mail (too early), turn the corner, and punch number nine in the elevator.

Carmen greets me at the door, and Loretta, who's sitting at the kitchen table with a deck of cards, asks me where I've been.

"I had a meeting with Omar at Canter's," I tell her as I set the bag down in front of her. "Here, hon, I brought you dessert."

CHAPTER 5

It's a rare day in June when I leave town and drive all the way out to Thousand Oaks. Actually, it's a rare day when I drive much beyond the confines of Hollywood anymore. There's Pete Zaslow in Pasadena, and I have an old music buddy who lives out in Venice; but other than that, there's no reason to move off the dime. Yes, Dr. Flynn, I know, I know. He takes umbrage at my inertia. Move or die. That's his schtick. Okay, so now I'm moving.

I call Omar, tell him where I'm going, ask him to please keep an eye on Rabbi Josef's house, then I head up Highland and get on the Hollywood heading north. Thousand Oaks is technically in Ventura County, just off the 101. The air's better in these parts, the sky is bluer, and my guess is that the people here somehow think they've found the best of both worlds—they're willing to sit for hours in traffic coming and going from LA where their jobs are; then on the weekends they get to live the life of Riley in the suburbs, mowing their lawns, waxing their cars, and yelling at their kids to stay the hell out of the street. When I was young, all I ever knew about Thousand Oaks was that it used to be nothing but rabbits as far as the eye could see. Rabbits and oaks, of course. Then later I learned that that's where they shot movies. *Tarzan. The Grapes of Wrath. Spartacus.* Lots of Westerns. Who knows? Maybe they still do.

I get off at Borchard Road. Right away I see that Thousand Oaks has come a long way since last I visited. There are some very swank condos and townhouses, which give way to a row of sleek one- and two-story professional buildings, most of them sand-colored, with red Spanish tiles on the roof. *Francis Crocker must be selling a boatload of snake oil to pay the rent around here,* I think. Rows of sturdy, well-nourished palm trees sway in the breeze. A quarter mile up, I pull into a parking lot. He's on the second floor of what's called the Penn Building. I take the stairs. He's the fourth office down, sandwiched between a certified public accountant and a wedding planner. The sign on the door reads Francis Crocker Organics. *Natural Remedies for Natural Problems.* Swell.

I turn the knob and find myself standing in a reception area. The space feels unloved. Or not unloved, but staged. The room is comprised of three fake black leather director's chairs, a colorless carpet, a half-dead cactus struggling in an orange clay pot, a rack of well-thumbed magazines, and desert landscapes adorning the walls. The landscapes are particularly stark and garish. I'm no art maven, of course—what I know about art could fit inside a tin of sardines with room to spare—but even so, I'm guessing Mr. Crocker picked this stuff up for ten bucks at a yard sale. If he paid more than that, he was robbed.

In front of me behind a glass partition sits a young woman at a desk. She has short, clipped blond hair, which at first glance makes her seem like a teenage boy. On second glance, I realize she's not, maybe she's twenty, twenty-five, and she's concentrating hard on a computer screen, typing rapidly.

"Can I help you?" she asks, looking up. She's got bright red nail polish on her fingers, as well as a cherubic face—a *sheina punim,* as we say in Yiddish—and I'm immediately drawn to her. I also feel a certain amount of pity for her, stuck in this miserable rathole. Does she know that the man she works for is a crook? That this whole setup is a charade?

"I'm looking for Francis Crocker," I say.

"Frank's not in. He comes and goes on his own schedule; I never know when he'll be here."

"Well, that must be maddening," I reply. "I mean, from a retail point of view. He must lose a lot of customers that way."

She wags her head from side to side. She sees my point. On the other hand. . . . "That's over my head. I'm just the go-between. I come in every day. Process the orders. Make sure the products get shipped. Everything happens at the warehouse in Inglewood. Would you care to leave your name and number? He does check in. Not every day, but most days."

"Well, I would, but I really need to talk to him face-to-face. I don't want to place an order. It's not so much about the drugs. In fact, it's not about natural remedies at all. It's personal, I guess you'd say."

"Gee," she says, "that's also over my head. Best thing you can do is leave your name and number. He just returned from Brazil last Thursday. He's on the road a lot, doing research, but he's pretty good about calling customers back." She leans forward. "What I mean is, if you don't tell him it's personal, he'll probably call you sooner. Just an opinion, you didn't hear that from me. I'm Sherry, by the way."

"Amos Parisman," I nod. My many years on the job tell me she's dying to know what this is all about, that no one like me has ever stepped into this office before. I could—in a few short sentences—magically make her day. But there are always these boundaries between strangers, aren't there? Etiquette. It's the whole reason Emily Post exists. I could give her my business card, but then she'd see my line of work. Instead, I pull out the trusty notepad from my jacket, jot down my name and number, tear off the paper, and pass it over to her. "Right. We never had this conversation. But if he could spare the time, I'd sure appreciate it."

I turn to go, then something else pops up. "You don't happen to have the address of the warehouse, do you?"

Sherry's lips tighten. She readjusts her bottom in the chair. This seems like a startling request. "I really doubt you'll find him there," she says.

"Maybe not, but I drove a long way to see him this morning, and Inglewood is a helluva lot closer to where I live than Thousand Oaks. It's worth a shot."

She takes out a pale-yellow envelope. It's got the warehouse's address printed on it. "They aren't open to the public," she warns. "I don't know what good it'll do you."

*   *   *

The remainder of my afternoon is wasted poking all around the internet for information about Dmitri Kuznetsov. Wasted, because nothing comes up. I'm used to mysteries, but Kuznetsov is an absolute black hole; he doesn't make a blip on the radar, and just plain old common sense would tell you that a billionaire, a friend of Vladimir's, would be listed: every gold-plated registry in the world would want him included. He's rich, and the rich are never anonymous. They can't help themselves. I keep scratching my head. Dmitri would have a lifetime box at the Bolshoi Ballet, he'd donate every month to the Writers' Union of Russia. He'd be on the board of a couple of gas companies. Hell, I can't even come up with a picture of him, though I'm sure Pete Zaslow's friends in Washington have dozens in their file.

I finally give up on Dmitri and call Harriet Reines to find out how she's doing with the security installation. There's a team coming tomorrow at 9 a.m. with sensors and alarms and a closed-circuit TV setup. "But they'll need someone to let them in," she says. "I left a message on the rabbi's cell phone. I'm still waiting to hear from him."

I tell her I'll follow up on that. Then I call Omar. "You seen the rabbi?"

"Not since he came back from the supermarket an hour ago."

"And his wife?"

"I don't know what she looks like, but no one's been in or out since I got here. Except for a ten-minute break, maybe, when I used the bathroom down at Goodwill. Sorry about that, I had no choice."

I fill him in on Dmitri Kuznetsov then, the mysterious Russian tycoon, and his love for things rare and old. I also mention my trip to Thousand Oaks this morning—that it was all a wild goose chase—trying to find his employee, Frank Crocker, the guy who ships homeopathic medicine around the world.

"I don't get it, Omar. They're such passionate people. But their interests are so different. Gas companies. Herbal cures from the jungle. Kinda weird, don't you think?"

Omar agrees with me, it all sounds weird. "So, you think he's our boy, this Dmitri?"

"He could be," I say. "He's got the cash to fund his hobby. Which means that maybe guys like Frank Crocker work for him not just here, but everywhere. Europe, Asia, South America. The triptych came from Italy. What we know for sure is that he has a ton of art in his house, and some of it doesn't belong to him. And he stays put in Russia, where he's protected. Even if he's not our boy, we've gotta keep him in the lineup."

After Carmen leaves to catch the last bus to El Sereno, I move Loretta over from the kitchen table to her favorite spot on the couch so she can watch the reruns of *Jeopardy!* She has a thing about game shows, and still has a serious crush on Alex Trebek, even though he's no longer around. In the old days she could answer half the questions he threw out just as fast as the contestants, and most of the time she got them right. Now I notice she doesn't respond, or if she does, it's with a whisper, as though she doesn't want to interfere. Once she's settled, I retreat to my office in our spare bedroom. There's a single bed tucked away here in the corner with a Mexican blanket on top, but Shelly's the only one who's used it in years—his wife threw him out one night and he couldn't bear being in a hotel all by himself. My desk is pretty rudimentary—just a computer, a yellow legal pad, a jelly jar filled with pens and pencils. There's a framed shot of my parents' wedding from 1938, the two of them standing on the steps in front of the rabbi's apartment in the Bronx. They're in their twenties, grinning at the camera. They're so young and proud and cocksure of themselves. They've been through the Depression, that's what their look says. They're tough, they can lick the whole goddamn world. Even so, they're too young to know what they're doing. And forget about the future. The pain and angst tumbling toward them, gaining momentum like an avalanche. They aren't thinking about that. There's also a photo of an eight-year-old boy, Enrique Avila. He lived in Alhambra and he disappeared on his way home from elementary school, years ago. My first case. The one that's still out there in the ether. The one I still need to solve.

Bill Malloy is probably done eating by now, I think. I tap his number and he answers on the second ring.

"How was dinner?" is the first thing I ask. I don't start with hello. By now I figure he recognizes my voice.

"Jessie made pot roast," he says. "My favorite."

"Yeah, but it's June, Bill. No one eats pot roast in June."

"I just did. Sue me."

He asks after Loretta, and I tell him she's busy watching *Jeopardy!* I tell him she's still so much smarter than me when it comes to stuff like that, and he says she was *always* smarter than me. We go back and forth for a while, old men pretending to be young again, wrestling gently with one another. Then he asks me what's up.

"I'm wondering if you could do me a favor, Lieutenant."

He pauses. "You never end a sentence with the word *lieutenant,* unless you want something from me."

"I do. I already told you. I need a little favor."

"Yeah, but when you say *lieutenant,* it's always official. It means you want me to cross the line, break the rules. That's not how it works, Amos."

"Hey, you haven't even heard what I want. Gimme a break."

Another pause. "All right," he sighs. "Spit it out."

"You have all those fancy machines down there in that building where you work, right? You can look things up? Look people up?"

"We have databases we can go to, sure. Arrest records. Convictions. Domestic disputes. Gun licenses. All sorts of things. I take it that's what you're talking about."

"Bingo. I want you to turn on your machines and run a name for me. Francis Crocker. Can you do that?"

"And just who is this Francis Crocker?"

"He's a mover, I guess you'd call him. A schlepper of goods."

"What sort of goods?"

"Well, supposedly, he's in the drug business. Herbal drugs, I mean. Not meth or heroin. Roots and plants and potions he gets from South America. He does a lot of shipping out of a warehouse in Inglewood."

"Inglewood, that's convenient," Malloy says. "Inglewood's close to the airport. But what are we really talking about? What does Francis Crocker have to do with you? And why on God's earth should I care?"

"You should care, Lieutenant, because there's a chance he's involved in the break-ins at Anshe Amunim. And of course, that could mean he also knows something about the murder of Luke Chandler."

"You didn't just pick his name out of a hat, did you?"

"No, not at all."

"Then where did he come from?"

Bill Malloy has never had the pleasure of meeting Pete Zaslow. I think they'd get along just fine; they're both cerebral, witty in their individual ways. But different, you know: Zaslow is a sponge. He reads the *New Yorker* and *Foreign Affairs*. He speaks three languages. He's got pen pals he still writes to in France, Japan, and India; he's a freethinker, an iconoclast. Malloy, he keeps to himself. Sometimes on Sundays he goes for a long walk down by the Los Angeles River, where he meditates and recharges his soul. At night, when he's not on the homicide beat, he sits in his living room, puts his feet up, and studies Irish drama and poetry. He used to read the Bible, he used to pray, too, he admitted to me once, but not anymore. He still believes in God, but it's just a habit now, a reflex, like the way he plays gin rummy on Friday nights with Jess. And he's loyal to the organization, the LAPD, sometimes to a fault. Anyway, I haven't connected them yet. It's like they're renting two separate rooms in my head.

"I can't really tell you that," I say. "It was a tip from an informant."

"You have informants?"

"I couldn't exist without informants, Bill. And neither could you."

He doesn't respond immediately. But I can tell he is taking it all in, letting it marinate. In the end, he can't disagree with my logic, even if it is against regulations.

"I'll see what I can do," he says at last. "But don't hold your breath."

* * *

Omar doesn't understand, and privately, I'm sure, he thinks I'm crazy; but I keep telling him the world is gonna end. You've been warned, amigo, you know that up front. But here's the rub: it never ends when you think it will. It's some kind of cosmic joke. As human beings, our timing is terrible. This is what I've learned from thirty years in the business—you're always getting caught with your pants down.

I was nowhere near solving this case; hell, maybe I was never going to solve it. That didn't matter. In a perfect world, all we needed was a little bit of time, just a few more hours for the security cameras to start rolling at Anshe Amunim. Is that too much to ask? Then, at least the Torah would be back in the sanctuary, the doddering old men and women could come and go on shabbos like they used to, they could bow and scrape before their God and there'd be no way possible for a gonif to break in and steal it. Mission accomplished.

My phone rings just as I'm turning in for bed. Omar sounds funny, like he's choking on his words, like he's practically out of breath.

"I went out to grab a snack from the market," he says. "I swear, Amos, I wasn't gone twenty minutes. And when I turned the corner, the rabbi was standing outside in his pajamas. Wandering back and forth on the curb. He was holding his head in his hands and he was screaming. 'They took it, they took it, they took it! God in heaven!' That's what he was yelling. Lights were going on up and down the block. I found the first parking place I could and started to walk toward him. But then I stopped."

"You stopped? Why?"

"Two cruisers pulled up out of nowhere, that's why. Everybody jumped out with their guns drawn. Four cops were shouting at him, flashlights pointing all over the place, it was a mess, and I—I got nervous. I just didn't feel like rushing into the middle of that. I wasn't afraid, you understand, but I know what happens when a guy who looks like me, who doesn't live there, doesn't belong in the neighborhood. . . ."

"I get it, Omar. It's okay. You did the smart thing."

"So I got back in my car and sat still and watched. The rabbi was pointing in the other direction anyway, I guess that's where he thought the thief went to, and one cruiser took off that way. One of the cops started checking out his head, see if he was hurt. And they must have called for backup then, because I heard sirens. That's when I decided it was time to leave."

I tell him to get some rest and meet me tomorrow evening around six here at the apartment. That we may have another little job to do.

"Sure," he says, "okay." But I know he doesn't care about tomorrow night. He's just focused on Formosa Avenue. "Aren't you going to go there? See how the rabbi's doing?"

"I'm sure he's doing terrible right about now, Omar. He doesn't need me. He needs a doctor. Besides, Malloy and his people will get all the details from him. That's what they do. We'll hear what happened soon enough."

I finish stripping down to my underwear then, turn out the lamp beside the bed, pull back the covers, and crawl in next to Loretta. A silvery moon high over Griffith Park is filtering through the blinds. It lights up her cheek. I lean over and plant a deliberate kiss there. She smiles serenely in her sleep.

I roll on my side, close my eyes, and try to do likewise. But of course that's not in the cards tonight. My brain is spinning like a dreidel. Somebody must have known the rabbi was taking the Torah back to his house for safekeeping. Someone maybe followed him home and waited for another chance to strike. But who? Even if he still had his head in the clouds, even if he didn't believe in keeping secrets from his congregation, Rabbi Josef hadn't had enough time to spread the word. Well, maybe a little, but not much. And you'd think, watching Luke Chandler die, he'd realize what was at stake; he'd be cold sober now after an experience like that. So, who would know?

I doze off, wake up, go back to bed, turn on the lamp, read a couple of chapters from this novel I bought a week ago at Skylight. The book is called *Fat City*, by Leonard Gardner. This Gardner fellow, he writes like a sonofabitch. I could have finished it by now, but I'm reading it slowly because I want to make it last. It's set in the fifties, and it's all about these boxers in Stockton, California. Young working-class guys down on their luck, living in fleabag hotels, struggling to find a life. It's a story about redemption, how you come to be the rose that miraculously grows through the crack in the sidewalk. Maybe that's why I like it.

*   *   *

I've got my jacket on and I'm getting ready to go downtown the next morning to meet with Malloy when the doorbell rings. There's my cousin Shelly. He's standing like a big balloon, all dressed up in a slate-blue suit and tie, a gigantic grin on his face. It's so big, it seems forced. "Boychik," he says, "this is your lucky day. I'm taking you to breakfast."

"Gee, I'd love to, Shelly, but—"

"No buts about it, man. I insist."

Then before I can say anything else, he wraps me in a bear hug. I feel his heart pounding away in his chest. Is he out of breath? Is the elevator out again? Did he hike up nine flights of stairs to get here? Nah, he would never.

"Shelly," I whisper into his ear, "Shelly, what's wrong? Ruth throw you out again?"

He starts sobbing on my shoulder and he can't talk. I grab him by the shoulders. "Listen to me," I say. "Listen, you want to stay here for a while, you can. Is that what you want? Spend the day. Spend the whole fucking night, I'm okay with that. The bed's still there. We're family, right? Mishpucha."

He nods, pulls a white silk handkerchief from his lapel and mops the sweat and tears off his face. "Thanks, Amos. I just need a little time out, know what I mean? Ruth and I—we're meant for each other. It's *beshert*, fated. She knows that. I know that."

"Sure, sure," I tell him. "You love each other." The truth is far more complicated than that, of course. They love each other; they also despise each other from time to time. It's a marriage, and I've only heard about it obliquely from Shelly. Shelly, who isn't a perfect human being. Ruth's his second wife. They've been together ten years and they call each other "dearest." As in: Dearest, please don't forget your raincoat. Dearest, take out the garbage, will you. Dearest, do me a favor—go to hell."

Loretta wanders into the kitchen just then, where Carmen is stirring her oatmeal on the stove.

"Well, hello, hello, hello," she says. Loretta has always had a soft spot for Shelly. I could never figure it out. He's not half as good-looking as me. Certainly not as reliable. Maybe it's just that he's the only blood relative I have left in LA. Or she likes the timbre of his voice. Or it's his aftershave. Whatever. She beams, points to my empty chair. He should sit across from her, talk to her, keep her company.

I move toward the door. "It's good to see you, Shelly. Make yourself at home. Relax. I'll check in with you later."

An hour later, I'm sitting in Malloy's private office, which is just part of a dozen open-air offices on the fourth floor. It's a sea of plain metal desks with neon lights hanging overhead, air-conditioning blasting, telephones ringing, and people staring at computer screens. Remo and Jason have desks of their own. They're sharing coffee in cardboard cups and a bag of pastries that Jason just brought in. They offer Malloy some, but he refuses; he's trying to cut back on sugar.

"You reach a point where you've gotta listen to the doctor," he says to anyone within earshot.

"You know something? You sound just like my parents," I tell him. "They used to say they worshiped at Kaiser twice a week. Rain or shine, they were there. Blood tests. Urine tests. It never ended.

Until suddenly it did."

"Yeah, well, I still need to keep things on an even keel. The doc says I'm pre-diabetic."

Remo's been listening in. He doesn't care for me much. I don't know what his problem is. I think maybe I remind him of his father. Maybe he hates his father, maybe the big man beat him and that's how he turned into a fat snake. "Why're you here, Parisman? What's the occasion?"

"I dunno, Remo. Do I need a reason? Bill and I are old friends. We were friends at the dawn of time. You're probably too young to remember the dawn of time."

"I don't know what the hell you're talking about."

"No," I say, "you wouldn't."

Malloy smiles. He has to keep peace in the family. "Remo, why don't you and Jason go down to that temple on Beverly, check on how they're coming along with the security setup?"

"But boss," Remo says, "the Torah's gone, you know that. What's the point?"

"They'll get their Torah back sooner or later. We'll find it. The point is, I want to talk to Amos. Alone."

Remo sighs. Jason downs the last of his coffee and gets up. Both men reach for their jackets. Malloy follows them with wary eyes. When they get to the elevators on the other side of the room, he turns to me. "So, you know what happened with the rabbi, don't you?"

"Sorta. I heard from Omar. He was cruising the neighborhood just afterwards. The cops were already on the scene. He thought someone must have mugged him, then whoever it was made off with the Torah."

"Something like that. Actually, two men showed up at his house about nine o'clock. His wife answered the door. They pulled a gun on her, put it to her head, asked for the Torah. She didn't want to tell them. She lied at first, told them it wasn't there, said her husband had left it with the police. They didn't believe her. One of them got heavy, slapped her face. Just then, the rabbi walked in. Saw what they were doing, tried to be a hero."

"They didn't appreciate that, I imagine."

Malloy frowns. "They clubbed him with a pistol. I don't know how hard. He's an old guy, though, it wouldn't take much. His head started bleeding and he collapsed. But he wasn't unconscious. I guess he recognized there was nothing more he could do. He told his wife to show them where the Torah was. She led them upstairs and opened the cedar chest. They'd hidden it beneath a bunch of blankets."

"What I'm hearing is, then, they knew generally where the Torah was. They knew for a fact he'd taken it home."

"I don't think so. More like they knew the rabbi could point to the Torah."

"That's what bothers me, Bill. The rabbi didn't tell his congregants, did he?"

"He swears he didn't breathe a word. I believe him."

"Then that narrows the field considerably, I would think."

"To who?"

I start counting on my fingers. "Well, there's his wife, but I'd rule her out. There's you, the police. Again, a non-starter. There's always me, I suppose, but my Hebrew's pretty rusty. And I have no use for a Torah."

We stare at each other. "That's it?" he asks, bewildered.

"Not quite. Let's not forget about Harriet Reines."

He twists around in his chair. "The one who hired the guard, the one who's paying for the cameras. Makes no sense."

"The one who hired me, too. I agree. But it could be a mole in her circle, just like it could be someone in the congregation's circle. One bad apple, maybe, that's who we're looking for."

Then I ask him if he's had a chance yet to check on Francis Crocker.

"That guy," he says. "I gave his name to Jenny downstairs, she was gonna see what she could find, get back to me."

"And?"

"That was just this morning. An hour or two ago. I've got nothing so far. You have to relax, Amos. The wheels of justice move slowly."

CHAPTER 6

Omar turns up around six thirty, which for him is early, and we take the Santa Monica west and meander down to Inglewood. It's changed a lot since I was a little kid. I came a couple of times, I remember, with Uncle Al. Inglewood was his go-to place. He took me to Randy's Donuts once, and we always went to Hollywood Park to bet on the ponies. Well, I didn't bet, he did. I went for the Coke and the hot dogs. I didn't think about where I was. It was just crowds of grown men and women standing around, smoking and drinking and shouting. And of course I didn't pay any attention to the fact that everyone was white. In the olden days, Inglewood was one of those towns. Working-class, but white. It had a reputation, I heard later on: the Klan was still in Inglewood, and Blacks and Mexicans, they kept their distance.

It's still warm, even at dusk. We drive around, past a few taquerías and a bunch of Latino businesses. Lavandería. Envíos y Correo. We stop at a red light; there's R&B music pumping out of a souped-up Chevy Impala, and a nice mix of people on the street. I've told Omar we're going to dip into the warehouse Francis Crocker operates out of.

"Por qué? You think you'll find the Torah there? It's gonna be that simple?"

"That'd be nice, huh?" We turn right then, at Hawthorne. "Tell you the truth, I'm not so sure we can get in. It's probably closed by now. But that's why I brought you. You're talented that way."

He looks at me, furrows his brow, shakes his head. On balance, I know, America has been good to him. Even living as a second-class citizen in Boyle Heights—even with his occasional run-ins with the cops—what he has here is so much better than the old life back in Oaxaca. But Omar's still very much a work in progress. There's a lot about this place he doesn't understand, and I'm the wrong one to educate him. I want him to grow up to be a model of propriety, to vote (as soon as he gets his papers), to hold his head high someday as a proud American. But right this moment, I need him to help me break into a warehouse.

The whole neighborhood here is a colorless moonscape. Row upon row of vacant, unloved buildings and empty parking lots. You could drive by and never see it. I glance at the yellow envelope on the dash, check the address. The warehouse is an older one-story cinder-block affair, set between two tall structures. They both feature a lot of glass. The one on the left has a big illuminated metal sign that reads Gramercy Appliances. On the right, it's Ortega Office Supply. The building we want has nothing, just a number and a buzzer next to the door. I don't know if it was always a warehouse, but it is now. There's a long bank of windows near the top, some of them cracked, some painted or taped over. The glow of what might be a neon light left on by mistake emanates from inside. No cars in the parking lot. I imagine Crocker doesn't need anything fancy to pack up little boxes of powders and vials—if that's what he does.

"Business must be slow," I say. I press the buzzer then, just for form's sake. There's no answer.

I pull out my flashlight and we walk around to the back alley. There's a green half-filled dumpster on wheels. Judging from the contents, it belongs to Gramercy Appliances. Lots of broken plastic, crushed cardboard boxes, bubble wrap. I swing the light back to Crocker's side. There are some grooves I notice in the cinderblock construction, slight irregular slots that, under the right circumstances, could be finger-holds for an agile climber. Whoever built this thing was in a hurry, or he did it on the cheap. He didn't bother to line things up properly.

I point these discrepancies out to Omar. "What do you think, young man? Could you pull yourself up to the roof?"

He spreads his hands. "Sure," he says. "But why?"

"Because I'll bet you a nickel there's a skylight up there you could unscrew or pry open with a crowbar if you had to. You could lower yourself down. Then all you'd have to do is let me in."

"You have a screwdriver handy?"

"I have a crowbar in the trunk. You wait here."

A minute later I'm back. I hand him the crowbar, he gives me a reluctant look, then he stuffs it through his belt loop and begins to work his way steadily up the wall. In twenty seconds he's reached the top. I go around to the front.

A moment later, I hear a small distinct thud from inside. Then an amber light flips on.

"Bienvenido," Omar says as he opens the door.

The warehouse is a warren of plastic shelves. It's not sterile, but it does remind me of the pharmacy on Pico where my aunt Esther once worked. Everything has been carefully labeled. Everything seems to have an Indigenous name. It's stuffy, and it all smells terrible at first, but you get used to it. I pick up the little white boxes, which are beautiful and quaint in their way; I study them one by one. *Ground Wasai* (Kidney), *Lapacho* (Cancer), *Tawari Tree Bark* (Cancer, Inflammation), *Sodo* (Addiction, Alcoholism), *Pusangade Motelo* (Anxiety). It goes on and on.

To the left of the front door is a long wooden counter with bins full of bubble wrap, cardboard shipping containers, a label gun, and white flat-rate boxes from the United States Postal Service. The counter itself has rolls of clear plastic shipping tape, scissors, and marking pens. There's an AM/FM radio, a small refrigerator, a water cooler, and, in the far corner, a red plastic electric coffee maker and an assortment of ceramic cups.

Omar looks at me. "I guess he's what he says he is." He offers me back the crowbar. "Okay, can we please go now?"

I can tell he's antsy being here—that in his head he's already hearing sirens in the distance—and he wants to leave pronto. "Let's just give this a quick sweep," I say. "Another minute or two, then we'll get the hell out."

Toward the rear of the building is a small office, and Scotch-taped to the door at eye level is a road map of greater Brazil. It has folds in it, which makes me think it belongs in a glove compartment, that maybe he picked it up at a local AAA. There are colored push pins in several towns along the Amazon Basin, and a couple nearby in Peru. The door is locked, of course. I usually have a tool that can handle that sort of problem, but I forgot it tonight.

"What if he stashed the Torah in there?" I ask.

"What if he did? You wanna bust the door down? Right now we can walk out the front and drive away. Nobody will know the difference. You break the door, you tip him off."

Omar makes a fair point. We're skating on thin ice just wandering around this place, and besides, now that we've had the tour, I don't really think the Torah's here anyway. *If* he took it, which is a long shot. I was just playing a hunch. The folks Pete Zaslow talks to in Washington are always hatching global plots. And that's good news for the movie industry maybe, but probably doesn't add up in a backwater like Inglewood. We make our way toward the counter. I'm about to switch off the lights, when I spot an official-looking register on the corner. I thumb through the pages. It seems to be a list of customers with names and addresses—most of them homeopathic doctors and health-food stores across the country—but also just individuals. Packages went out today via UPS Ground to drugstores in Salem, Oregon, Boston, and Maryland. And one lone package was sent to a post office box in Montreal. A man named Armen Sokolov. His went express. The weight of each shipment is also listed. Most of them are in the five-pound range. Sokolov's package clocked in at fourteen and a half. That's a lot of tree bark, I think. The poor man must be suffering.

I take out my notepad and scribble down his information. "This could matter," I say, "you never know." Then I yank my handkerchief from my breast pocket and wipe down any latent prints I might have left behind, kill the lights, crack open the door, and Omar and

I walk cautiously into the still-warm Inglewood night.

He's visibly relieved to be safe in my Honda and back on the road again.

"You did real good," I tell him. "We both did good."

"We didn't do nothing," he says, "not a goddamn thing. Not as far as I can see." He rubs his hands together, trying to scrub the dust and dirt from the climb. He has very large and powerful hands. Every time I look at his hands, I can't help but think he missed his calling: he should have been a piano player. "I coulda got myself busted back there, Amos. And for what? A bunch of voodoo medicine from the Andes?"

"Amazon," I correct him. "Although there may be some stuff there from the Andes too, I dunno."

"Whatever," he says, glumly.

We're almost to the on-ramp for the 405. I tap my fingers gingerly on the steering wheel. I'm trying to stifle it, but I've got an urge to launch into my standard speech about the nature of our work. What a detective really does. That it's about patience. Being meticulous, turning over each and every stone. Asking the same damn questions again and again until the sound of your own voice makes you yawn. I've told him these things before, but he's a young man, and young men have their own ideas. It's not that they don't listen. They do. They're smart—more competent than me, many of them. They sail on with their big plans. They're always gazing off into tomorrow, at what's next, they're so sure, and they lead such busy lives. But a cup can't be filled unless it's empty. That's all I want to say to Omar. It's a simple proposition. Will he hear me?

*   *   *

Shelly isn't there when I get home. There's an envelope with my name on it propped up between the two brass candlesticks on our dining room table. *Talked it over with Ruth. All is forgiven. Thanks, Shelly. PS Your wife was sleeping like a baby when I left at ten.* There's also a crisp one-hundred-dollar bill inside, with a Post-it on it that reads, *Because I'm such a fucking nudnik.*

I shake my head, tuck the money in my wallet. What can you do with a relative like that? When I was growing up, Shelly was like my older brother. He watched out for me, fought off the bullies on the playground, taught me things, good and bad. Shelly showed me how to flick a marble with my thumb, how to use chopsticks, how to smoke a cigarette the way Bogart did. I learned about girls from Shelly—well, from his *Playboy* collection really; what they look like without any clothes on. And later I became a patriot, a reluctant one, I suppose, because of him. He didn't have an opinion about what was going on in Vietnam—politicians get it right, they get it wrong, it's always a crapshoot—but America is always worth fighting for. He argued for that in a high-school debate once, and he believed it with all his heart. Which is why it pained him so much when the Army rejected him because of his flaming ulcer, and maybe why he talked me into joining the Marines a few years after that, to compensate. Shelly and I go way back, and even though there've been plenty of times when I've felt like I've had enough, when I'd much prefer that he stay the hell out of my life, I can't tell him that. I swallow my pride. I take his bad jokes and his bags of pastry and his monetary gifts, and I keep my mouth shut. There's an ocean of good feelings sloshing around in my crazy cousin's heart. I know that. He loves Loretta, he loves me. He's also impossible.

In the morning, as soon as Carmen arrives and Loretta is settling into her breakfast, I throw on my sports coat and tell them I'm going to run a quick errand.

"Where are you going?" Loretta wants to know. She raises her eyebrows. "To see Shelly? Will you bring him back?"

I squeeze her hand. "You miss him, don't you?"

"He was here last night. He always makes me laugh."

"You know what? Shelly's gone home to Ruth. They had a fight, but now she said she loves him again. Everything's fine."

"I'm glad," she says. She turns back to her oatmeal, sticks her spoon in the bowl, gives it a stir.

Loretta's met Ruth many times, but I don't know if she

remembers which wife she is. She was a lot closer to Sally. They belonged to the same book club at one time, on weekends they'd grab lunch at the Farmers Market, and Sally used to think of her as the sister she never had—that is, until she divorced Shelly and wrote off our entire family.

Carmen is reaching for the deck of playing cards we keep on the shelf next to the spices. She's already planning a game of gin rummy, something they haven't done in a while. Loretta has forgotten some of the rules, but Carmen is very forgiving. "You go on," she beams up at me. "We'll be fine."

*   *   *

I drive over to the rabbi's house on Formosa. He knows I'm coming. Still, when I ring the doorbell, he only opens slightly, and I see that he has kept a gold chain lock attached as a precaution. "Oh, it's you," he says, and unhooks it. "Come in, come in."

He leads me into the living room, which is really more akin to a library, a smaller, less airy version of Pete Zaslow's place. Half the books are in Hebrew. I notice that the back of his head still has a small bandage on it from where they hit him with the pistol; it doesn't seem serious, though, not today. We settle down on his sofa, and his wife appears from the kitchen, wanting to know what we need. "Tea? Coffee? I can make both." He shrugs. I shrug. "Nothing, then," she mumbles, and vanishes.

We sit in silence for a moment. Then the rabbi asks, "So, on the phone, whatever you said led me to believe you've made progress. Does that mean you've located the Torah?"

I make a little motion with my hands that suggests you can only do so much. "We've made inquiries," I tell him. "We've got some theories."

"And what would those be?"

"Well, one theory is that a member of your congregation, or more likely an acquaintance of one of your members, got wind of the Torah's existence somehow and absconded with it."

"I don't think so," he says, shaking his head.

"Somebody knew it was at Anshe Amunim," I say. "That's obvious. And it's been there a while, right? A few years?"

"Five years, we've had it."

I take out my pencil and notepad. "And in all those years, you didn't advertise that fact, did you, Rabbi? You didn't have an interview with the *LA Times*? Nobody wrote a story for a magazine?"

"No," he says, "but we took our responsibility seriously. To keep it to ourselves. The whole congregation knew."

"All twenty-five of them."

"There were twenty-eight, but two families moved away. And another fellow, who lived all alone, he died."

"I'm sorry."

"Yes, well, you know. That's life. Death, I mean."

My eyes glance around the room. He has swaddled himself in books and human kindness. It feels like a sanctified place we're in. If he wouldn't buy the insider theory, there's not much point in telling him about a greedy oligarch in Russia. That's even more far-fetched; I'm not even sure I'd buy it now. "Tell me what you remember about the robbery itself. The people who barged in here, what'd they look like?"

He shrugged. "I've already explained this to the police."

"Yes, but I need to hear it, Rabbi. I'm not with the police."

A sigh. "There were two gentlemen," he begins, then immediately rephrases it. "Okay, not gentlemen. But two men, anyway. They both had blue sweatshirts on, the kind with zippers and hoods. Oh, and sneakers. One of them, I'm thinking, was Mexican. Or maybe Filipino. He was short, he looked strong, tough, you know what I'm saying? Like he works out in a gym."

"Just how'd you figure he was Mexican? He say anything?"

"No, not a word. But he wasn't a blond, blue-eyed Aryan, I'll tell you that. His complexion was darker. Black eyes, thick black hair, from what I could see. Okay, maybe not a Mexican. I could be mistaken. People are people. You shouldn't generalize, right?"

"Which one hit you with the gun?"

"The Mexican. I know because I was talking with the taller one. Well, not talking: I was yelling at him. I lost my temper, I guess, but who wouldn't, huh? I told him to take his hands off my wife. I didn't really get a look at the Mexican until I was down on the floor."

"Anything else you noticed about the way they looked? Did you hear an accent? Did they have any jewelry? Rings? Chains? Watches? Scars? Tattoos?"

"It happened so fast," Rabbi Josef says, with a dismissive wave. "I wasn't studying their faces. I was worried about Shayna."

"Of course you were. All right, what about the other fellow, then, the taller one?"

"Don't get me wrong. He wasn't a string bean, not extremely tall. Just taller than the other guy."

"How tall?"

"I'm five-six. He had to be what—? Five-eight, five-nine. And he did all the talking. It just seemed like he was the man in charge. He'd neglected to shave, I remember that. He had a couple of days' worth of beard."

"What color was his beard?"

"I don't know," the rabbi says. "Black? Gray?" His eyes light up. "Yeah, it was a little bit gray, I think, around his chin. Is that important?"

"Could be," I say. "It says something about his age."

"Good point," he agrees. He leans forward, rubs his fingers over his lips, looks at me intently. "You're a clever man, Mr. Parisman. The two policemen, when they were here, they never asked me about his beard."

I nod. He's a diplomat, this fellow. Clever. Praising me, while not openly attacking the LAPD. He knows how to manage alliances, or at least how to paddle on both sides of the canoe. That's what rabbis are trained to do, I guess.

"And you'd never seen either of these people before?"

"Never."

"But still, the taller one, the one who talked to you, he knew you had the Torah in the house?"

"Well," the rabbi says, "that's a question. In the house? Not in the house? Let's just say he wanted the Torah. And he knew we could direct him to it."

Shayna ambles in from the kitchen then. She's a sturdy, ruddy-cheeked woman—not unattractive, but not a raving beauty either. The word that comes to mind is *practical*, or maybe *capable*. A worker. I could see her handling a tractor on a collective farm. She'd look good in a babushka. She's about the same age as her husband. Unlike Harriet Reines, she hasn't dyed her hair or had any work done on her face. What you see is what you get. Sensible shoes, no lipstick or makeup, and, except for a thin gold chain around her neck with a star of David, she's not wearing any ornaments. She carries a plate of almond cookies.

"Imported from Israel," she says as she sets it down in front of us. "You didn't want my tea or coffee. So, try one, it won't kill you."

I take a bite of a cookie, it's delicious. I nod appreciatively. She purses her lips, settles into a plush maroon chair opposite us. "All right," she says, "now, what did I miss?"

"He was quizzing me once more about what happened," Rabbi Josef says. "He thinks it could be someone in our congregation. Someone we know. Can you imagine, Shayna?"

"I didn't say that," I say. "But the police probably think that. Which reminds me, have you given them a list of everyone who belongs?"

"They asked," he says. "They asked, and I'm preparing one. It may take another day or two."

"It's only twenty-five names," I say.

"Twenty-five names *plus* addresses," he corrects me. "And telephone numbers. Some of them have moved. Some of them use only cell phones now. It's a new world." He makes a little iffy motion with his shoulders, which suggests both that he's doing the best he can and that the new world is not for him.

"Tell me, Rabbi, do you happen to own a computer?"

"I bought one once, but I couldn't understand all the language they were using. Do this, do that. Jiggle the mouse. It gave me a headache, so I took it back to the store."

His eyes narrow then, as though I've touched on a difficult subject.

"The only reason I mention it is, you could keep track of your people that way. It wouldn't be that hard."

"He doesn't do anything *unless* it's hard," Shayna says. "He's a stubborn old man."

"I am not!" Rabbi says, louder than necessary, since she's only two feet away.

She beams at him. He glares. They've been married a long time. This is how they communicate.

"As I understand it," I say, "after your husband was knocked down, he told you to show them where the Torah was hidden."

"He was worried for my safety, yes. And it's true, they had guns. So, I led one of them—the tall one—up the stairs to our bedroom. I opened the cedar chest, lifted the quilt it was under, showed him."

"And what happened then?"

"What happened? He took it and left. Both of them just waltzed out the door. No, wait. First, he stuffed it back into the Trader Joe's grocery bag where I'd hidden it, then he waltzed out."

"What kind of bag was it?"

"Just a cloth tote bag, you know. With their label. I think it had a coconut on it, maybe."

"Okay. Can you describe the tall man for me? Was there anything special you noticed?"

She thinks for a second. "Yeah," she says. "He smelled bad. He had that smell, like an old cigar. My grandfather from Spain used to smoke cigars, and it stayed with him, it was hiding in his clothes, on his hands, everywhere."

"Anything else? Do you remember what color his eyes were? Did you see his hair?"

"He had a hood over his head, so I couldn't tell you much about that. He had light-colored eyes, blue or gray. High cheekbones. Oh, and he needed to shave."

"I told him that already," the rabbi says.

"He was talking to me," his wife replies. Again, she beams.

"And did the police ask if you could maybe describe these men for one of their sketch artists—whether you thought that might be worthwhile?"

"There was some discussion of this, but in the end we decided not to. It happened so quickly," she says.

The rabbi looks at me to remind me that he also said it happened fast. But this time he knows enough to keep quiet.

"Did you get a good look at the guns they were carrying? Could you tell me what they looked like?"

"I've just seen them on television," says the rabbi's wife by way of apology. "They all look the same."

I fold my notepad, tuck it into my jacket, and stand up. "Well, folks, I think that's about all I have at the moment. Like I said, there are a few possibilities we're following up on. You'll hear from me again. Meanwhile, I'd also like a copy of who's who at your synagogue, Rabbi. That is, when you get it together for the police."

"I'll try to finish today," he says.

I nod, head toward the front door, then stop. "Oh, one more thing. Just out of curiosity, how much did that Torah weigh? Do you remember?"

He cocks his head. This seems out of the blue to him. "They all weigh about the same," he says at last. "Twenty to thirty pounds. Like a small child."

CHAPTER 7

Carmen and Loretta are still sitting around playing gin when I get back to the apartment, though Loretta is obviously getting sleepy. She's holding her cards, but sloppily; she's yawning and leaning forward. You can see practically everything she's holding.

"I think maybe you should take a nap now," Carmen says, lowering her cards. She studies the scorepad in front of her. "Besides, you've already won."

"I've already won?" Loretta asks. Her eyes go wide. Even before she got sick, she always enjoyed it when she won. "So why are we still playing?"

"Exactly," says Carmen. "Come on, señora, let's get you into bed. Just for a little while, you know. And then, when you wake up, we'll have lunch. Grilled cheese."

She gently maneuvers Loretta toward our bedroom, cooing to her softly all the while, sometimes in English, sometimes in Spanish. They're like lovebirds, I think, as I take off my jacket and loop it on the wooden peg by the door.

I take Loretta's seat in the kitchen, which is still warm, and punch in the phone number for Pete Zaslow. "I've been homing in on the elusive Francis Crocker," I say. "And you're right, Pete, there's something strange about the whole operation."

"You talked to him?" I hear incredulity in his voice. Pete is what I like to think of as a theoretical sleuth; he analyzes all the possibilities, weighs what might happen in any given scenario, then he subtracts it from what couldn't possibly happen. But in the end, it's all in his head. He rarely if ever steps out of his living room.

"No, we haven't laid eyes on him. Not yet. He wasn't at his office in Thousand Oaks. But his secretary was kind enough to give me the address where he ships stuff out of. It's a warehouse. Not the classiest part of Inglewood. We visited the other night."

"And?"

"He wasn't there, either. Nobody was, in fact. But we had a good look around."

"Who let you in?"

I don't answer right away. Then I remember that Pete's a civilian. He lives by some moral code, that's for sure, he's as decent as the day is long, but he's not sworn to uphold an oath. "If you wanna know, we let ourselves in. It was after hours. What can you do?"

"That's very quaint," he says. "You let yourselves in. I'll withhold comment. But tell me, what did you find?"

"Apparently it's just like Crocker says, Pete: he ships herbal remedies all over the place. I had no idea there was such a market for that kind of stuff. I guess if you're sick and desperate, and Western medicine isn't doing the trick, Francis Crocker's little white powders might be your salvation. But we were hunting bigger fish."

"Such as?"

"You heard about the shoot-out at the synagogue, right?"

"It was on Channel 4 this morning. Too bad about the guard."

"Yeah. So, after that, the rabbi took the Torah home with him for safekeeping. And the very next night, two goons knocked on his door. They hit him with a pistol, threatened his wife. In the end he gave them what they came for."

"I see," Pete says. His voice has a measure of gravity in it now. "And you put two and two together and guessed it might have ended up in that warehouse."

"It was worth checking out, don't you think?"

"In a perfect world, yes. You could have gotten lucky."

"But we didn't. We looked just about everywhere, too. Nothing."

"Like I said before, this whole business with Kuznetsov and Francis Crocker, we're speculating here. They're both crooked, but they may not be the crooks you're after."

"I get that, Pete. Oh, one more thing: I found a list of people they'd shipped to on the day we visited. There weren't that many, but one caught my eye. A fellow named Armen Sokolov. Lives in Montreal."

"And?"

"Well, the reason I paid any attention to him was because all the packages they sent out had more or less the same weight—four to six pounds. Sokolov's weighed in at fourteen and a half."

"And you think that might have been the Torah?"

"No," I tell him, "no way. Your average Torah weighs twenty-five, thirty pounds. The rabbi told me. But Canada may not be monitoring things as closely as you guys do. And Dmitri could be moving other goods around besides art, right? I mean, there are all kinds of commercial products they're lacking in the old country."

"Definitely. Sokolov could be another way station on the road to Moscow. What's his address?"

I read off the street in Montreal, and Zaslow promises he'll check into it.

*   *   *

The next morning, I'm back at the Biltmore, sipping French press coffee and chatting with Harriet Reines. Well, I'm not chatting, exactly. This time she's let me into her private suite, which is pretty swank, if you like large modern hotel rooms with tall windows and heavy chintz curtains. I figure she's gonna be upset when I finally get around to why I've come, to explain how the Torah's gone AWOL. But she's on her third cup of coffee, talking a mile a minute, and not in any mood to listen.

"The security system will be installed this afternoon," she assures me. "Everything's settled. Cameras, sensors, new locks, the works. We won't ever need a guard again." She shakes her head. "That poor

Mr. Chandler. I feel so awful for him. And for his daughter."

Her secretary, Anna, paces back and forth in another room, talking in hushed tones on her cell phone. She's a wiry woman with a white frilly top and black pants. Short straight black hair that stops precisely just below her ears. Some kind of accent I can't place. South African? Australian? She has a small, well-shaped mouth and green-framed glasses that dangle from a chain around her neck. The glasses look expensive; in fact, every aspect of Anna looks more than I can afford.

"Chandler was a good man. I'm sure that when he clocked in, he didn't think that would be his last day on the job. Quite a surprise. But that's a gift, you know, in a way. To die like that."

"Yes," she says, and takes a sip from her cup. I doubt she has the vaguest notion of what I'm trying to say. Sure, she's a widow, but what's that mean? She's not familiar with all the many varieties of death. I go back to my time in the service. To what happened to Marco. He was on point that day. To be taken down by a single shot when you're just ambling through a rice paddy, and it's a beautiful Sunday afternoon and you only have one more week to go and Charlie's not supposed to be anywhere near and you're daydreaming about your girlfriend back in Ohio. Then boom! Just like that, it's over. That's terrible, of course, but not the worst. I've seen much worse.

"Unfortunately," I say now, "all that cash you've shelled out on security may be for naught, Mrs. Reines. Someone attacked the rabbi and his wife last night in their home. The Torah's gone."

"Oh, no!" she says, bursting into tears, and Anna, who had her back to us, swivels around suddenly to hear what's going on. "They're not hurt, are they? Tell me they're all right. Please."

"They're okay," I say. "A little shaken, you know, but they'll be fine."

She nods, reaches for a Kleenex to daub her eyes. "And they've talked to the police?"

"The cops are all over it, Mrs. Reines. They're hunting for DNA. They're lifting fingerprints they found at the rabbi's, comparing them with whatever was at the synagogue. They're pretty good with technology nowadays. Something will turn up before long." I say it all with a straight face, with perfect confidence. I say that, even though in my experience it's rare when they find a decent print and match it with the millions of prints they have on file. It happens sometimes in real life, sure; but mostly that's just the stuff you see on television. On TV, the crime is always solved in under an hour, and that's leaving plenty of room for commercial breaks.

"So where do we go from here, Mr. Parisman?"

"You want the truth? The truth is, we wait. I'm going to check in with Lieutenant Malloy to see what the forensics team has come up with. Also, I'm anxious to start eliminating suspects from the rabbi's congregation; but for that, we need a list of names and addresses. He keeps promising, but he's not exactly Johnny-on-the-spot."

"What about the cameras and sensors? Should I cancel? Tell them to wait?"

"No," I say, "I'd still go ahead with that. It can't hurt to have extra security. The Torah's gone for now, but that doesn't mean we won't track it down sooner or later. And in a sense, this is about more than the Torah. I'm looking at this as a hate crime."

"Well, you're right on that." This morning's *Los Angeles Times* is heaped at her feet. She reaches down, thumbs through it until she comes to the page she wants. There's a short article above the fold about the break-in and the death of Luke Chandler. The headline reads *Hate on the Rise in Hollywood*. No mention of the Torah, or why a two-bit little temple on Beverly with folding chairs would need a security guard in the first place, but that's okay. The reporter did a quick-and-dirty job; she only interviewed Lieutenant Malloy, it appears, and he was pretty tight-lipped.

My phone rings then. It's Omar. "Excuse me," I tell her, pointing to the phone. She doesn't seem to mind. I get up and walk off into another nearby alcove, which turns out to be a spare bedroom. Pastel walls and a small, tidy bed with lots of pink throw pillows on it.

"Hey, what's up?" I say.

"I've been walking the neighborhood," Omar says, "and I talked with a dude who owns a fitness center in the next block. He said that he's had a couple of run-ins with Leo Schmidt, the guy next door at Oldies but Goodies. You know, the thrift store. He says Schmidt has some pretty interesting ideas about Jews."

"Like what, for example?"

"Like he hates them. For starters, he thinks Jews have all the money, that they run the banks, newspapers, the movies, the federal government. Stuff like that."

"That's what Schmidt believes?"

"Yup."

"Gee, I wish to God he was right, Omar; I'd love it if we ran everything. The world would be a much sweeter place."

"Yeah, well, maybe," he says. "But the fact that he's talking that trash and he's just next door to the temple, and he was aware of the Torah being there—"

"He was?"

"You bet. Almost every merchant I talked to on the block seemed to know. They didn't all get how important it was, or that it came from Africa, or that it might be worth a lot of coin, but they knew."

"So much for keeping it a secret, I guess."

"Exactly," Omar says. "And we probably don't have to bother interviewing his congregation, do we? They're more likely to keep their mouths shut than these merchants are."

I tell him he's done good work, that now he should zero in on Leo Schmidt directly, feel him out. Maybe he had some specific beef with the rabbi, maybe Leo was trying to get back at the rabbi or the temple for some slight, some insult.

"Treat him gentle," I say before I hang up, "and don't let on that you've been hired to look into this. Just get him talking. Say you have some beef against the rabbi or the Jews who worship there. Or just Jews in general. You don't have to say much, especially if he already thinks like that himself."

"I can do that. I'll just close my eyes. Close my eyes and think of you."

"You're a funny guy, Omar. You are, you're sharp, like a whip. But just remember: I'm the one who's paying your salary."

"Hey, is that all you people ever think about?"

*   *   *

I do a leisurely drive past the rabbi's house on my way back from the Biltmore. There's a police cruiser parked out front, and a young uniformed officer sauntering up and down the block. His shoes are shiny, and he seems bored. Maybe he has a high opinion of himself and he thinks he's destined for better things. He also seems slightly uncomfortable—not accustomed to wearing so much weight around his middle—the leather duty belt with the gun, handcuffs, taser, extendable baton, gloves, and ammo. I'm guessing he's probably a rookie—first week on the job—and, for whatever reason, they're just breaking him in slowly. I could be all wrong about that, but still, that's what a detective is trained to do—take a quick look and make a guess.

The presence of this cop in front of the rabbi's also makes me suspect that Malloy is worried now, which he ought to be. The rabbi and his wife were witnesses. And given the brazenness of the last couple nights, the two morons who took the Torah might want to come back yet again, this time to eliminate them. *But don't call them morons, Parisman.* My guess (there I go again) is they're just working stiffs, hired to do a job; they have no real interest in the matter beyond getting paid for their services. I think back to how the rabbi described them. There was something extra brutal about how they arrived in their hoodies and pushed their way in the door, how they pistol-whipped the old man, shoved a gun in Shayna's face. Something low-life and excessive. They didn't need to terrorize them to get what they wanted. They could have been straightforward about it. But terror ended up being a big part of the show. Terror is the tool of novices and bullies, not professionals. My gut tells me these guys were out of their depth, that they may only have had the vaguest idea of what a Torah is. They were sent to do a simple mugging, and they felt like they had to show off, pull out all the stops.

I am brought back to the present as I approach, and one of the guards—a new guy I don't recognize—raises the barrier and waves me past the gate at Park La Brea. I make my way around through the maze of towers, find my assigned spot—the one marked 114— in the shadow of our building, and kill the engine. I find myself just sitting and staring. I know I should go inside, press the elevator button, and check and see how Carmen's getting on with Loretta— whether Loretta's up from her nap, whether she's cranky or in a sunny mood, whether Carmen remembered to give her her pills, whether Carmen fed her lunch, whether Carmen could use a break right about now. The irony is, she never takes one when I offer. Is that a cultural thing? Maybe she doesn't want me to see her slacking off on the job, maybe in her heart she has this unspoken fear that I'll fire her if she gets too relaxed, find someone who works harder. None of this is true, of course. Carmen is a Godsend and I'd run across a freeway to keep her if I had to.

Out of the corner of my eye, I spot Mr. Wu heading for the glass doors. Mr. Wu is my neighbor on the ninth floor. He's a quiet old bachelor. He looks to be in great shape, which may be because he doesn't own a car and walks everywhere. I suspect that English is not his first language, but that's hard to tell. In all my years here we haven't actually exchanged a complete sentence between us. It's always just, good afternoon, Mr. Wu, good afternoon, Mr. Paris- man. He's an enigma. I've never once set foot inside his apartment; but when I think about it, he's the closest thing I have to a friend around here. I roll down my window, give him a wave. He's carrying two hefty paper sacks of groceries, which I'm guessing he bought at Ralph's down on Wilshire. A bunch of carrots are poking out the top of one of them. His hands are full, so he can't wave back, but he nods graciously.

My cell phone rings right then. It's Malloy.

"Why'd you go by the rabbi's house this morning?" Bill asks. "It's not the normal way you go home."

"The rabbi? How'd you know that?"

"One of my men was on duty there. Took down your license plate. You slowed down, like you might be casing the joint. You looked suspicious, apparently."

"I am," I say. "I suspect everybody. Is that really why you called, Bill?"

"No," he says. "I wanted you to know the rabbi finally gave us his membership list. Twenty-four families. A grand total of ninety-six individuals."

"Any children there?"

"We counted ten under the age of eighteen."

"Well, you can eliminate them right away."

"Shit, Amos, we can eliminate the whole lot. Most of them are drawing Social Security. Two are legally blind. Four need a wheelchair to get around. And the rest probably wouldn't have the strength to lift a crowbar."

"What about the parents of the kids?" I say. "You must have some middle-aged dads there, right? They can't be decrepit."

He pauses, like he's running his finger down a sheet of paper. "Let's see here, we're talking about just three families in all. There's a produce manager at Gelson's on Sunset, one's a radiologist at Cedars-Sinai, and the last guy is with the DA's office downtown. I've actually met him a few times, in fact. His name is Cardozo. Sweet man, four children. Does a lot of pro-bono work. Whenever I see him I always tell him how tired he looks."

"He must enjoy that."

"No, he agrees with me. His kids wear him out."

Then I relate to him what Omar had told me, about how virtually all the merchants in the neighborhood were aware of the Torah's existence, which makes his list, or whatever he's holding in his hands, worthless. I also drop Leo Schmidt's name, the proprietor at Oldies but Goodies. "He's a possibility. It's all circumstantial, but you might want to do a deeper dive into him," I say.

"And why's that?"

"Well, number one, he's right next door. Number two, he's a big healthy guy. Number three, the word out on the street is that he hates Jews. I dunno, I guess we rub him the wrong way. Go figure."

"We interviewed him. Remo did, anyway."

"And what'd he say? Did he have an alibi the night Chandler was killed?"

"I don't know," Malloy says. "I'm not sure Remo asked him at the time. He was probably just hoping he'd witnessed something. I'll have to go back and check his notes."

"I'd do that," I say. "And then I'd talk to him a second time."

Malloy thanks me, says he'll do a follow-up. We're about to end, when I ask if he's learned anything new about Francis Crocker.

"As a matter of fact, we have," he says. "Wait a sec. Let me see where I put that report."

A few seconds later, he's back on the line. "Crocker, Francis James. He's had his fingers in a couple of pies. Fraud. Theft. Racketeering. Prosecutor couldn't make a convincing case for the racketeering, though. That was dropped before it ever went to trial. Crocker did do eighteen months in Chino. Released on good behavior six years ago. Clean since then."

"Tell me more, Bill. Who was the victim?"

"A company he worked for, called Orinoco. They're based in San Jose. They sell natural products from Peru and Colombia. Looks like Crocker was stealing from them on the side, then repackaging their products under his own label and selling them back to Orinoco's customers, only much cheaper."

"Clever lad."

"Not clever enough. Management suspected something was wrong, one of their staff spotted him loading up his van one night and followed him home. Later on, when the cops arrived, they found a whole shipping operation in his garage."

"Funny," I say, "that's what he's doing now in Inglewood. I mean, I don't think he's stealing the merchandise anymore, but otherwise."

"Clearly a man who loves his work."

"Yeah."

"What I don't understand is, why are you so interested in him?"

"Oh, I dunno, Bill. His name just popped up on the radar. A

friend of mine has this weird idea. He thinks it might not be a strictly local outfit that stole the Torah. Something that old, it could sell for a lot in the right market."

"I'm not sure I follow you, Amos."

Once again, my mind debates whether to tell him about Zaslow and his international conspiracies. They're not so crazy, I think; they're within the realm of the possible, but I know Bill Malloy. Not a fan of James Bond movies. He's a bricklayer, he works from the ground up, step by step. He needs clues. Tire tracks. Shell casings. If I tell him about Zaslow and his fancy friends in D.C., he'll roll his eyes.

"It's nothing," I say finally. "You know me, Bill. I was just pulling on a loose thread; I thought it might lead somewhere interesting. Let it go."

"Sure," he says, a little disappointed. Then there's a thunk and it's like he's distracted, talking to someone else. I hear a muffled back-and-forth conversation, and Malloy's voice saying clearly "Well, will you look at that," and all at once he's back on the line. "Guess what Jason just laid on my desk, Amos?"

"Is it heavy?" I ask. "It sure sounded heavy."

"Heavy enough," he says. "It's an MK25. The same kind that was used on Chandler. It's also—I don't know whether you follow this kind of thing—the official gun of the Navy SEALs. That might be important. They found it in a trash can on Alta Vista. Could be our break."

He sounds excited, and Bill Malloy doesn't get excited too often, so I let him go on. I don't rain on his parade, I don't snipe, I don't tell him what he likes to tell me—that there are a million loose guns in greater LA; that, if he wanted to, he could walk down any street in Watts or Compton or El Monte or Pacoima and come back with a loaded gun in fifteen minutes. Chances are it'd be stolen, of course, but so what?

"Could be," I agree, "but first forensics has to sink their teeth in."

"No question," he says, "and that's where it's headed—to the lab. I'm just thinking about proximity, Amos. It was right around the

corner from where the rabbi lives. And not that far from the synagogue. I imagine we'll hear before long."

"You'll let me know as soon as they learn anything, won't you?"

"Of course," he says. "Be happy to. Just as soon as you tell me
why you were so damn interested in Francis Crocker."

"It was a blind alley, Bill. Come on. Every detective makes a mistake now and then. Don't tell me you've never wandered down a
blind alley. You must have."

"I keep my nose to the grindstone, Parisman. You oughta try
it sometime."

CHAPTER 8

Shelly drops by unexpectedly with a couple of meatball pizzas from Mozza on Melrose. He also has a bottle of chianti tucked under his arm. "I was feeling nostalgic," he explains. It takes me a few minutes to figure out what's really going on: tonight is Ruth's book group and Shelly can't bear to eat alone. Loretta gives him a warm hug and we sit down, but she won't touch the meatballs, they're too spicy for her. She picks them quietly off the pizza, parks them on the side of her plate, and devours the cheese-and-tomato crust instead.

About three slices in, he turns away from Loretta and asks me how my career as a gumshoe is going.

"Oh, you know, Shel, up and down." He doesn't really want to know. Talking about my career is a cheap way for Shelly to feel good about himself. He has a substantial career—that is, he makes a substantial amount of money leasing and selling high-end cars in Beverly Hills—and though there's never any mention of it, I can see the wheels turning in his large bald head. His eyes are bulging and he's calculating and comparing his house in Bel Air, his six-figure income with mine. Somehow, mine never measures up. That's one side of Shelly. But there's another side, too. The other side is in love with my career, because deep down, ever since he was a kid, he's yearned to be a detective. The Hardy Boys and Nancy Drew, Sherlock Holmes, Lew Archer, Dashiell Hammett—he read everything the public library had to offer.

So I always have to take a step back when he comes in here bearing gifts. There's a huge imbalance between us, and I just need to listen: He's lonely. He pities me. I am so poor, after all. But somewhere deep down in his soul, he would dearly love to be me. It's complicated.

I tell him about the murdered security guard, the missing Torah. The Sephardic temple on Beverly.

"I didn't know there was one," he says. "Are they different?"

"Than us? Maybe," I say, "around the edges. I read somewhere that in some places—Yemen and Turkey—they slip their shoes off when they enter the *shul*, kinda like a mosque. I bet they don't do that here, though. And the Torah is the same as ours."

He nods, takes a swallow of wine. "What are the odds of you ever catching this guy?"

"Hard to tell," I answer. "People like to talk, you know, about committing the perfect crime. It's a great parlor game, right? And some crimes are never solved. But this one?"—I shake my head— "In my book, this ain't perfect. Trust me, whoever did this will get caught. It's just a matter of time. And luck."

"Luck?" The word lights him up. Like me, Shelly learned his poker skills sitting around the table with Uncle Al. Unlike me, he still believes he can win. "What's luck got to do with it?"

"Most human beings are slobs, cousin. They make mistakes, they leave little traces of themselves wherever they go. It can't be helped. For instance, the rabbi and his wife have a vague idea about what the thieves looked like. Yeah, they were scared, and everything happened fast, but if they see them again in a police lineup, who knows? Also, the cops now think they may have found the murder weapon. They're checking that out. That might lead them back to the person who owns it. Maybe it was stolen, maybe not. Maybe that guy knows something. It's a process."

"Yeah, but where does that leave you?"

"Me? I'm chewing on the other end of this. Why would anyone want a two-hundred-year-old Torah in the first place? What's the angle? And who'd want it so bad that he'd be willing to kill for it?"

"A collector," Shelly says. He lowers the slice of pizza he was about to put in his mouth, and starts pointing with his finger. "I once knew a guy like that, Ed Schumer, we worked the floor together when I was first selling Lincolns. He was all obsessed with salt-and-pepper shakers. You know those things? Little ceramic bunnies, and carrots and cucumbers, little clay gnomes, little plastic devils and angels, there's no end to them."

"I'm familiar."

"Yeah, well, in the beginning, his wife didn't mind. She thought it was a cute hobby. An extra salt shaker here and there? She was okay with it. But then every weekend he'd take off. He'd go out to flea markets and yard sales, come back with more. He couldn't stop buying them. After a while they were everywhere. The kitchen, the living room. Little by little they took over the house. It was . . . it was like a disease."

"So, what happened?"

"She left him," he says, throwing up his hands. "Had enough. Walked out the door one day and filed for divorce."

"Wow, that must have hurt," I say.

"I don't know," Shelly says. "He was pretty philosophical about it. I mean, he got to keep all the salt shakers."

*　　*　　*

The next day, I meet Pete Zaslow at Mijares in Pasadena for lunch. Mijares is a family eatery with a long lineage. It's got white plaster walls and red octagonal tile on the floor—and it's probably been around since the good old days when the Mexicans still ran California. They've upgraded it since I was last here, which was years ago. Now we sit out on the patio under an umbrella. The warm air feels good. There's mariachi music playing somewhere, and the waitresses are sweet and dark-eyed and efficient. Margaritas and chile relleno. I could get used to this, I think.

"Lunch is on me today, Amos. I wanted to thank you."

"For what? I didn't do anything."

"Actually, you did. You gave us Armen Sokolov's name and address. He's a good little handler for the other side. A critical link in the chain. At least he was."

"What do you mean 'was'?"

"The Royal Canadian Mounted Police paid him a visit last night. I guess he wasn't expecting them."

"They didn't happen to find a Torah there, by any chance, did they?"

"Afraid not. But there were all kinds of wonderful classified devices in his bedroom that at one time belonged to the U.S. Navy. How Mr. Crocker got his hands on them, we may never know; but they were boxed up—ready to be shipped off to Serbia."

"Serbia? What's there?"

"You mean *who's* there. Another link in the chain, like Sokolov. A man named Becic. We've known about him for a while, but we have to tread more carefully in that part of the world. Serbia is the Russians' back yard. We can't call in the Mounties. Not there."

"I see. So now they have to find another intermediary to do their business."

"Yeah," Pete says. "And that'll take time. They need to worry about how much Sokolov knows, how much he'll cough up to the Canadians. I expect a guy like Frank Crocker will be hard to locate once he hears the news."

There's a bowl of tortilla chips in front of me and I take one, then another. You can't eat just one, it turns out. "Wouldn't now be a good moment to bust him, then, before he takes off?"

"Bust him for what?" Pete asks. "You didn't find anything incriminating when you broke in the other night. There's still probably nothing worth looking at today. No, the best thing we can do is try to keep an eye on him. Like I say, I think he'll make himself scarce. But even if he doesn't, after what happened to his pal in Montreal, the Russians aren't going to hire him for anything important again. He's radioactive."

The waitress interrupts our conversation with platters of warm food, and we smile and dig in.

I tell him the cops found a gun they think might be the one used on the security guard, that it's an MK25, an automatic favored by Navy SEALs.

"That would make sense," Pete says. "The devices Sokolov was about to put in the mail probably came through them. So maybe we have ourselves a traitor. Or someone looking to make a little extra cash on the sly."

"Jesus, Pete, it sounds like I've been a gold mine for you today. Hell, I'm a goddamn hero."

He tilts his glass in a toast. His eyes twinkle. "You are, Amos."

"A cheap one, too. All you had to do was buy me lunch."

We spend the rest of the meal talking about our wives. Or, rather, I spend a whole lot of time giving him the latest on Loretta's condition, and he graciously listens and nods every so often. Part of me envies him that Muriel has nothing wrong with her, that she still goes to salsa classes and reads books and bakes amazing things in the kitchen. That she has a life. That they have a vibrant life together. And, of course, I'm sad about Loretta, that our time is coming to an end and we seem to be on the downward slope.

Pete signals our waitress. He orders two coffees and flan for dessert. *You like flan, don't you, Amos?*

The question rushes past me. I'm in another world and now I can't seem to stop talking. Dr. Gupta, Loretta's gerontologist, had some very hopeful things to say to us last week. She's always brimming with hope, that woman. Upbeat. They're publishing new studies in England and in Israel, she said. New drugs are in the pipeline. New therapies. She's excited for the long term. We could be on the cusp of a whole new age. Okay, that's possible. Anything's possible. You have to believe in the future, right? The future's our salvation. But I'm still not jumping for joy, I tell Pete. I see the way she is. I see how she is—and I remember how she used to be. It hurts. It breaks my heart, and it's as clear as day.

*   *   *

Malloy calls me the next night, says he's in my neck of the woods and asks if it would be all right if he came by. I tell him it's not a problem. After we hang up, I make a quick call to the security gate so they have a heads-up and know who to expect. They do everything by the book here at Park La Brea; it's one of many things that bug me about this place. There aren't a lot of secret visitors—guests need to be announced in advance—although Malloy could probably just flash his badge and that would be enough.

I have to credit Malloy on his timing. It's impeccable. The dishwasher is humming and I've just tucked Loretta into bed. She's had a long day; I figure she'll be fast asleep by the time he rings the doorbell.

Ten minutes later we're sitting in the living room. Bill is still in his tan business suit and blue silk tie; he had a late meeting with the captain, he says. That's one reason he's all dressed up, but the truth is Bill Malloy has always liked to look sharp, no matter what he is doing.

"You want something to drink, maybe?" I say. "It's a little late for coffee, but—"

"Oh, no, thanks," he says. "Coffee would just keep me pacing the floorboards at this stage of the game, and, as you know, my days of debauchery are over."

"I wasn't going to ply you with alcohol, Bill. I was thinking like, ice water, or, you know, ginger ale. Nothing too sexy."

"Ginger ale, then." He smiles as if it sparked a memory. "I haven't had that since I was twelve years old."

I get up, go to the refrigerator, and bring us both back a glass. I've been buying a lot of ginger ale at Ralph's lately; Loretta likes it, says it settles her stomach.

"So, to what do I owe the pleasure?"

"I wanted to let you know. We got the report back from forensics on the gun. It was the one that snuffed out Luke Chandler."

"No fingerprints, though, I don't suppose."

"No, it was wiped clean, but we did manage to trace it back to the owner. He's an ex-Navy guy—Lieutenant Junior Grade.

Richard Sykes."

"He wasn't a SEAL, was he?"

"No, but it's funny you ask: his last tour was at a special facility that taught them. Coronado, if I remember correctly. Says he bought the gun for protection when he quit the Navy."

"When was that?"

"I dunno. A year or so ago. He moved to West Hollywood to be closer to his mom. She was in a nursing home there. Then, three months ago, someone broke into his apartment on Sweetzer in broad daylight. That's when he reported the gun missing."

"You've checked all this out, I assume."

"He filed a burglary report. Listed the gun, among other things. And the mother was in a nursing home, yeah. She died last month."

"So that leaves us back where we started."

"Not quite," Malloy says. "There was a camera that caught sight of the burglar. It's a little blurry, but we froze the frame and enhanced it. Then we showed it to the rabbi and his wife. He confirmed it was the same guy who hit him that night when they came for the Torah."

"Great. But you still don't have his name."

"Actually, we do. His name is Marquez. Jesus Emilio Marquez, and he's been working the West side for the better part of a year. Often poses as a gardener or a janitor. Once he pretended to be a handyman. He always brings tools along."

"How'd you get his name?"

"That's the curious part. Last month, he came to an apartment complex over on Ogden dressed like a gardener. One of the tenants saw him fooling around with the sprinkler system. She got suspicious, told him the sprinklers were working just fine. He said well, that might be true, but that he'd been called out to do a job, and she said okay, she was going to talk to the manager later that day and she asked to see his driver's license."

"And he showed it to her?"

"Unbelievably, he did. What else could he do? His truck was just sitting there. And she wrote down his name, but nothing else."

"And you still weren't able to track him down with that?"

"No," Malloy says, "the address the DMV had for him was four years old and he's never been busted, at least not around here." He pulls out an enlarged duplicate copy of a driver's license from inside his jacket and hands it to me. Jesus Emilio Marquez. It lists an address on Lucretia Avenue in Echo Park. Hair: Black. Weight: 165 lbs. Eyes: Brown. The date of birth would make him twenty-six years old now. He has thin lips, a resolute jaw. Most young men, when they get their first driver's license, they smile. It's a happy occasion; they're free. Not him. He's staring straight into the camera, like he's trying to show you how macho he is, like, if you chose to, you could use this as his mug shot, no need to bother taking another.

"Can I keep this?" I ask.

"Absolutely. It's one of the reasons I came by."

Somehow, though, I don't believe it's the main reason he's here. He didn't have to make a special trip. This picture of Marquez is a peace offering, a tangible sign that he cares about the missing Torah, and he wants to help me with my end of the investigation. It's also a silent request for me to be a little more forthcoming about my sources.

I set the photo down on our coffee table. "You're making headway, Bill, and if you ever catch up with Marquez, maybe you can put this all to bed. But right now, if I were you, I'd do a much deeper dive into Richard Sykes. Lieutenant Junior Grade."

"Because?"

And that's when the dam breaks. I realize I'm never going to crack this case without his help, I'm in the wilderness. So I open up and tell him all about my friendship with Peter Zaslow. How he does consulting for certain people in Washington, D.C.—I don't wink when I say this, but he knows what I mean. I tell him Pete speaks several languages, how he travels in very special company. How not everything he says is accurate, but that it's often in the ballpark. A couple weeks ago I asked him to look into his crystal ball, to speculate on what kind of individual would fancy an ancient Torah. And Pete gave me Francis Crocker's name.

"Crocker is someone they have their eye on in Washington?" Malloy's eyes light up. "He's that important?"

"I don't know," I say. "In Washington, they think Crocker works for an oligarch in Moscow, Dmitri Kuznetsov, who has a dacha full of stolen art from all over the world. And Kuznetsov *is* that important. He's friends with Putin, he loves old things, and he has the money to pay for them. From time to time, Crocker also helps ship other stuff, vital information, I don't know what, to the Russian government. Part of a chain."

Malloy listens to my spiel. "Okay," he says when I stop, "I'm willing to believe that. But tell me, how does this connect to Richard Sykes?"

Now I'm really going out on a limb, and I hope he accepts my version of things and doesn't ask too many questions. "Omar and I visited this Crocker's warehouse in Inglewood," I say. "I got a peek at the shipping roster. Most of the addresses he sells to look legitimate—naturopathic doctors, health-food stores. But he also sends packages to other places, to a friend of his in Montreal, a guy named Sokolov. The day after I mentioned this to Zaslow, the Mounties raided Sokolov's apartment. They found some classified devices lifted from the Navy. Stuff only a SEALs team would use. It was all packed up nice and neat and set to be mailed off to Serbia."

"And you think they originated with Sykes?"

"One way or another, yeah. Sykes either gave them or sold them to Crocker. And now there's the pistol, which was probably Navy-issue and purloined as well."

Malloy doesn't speak for a while, but I can see he's thinking hard. On the one hand, what I've given him is circumstantial. On the other hand. . . "This is above my pay grade, Amos. We ought to be talking to the FBI."

"They may be aware."

"Did your friend Zaslow tell you they've been contacted?"

"No, but—"

"Then I'm going to call Chuck Costello right now."

I stand up. "Fine, then, go ahead." I leave Malloy in the living room while I go off to see how Loretta is doing. This could turn into a lengthy conversation, and he'll want some privacy anyway, I expect. Charles Costello is the FBI's point man here in Los Angeles. He gets interviewed when there's a bank robbery or a kidnapping, stuff like that. You don't call him unless it's serious. He doesn't know me from Adam, and Malloy has probably only met him once or twice.

Loretta has let all the covers slide off the bed. They're lying in a heap and now she's slumped like a pretzel with her face jammed between the pillows. I reach down to the floor, pull them over her, and tuck them gently around her shoulders. She grins. She whispers something unintelligible in her sleep. I sit with her for a while, then I plant a kiss on her cheek and tiptoe out, shutting the bedroom door.

Malloy is just finishing up with Chuck Costello. When he says goodbye, I give him an inquiring look. "So, nu? What'd he think? Am I crazy?"

"No, you're not crazy, Amos. He did wonder how you'd heard about Francis Crocker, though."

"You mentioned Zaslow, I hope."

"I did."

"And?"

"He said that explains it. Zaslow knows his way around spies and international banking and money laundering. It's not Costello's bread and butter, mind you, but they've spoken now and again. Anyhow, the Bureau is aware of Crocker. That's the important thing. They've been monitoring his movements."

"Monitoring? What the hell's that mean?"

"It's not round-the-clock surveillance. They're keeping tabs on him, is my guess. Off and on. They take his temperature, but they don't follow him everywhere. He spends a lot of time in South America, evidently."

"Right: that's his cover story, buying roots and herbs. When he's not busy trafficking in other things."

"Yes."

"Okay, forget about Crocker. What'd he say about Sykes?"

Malloy loosens the knot in his tie, tilts his head. "Aah. Now,
Sykes was news to him; they're going to follow up with the Navy."

"Terrific," I say. He gets my concern. And I can see in his eyes
that Bill feels the same. All these outfits do it differently. But his
tone suggests Costello may not be thinking of this as a three-alarm
fire. Maybe just another leak in the ship, and the ship already has
so many.

CHAPTER 9

The next morning, Omar is seated across from me in a booth at the International House of Pancakes on Wilshire. I've brought him up to speed on what's happened to Sokolov in Montreal. For a minute, I'd thought about keeping that information under lock and key; that's what Zaslow and his friends in Washington would have preferred. But that's not who I am. Omar's my brother, we've saved each other's lives, and I want him to feel like an equal partner in this; I also want him to realize our little adventure in Inglewood has now produced a tangible result—even if we didn't exactly plan on it, Sokolov's behind bars and heads are starting to roll.

Meanwhile, I'm pounding away on my French toast. There're two eggs over-easy and a waffle on his plate, but he's not touching it, just a mug of black coffee. Omar is working off a hangover from last night, when he went out dancing with his new girlfriend, Lourdes. Normally he doesn't drink much, but something about Lourdes excited him, gave him butterflies, and for some reason he felt impelled to perform. That involved downing an unspecified number of beers followed by a short fistfight.

He's not about to throw up, but there's no color in his face and his eyes are having a hard time focusing.

"You look just awful," I say. "I'd tell you to eat something, that was always my mom's advice, but I think I know how that would end."

"I'll be okay," he says, squinting. "Don't worry about me, I'll get through this."

"You got a headache, Omar? Want some aspirin?"

The question startles him. "You have aspirin?"

I lift a little yellow tin out of my jacket pocket and push it with two fingers across the table. "Doctor's orders. I keep them handy, just in case. Nothing's happened to my heart yet, but at this stage of the game you can't be too careful."

"Thanks, man," he says. He pries open the tin, removes four tablets, pops them into his mouth, and gulps his coffee.

"You only need two."

"I gotta headache, man."

"Yeah, but too many'll make your stomach bleed."

"I don't care."

"Okay, so let's forget about last night."

"Believe me, I'd like to," he says.

"What I want to hear about is Schmidt. You had a chat with him yesterday morning, right?"

"I went in just after they opened at ten. Wandered all around. He wasn't out front. The clerk there kept giving me the evil eye the whole time, like I was some kind of shoplifter. But I was dressed sharper than him. You shoulda seen this kid, Amos. Tattoos on both arms, heavy metal T-shirt, black jeans, Doc Marten shoes. He looked like he coulda been out shooting smack in an alley, and he was the one in charge."

"At least he had a job, Omar."

"Yeah, well, I wouldn't have hired him. Anyway, he told me the boss was out, that he doesn't come till noon, and he was just covering for him."

"So you left?"

"What else could I do? I said I'd be back, and after lunch when I walked in, sure enough, there he was, sitting behind the counter."

"And?"

"We got to talking. We were the only ones in the store. The kid was long gone, the clock on the wall was ticking, and Schmidt looked bored out of his mind, like he didn't have anything better to do. I mentioned reading about the murder next door, and he said 'Yeah, yeah, it was unfortunate, but even worse than that, it was bad for business. Customers stop coming around when someone dies. What are they afraid of?' Those were his words. He kinda meant it like a joke, but he was also serious. He's a big, heavy-set guy. Reminds me of some of the brawlers I used to go up against in Mexico. I'm not sure he knows how to tell jokes."

"So, what did you learn?"

"He didn't want to say much; I dunno, maybe he thought I was a reporter, but I just kept it light. At some point I brought up the rabbi, I asked him why they'd even need a security guard in a run-down place like that. And he said he heard they had a fancy Torah there, that it was probably worth a fortune. Then right after that, it was like he had turned some kind of key in the ignition and he started rambling all on his own."

"About what?"

"About Jews, what else? He said he's had dozens of run-ins with Jews. That he used to hate them, but not anymore. Now he's beyond that, he just feels sad. He told me they deserve whatever happens to them. Not because they killed Jesus or spread disease or control the stock market. No, that's crap. Jews aren't evil or grasping, he said; the problem is, they're stubborn: in two thousand years they never learned how to fit in. They have no sense of style. 'Style?' I said. I thought he was kidding. 'What the fuck does that mean?' And he said, 'Well, take the Torah next door. That's a perfect example. It's special. It's rare. Doesn't belong in a dump like that. No one wears pearls in a soup kitchen, understand? It's just not done.' And then he grinned, and shook my hand, and that was the end of it."

"Well," I say, "Leo Schmidt is a little bit more scintillating than I expected. But between you and me, he's just your garden-variety antisemite. He's got a big mouth, but I don't think he's our man. I've seen classier bigots at last call in some dive bar."

"So where do we go from here?"

I bite my lip before I tell him. He's not going to like it. Ever since his close encounter with the police when he landed in Boyle Heights, Omar leans more and more conservative. He's not afraid of anyone or anything, that's still not part of his genetic makeup, but he's cautious. "I want another crack at that warehouse in Inglewood."

"Oh, man, c'mon. We've been there, done that."

"True, but we never got into his office, remember. That was the one place we didn't search. Also, they've only just picked up Sokolov. I doubt very much whether he's had a chance to tip off his friends."

"So let me get this straight," Omar says, cupping his hands around the coffee mug. "What you're saying is that *if* Crocker stole the Torah—for which we have no evidence—and *if* he was still in the dark about Sokolov getting busted—about which, tell the truth, you have no idea—and *if* the plan all along was to ship it to him and not somewhere else—and that's just a fucking wild-goose-chase guess—then odds are it's still sitting there in Inglewood. Am I hearing you? Is that about right?"

I nod. "It's a long shot, I know. But what do you think?"

"You wanna know what I think? I think you're loco, man. That's a whole lotta ifs. And now you want to go break in there again and risk me getting killed? For what? For some stupid James Bond story your friend Zaslow told you?"

I lay down my fork, look him in the eye. "You don't want to come, Omar? Just say so."

"I don't want to come, no."

"Fine," I say. "I'll go by myself." I signal to the waitress for our check.

"You can't go there alone," he says. "You'll get hurt, pendejo."

"Hey, don't worry," I tell him. "I've got a pistol. I've used it before, Omar. I'll be fine."

The waitress drops our bill on the table, and I take out a couple of twenties and hand it to her. "You keep the change," I say. "My friend here is sure I'm gonna die before the day is out. He might be right. So go on, sweetheart, enjoy yourself."

She stares at me, delighted, but also confused. In her experience, the International House of Pancakes has probably never been much of a forum for weighty, life-and-death discussions, certainly not before 9 a.m. "Really? That's such a big tip!" And as she walks off, she turns back toward us. "I hope you enjoyed your breakfast. I hope . . . I hope you don't die."

Omar shakes his head and frowns at me. "All right, mother-fucker, you've made your point. I'm going with you."

* * *

We agree to take separate vehicles and meet at the warehouse at seven. I tell Omar I'm bringing my gun, and also my special tool for picking locks so he won't have to scamper up on the roof again. Omar doesn't own a gun, though I'm sure if he had to, he could score one in a hurry. It won't be getting dark until closer to eight, and chances are most, if not all, the employees will have left the building. I don't tell him what I'm really hoping for—that Frank Crocker will be there so we can finally meet in person.

I spend the rest of the morning playing checkers with Loretta while Carmen vacuums and cleans out the refrigerator. I would do these chores myself, but Carmen insists I don't know how, that men never listen and are hard to teach. I think she's telling me this in part because it's true, we do have lower standards of cleanliness. And yeah, we're set in our ways. But also because if she really allowed me to do what she does, she knows she'd be out of work before long. So, I give in and just sit and play checkers.

Loretta beats me pretty consistently. She really likes to win, she particularly enjoys it whenever she jumps my men; she says it's like riding a pony. I don't know what that means, maybe some kind of childhood memory playing out in her brain; but whatever, if it makes her happy, I'm good with that. We're wrapping up the last game when my phone rings.

It's Lieutenant Malloy. "Some good news," he says. "I thought you'd like to know that we found Marquez."

"Oh, yeah? Great! Where is he?"

"Well, right now, he's lying on a plank in the morgue. Somebody stuck him several times with a knife."

"Jesus! How'd you find him?"

"That's the curious part. He was in a parked car on Fountain near Tamarind. All hunched over the steering wheel, you know, face down, like he was sleeping off a bad night. It's a thirty-minute parking zone there, and one of our officers came by and was writing out a citation; she couldn't help but notice. Thing is, he wasn't just sitting there dead in broad daylight, either; that would have been bad enough. But the car—it's a brand-new Buick—was stolen. We were already on the lookout for it."

"Gee, it doesn't sound like they were trying too hard to cover their tracks, now, does it? I mean, you don't leave a hot car on a busy street like Fountain, not with a body inside. Not if you're thinking clearly."

"Maybe not," Malloy concedes. "Maybe his killer panicked, ran off. Maybe the sight of blood makes him squeamish. I could believe that."

"Or maybe he didn't care. Maybe he was making a statement."

"You think?"

I roll my eyes. "What about his wallet? He have any cash left? Credit cards?"

"That's the thing, the wallet hadn't been touched. Eighty bucks still inside, plus his driver's license, a Shell gas card, Triple A, all that. Even a ticket from a dry-cleaner over on Santa Monica. But it wasn't a stranger who did this, Amos. You can tell. Whoever did this wasn't after his money. This was emotional."

"Huh. So what was going on?"

"Hard to say. Whoever he was with—probably the same guy who helped with the Torah—his partner could have turned on him. Just snapped, something like that. But they at least must have known each other. It wasn't some hitchhiker he picked up. And we think it was the same vehicle they used when they grabbed the Torah. The Buick was taken from a lot on Olympic two nights before. That would fit with the timeline. We also found a little blue notebook on his body. He had a solid work ethic, this Marquez, very systematic. Kept a list of dates and apartments he'd knocked off. Like he was proud of what he'd done. Building a résumé. We found the rabbi's address on Formosa at the very end."

"But no Torah in the trunk, I don't imagine."

"No. Lots of blood all over the front seat. Cigarette butts in the ashtray, so someone was a smoker. Maybe they both were. Other crap, too. They ate a lot of fast food—French fries, burritos, plastic cups and spoons, that sort of thing. Whoever his companion was is sure to have left a few personal souvenirs behind. Forensics is working it. We're hoping, anyway."

"Okay, Bill. You've got a suspect now, even if he's no longer with us. That's not *bubkes*. But we're still short on a motive."

He pauses there. "Both these guys were hired hands. That's how I read it. Marquez, at least. He had no background in fine art, stolen relics. He liked whatever sparkled. Rings and watches. Also cameras, computers, stuff he could move quickly on the street."

"What about his partner?"

"Him, we don't know about, not yet. He might turn out to be more sophisticated. That's for the scientists. It's one stone at a time. That's how we work."

I remind him gently of Francis Crocker and the Russian connection.

"Tell me," he asks after a long considered silence, "what does your friend Omar think of that idea?"

"Omar? He's like you, he's not thrilled with it. He thinks I'm a *luft-mensch*."

"What's that?"

"A cloud person. A dreamer. Actually, he said I was crazy. Kinda hurt my feelings for a second."

"Well," Malloy says, "he shouldn't have done that. That was inappropriate. Maybe cruel. But if you ask me, he's right. You are a dreamer."

*   *   *

I pull up a little before seven and park in the lot, which, in the deepening shadows, is already looking desolate. Just two other cars in a space the length of a football field. The neon lights are still flickering inside the warehouse. Gramercy Appliances and Ortega Office Supply are dark. Omar Villaseñor's black Camaro, the pride of Boyle Heights, is nowhere to be seen. I sit for a minute or two, pondering. I could wait for him. In fact, I probably *should* wait for him, that would be the smart thing, the prudent thing to do. But of course that's not how I roll. I did tell him I could handle this matter on my own, didn't I? I wasn't bluffing.

Looking back, I wonder, was I always trouble, even as a punk kid? Even from the beginning? My grandmother, she used to yell at me, called me a *paskudnyak*. A rascal. Maybe she knew what she was dealing with. Maybe that's where I got this confidence in my ability to land on my feet. There was that summer day when I was six or seven, when me and Shelly found an abandoned baby carriage in the alley behind my house, and just for fun we lit it on fire. Sure, when my dad got home we both caught holy hell for doing that, but we survived. Thing is, I'm not a little punk anymore. Why do I keep acting like one?

I climb out of my Honda, stop for a moment to check the safety on the Glock in my shoulder holster, and amble slowly toward the entrance.

A muffled conversation is going on inside. I twist the knob, the door swings open, and there are two Latinas in tight blue jeans and sweaters. The one nearest to me is short and sturdy, more no-nonsense; but in this shadowy, industrial setting they sort of look alike. She might be the mom, I think. Or she might be the older sister. She's taping bubble wrap around a bottle of capsules and stuffing it, making sure it fits snugly into a mailer. The other one is pouring some kind of liquid from a gallon jug into a row of smaller vials, using a red plastic funnel. There are maybe a dozen vials set in front of her, and she's been going from one to the next, pouring like a pro. She's on the last bottle. The minute they sense my presence, they both stop and look up, startled to see me.

"Oh, hi," I say. "I'm glad you're still open."

"We're not open," the one who was pouring liquid corrects me. She lowers the gallon jug she's holding. Her dark eyes narrow. "Not to the public."

"Oh, I realize that," I say, and, to underline the purity of my intentions, I toss in a smile. "Sure. But I just came by, you know. Spur-of-the-moment thing. I was hoping to see your boss. Mr. Crocker? Is he in?"

She glances over anxiously at her sister or her mom, whoever, as if looking for permission, then tilts with her head toward the back room, the place Omar and I never managed to search. "He's in his office," she says. "We're just about to leave."

"That's okay," I say. "Don't let me stop you. I won't take up too much of his time."

They nod. I can't tell what they're thinking—whether I've scared them by barging in like this, or whether they've collectively decided this is none of their business. They quickly organize their boxes and bottles, get ready to start again tomorrow. Then they walk around, flip off the three sets of lights illuminating the merchandise, but deliberately leave the last one on over the shipping counter. I watch as they grab their jackets and purses and make for the exit. They don't say goodbye to me. That I can understand. But I'm struck that they don't say goodbye to their boss, either. Maybe he's hard to work for; maybe there's not much love lost between them.

I wait a few seconds until their footsteps fade and the room grows quiet. Then I knock on the door, the one that's plastered with the map of Brazil.

A plainly irritated man's voice inside says, "Yeah? What is it, Luisa? You want something, come in."

I push open the door, and he glances up from the muddle of his desk.

"Who the hell are you?" he says. "Who let you in?"

"No one," I say, with as much pleasantness as I can summon. "I let myself in. The two girls out front told me where I could find you. You're Francis Crocker, am I right?"

He stares straight at me, trying to size me up. He's shorter than I expected somehow, at least that's how he appears, coiled behind a desk as he is. *Diminutive* is the word that comes to mind. Pale blue eyes that might have been considered cute once upon a time when he was a baby, but not anymore. A face that's tanned, weary. North of forty, but probably south of fifty-five. Still in the game. He's got on a blue Henley shirt with both sleeves bunched up almost to the elbows. A sporty wristwatch. His blond hair is thinning, and there's a filtered cigarette burning in a nearby ashtray. In fact, there are the remnants of several cigarettes in the ashtray, and his desk is a nightmare: manila files, receipts, legal pads, pencils, leftover paper plates and cups from takeout eateries. I get the distinct sense he doesn't much like his work: this part of it, anyway—that he feels trapped in this shabby box, that he'd do anything to be outside, hiking around in the verdant rainforest. I could be wrong about that, first impressions being what they are, but I don't think so. There's an old ceiling fan spinning slowly overhead. I take a quick survey of the tiny room. If there's a Torah stashed in here, I have no idea where it could be.

I ask him again if he's Francis Crocker.

"Who wants to know?"

"My name's Parisman, Mr. Crocker, Amos Parisman. I tried to visit you a few weeks back at your office in Thousand Oaks. You weren't available."

"I'm on the road a lot."

"Yeah, so I've heard. South America. Never been there myself, it must be lovely." The door is wide open. I point backwards with my thumb at the white cardboard boxes stacked on metal shelves. Even in his office, even with the fan, the smell from the other room permeates the air. I don't know how to describe it. Sweet, but dense. Like standing in a bog after a heavy downpour. "Is that what you bring back? Roots and herbs? Strange potions?"

He frowns. He's not quite as wary anymore. I'm obviously another dolt who needs enlightenment. "Western medicine has a lot to learn from Indigenous people. We throw billions of dollars at cancer and heart disease, we put up huge hospitals, research centers. We think if our scientists would just work a little bit harder, maybe someday they'll come up with a cure."

"And sometimes they do."

"They come up with treatments," he replies. "Their business is buying time. They postpone the inevitable. I wouldn't call that a cure. I call that hubris."

"And your Indigenous friends, they know better? Is that what you're saying?"

He shrugs. "They look death in the eye. They take what's available from the natural world, whatever the forest has to offer. It's all a gift to them. They're grateful." He leans back after his little lecture, and once again his face hardens. Francis Crocker may be doing God's work, but he's not a happy man, I think. There's a yawning gap between what he has and what he wants. "You still haven't told me what you're doing here. I take it you didn't come to buy."

"No," I say. "No, those Western doctors still keep me tied up in knots. I'm actually here to talk to you about one of your customers. A Canadian named Sokolov."

"Who?"

"Armen Sokolov? Lives in Montreal. I noticed him on your shipping log. He's a regular, which, to me, is kinda curious."

"And why's that?"

"Well, I mean, you have to figure that a guy like you sells almost entirely to naturopaths and new-age pharmacies. I get it, I do, they're your audience. You need each other. But Sokolov? He's a different animal. First off, he's not in the drug business. Just a private citizen. Second, he lives what—? Thousands of miles away in the frozen north. And still he shops here. Now what does that tell you?"

"I don't know," Crocker says. He scratches the side of his head. He doesn't know what to make of my intrusion, but he's also not ready to be combative. "What does it tell *you*?"

"It's gotta be one of two possibilities," I say. "He's either insanely loyal, or he just doesn't fit. That's your choice. By me, he's a misfit." I'm looking steadily at him. I'm sure I've upset him, but his expression hasn't changed one iota, and his hands are still where they were, still visible on the desk; he may have a pistol sitting in the top drawer, but he's not reaching for it, not yet.

"And just what were you doing, snooping around, looking at my shipping log? I—I don't understand."

"Yes, you do. Granted, I probably should have asked your permission first. That was rude. Sorry about that."

"Who are you?" he asks. Now his blue eyes are squinting at me. I've trampled on his turf, I've crossed the line and he's plainly offended. "Let's stop this little dance, shall we? Are you a cop? Is that it? I like to know who I'm talking to."

I smile. "You're close, Crocker. I'm an investigator. But you want to know why I'm here? It's like this: I got a phone call the other night from some friends of mine north of the border. They've been watching Sokolov, these folks, shadowing him around, filming him, you know, from a discreet distance. Well, that gets old after a while. Finally, they threw up their hands, said enough's enough. So they paid him a visit. And guess what they found?"

I hold it right there. I wait, let him fill in the blank.

He doesn't answer. His lips are pursed.

The silence grows deafening. This would be a perfect time for him to lose it, to reach into his top drawer. But his hands stay poised where they are. We stare at each other. I don't mind telling a fib or two about my friends north of the border; I don't have any, of course, but it's always better to imply you aren't alone, that you have allies waiting in the wings. Sometimes you have to embellish things to get to the truth. And sometimes you have to keep talking, just to stay alive.

"Now," I continue, "I don't know what's wrong with him exactly. I'm not a doctor, but I have to tell you, Francis, that stuff you've been shipping him? The stuff they found in his apartment?" I shake my head disapprovingly. "Number one, it's not organic. And number two, it's not doing him any good. Not from where he's sitting in his jail cell."

He sneers then, lifts his hands in mock surrender. "What do you want from me, Parisman? You're not a cop, so you're not here to arrest me. You come barging into my place of business spouting all this bullshit. I don't appreciate it when someone threatens me like that. It's a two-way street."

"I understand."

He sighs. You can't get mad at someone who wants to meet you halfway, who says he understands, can you? Anyway, it seems like, for the moment at least, we've reached a strange kind of truce. "I don't need to tell you this," he starts, "but for your information Mr. Sokolov suffers from anxiety and depression. For years now, we've been sending him a tonic called Pusangade Motelo. It's not illegal, but it does have certain psychotropic qualities. Some people claim it makes them happy. Nothing wrong with that, is there?"

"No," I say, "guess not."

"He claims it's the only substance that lets him lead a normal life. That's what we send him. I don't know what your friends in Canada discovered at his house. I don't know, and, frankly, I don't care. It has nothing to do with me."

He pushes his chair back from the desk and stands. He looks me in the eyes one more time, as if to say *I'm through talking.* "Now, if you don't mind, I'm going to lock this joint up and go home. It's been a long day. You know how to find your way out, I'm sure."

I lay my business card down in front of him. "Thanks for the time, Francis. You've been real helpful, and I didn't mean to come on so strong. I'm sorry about that. It's just, well, in my world you meet all types."

"I suppose," he says. He could clearly not care less about my world. He reaches behind him for his tan sports coat and slips it on. I can feel his eyes watching me as I leave.

Outside, in the parking lot, I spot Omar waiting in front of his car. He's wearing a leather jacket and running shoes. He looks like he's dressed for a fight.

"You were in there a long time, amigo. I was about to go in and rescue you."

"I'm glad you didn't, Omar. Mr. Crocker didn't care much for me. He probably wouldn't have been too keen on you, either."

"You learn anything useful?"

"Just that he's a capable liar, which doesn't surprise me. Listen: he'll be walking out the door in another minute or so. I'm gonna make myself scarce, but I'd like you to tail him home. I tipped him off that Sokolov's been busted, which I'm sure will send him scurrying every which way."

"You told him? What for?"

"He'd find out before too much longer. But now I've set off all kinds of alarm bells in his head. He doesn't know whether to believe me. If he does believe me, he doesn't know what Sokolov's told the Canadians. What they've already passed along to the folks at Langley. Right now he's scared. I mean, I walked in, out of left field. If *I* know about him, who else does? Who's watching him? People do weird things when they're scared. They make mistakes. This may be our chance."

CHAPTER 10

I still have that photocopy of Marquez folded up in my side pocket, and so, on my way home, I drop in on the rabbi and his wife. It's possible that Malloy or one of his people has already been here to verify, but maybe not; the LAPD is not unlike any large bureaucracy. Different people are in charge of different things, and it's not out of the ordinary for small details to get lost in the shuffle.

Tonight is a warm night. There's a cop in shirtsleeves barring the door, a big, burly fellow I don't recognize whose name tag reads McCollum. I show him my investigator's license, tell him I'm also working on the case of the stolen Torah, that we are brothers, but apparently that's not good enough for him.

"I gotta call inside, see if they feel like talking to you," he explains. He punches up their number, gives my name, and nods several times.

"Okay," he says finally, standing aside, "you can go ahead and ring the bell."

"Thanks," I say, and do as he instructs.

A minute later, I'm sitting in a BarcaLounger in their living room and Shayna is bustling around, straightening the pillows, picking up a stray newspaper from the carpet, saying she knows it's late but asking would I like some tea. "Herbal tea? I've had it at three in the morning and you still go right back to sleep. It's a miracle."

"No," I say, "I just have a few more questions for the two of you.

Then I'll be headed home myself."

She joins her husband on the couch. They weren't expecting company this time of night, that's plain to see; they're both wearing ordinary house clothes: he's in an oversized T-shirt and sweatpants, barefoot. Not your standard rabbi attire. She's got an old yellow housedress on, just a rag, really, a *schmata*, as we used to call it, and a pair of cheap but well-loved slippers. I pull out the photo of Marquez.

"First of all, I'd like you to tell me if you recognize the guy in this picture."

The rabbi takes his reading glasses from the side table, pulls the photo close to his face. "Maybe," he says. "It looks a little like the one who hit me on the head, but he's so much younger here. I dunno, could be his kid brother."

Shayna also looks. "That's him, no question. I can tell by the eyes." Then she reads the fine print underneath. "Marquez, Marquez. What is that, a Spaniard?"

"My guess is he's Mexican," I say quietly. "But don't worry. He won't be bothering you anymore."

"He's been arrested, then?" the rabbi asks, with undisguised hope.

I shake my head. "No. Unfortunately, somebody stabbed him."

They are both startled and disheartened. Which doesn't surprise me, frankly. As a rule, Jews don't jump up and down with glee when their enemies die.

"Oy," the rabbi says. He rubs his forehead.

"So young," Shayna says. She gives me back the photograph and, with great effort, pushes herself up off the couch. "I'll bring tea. The water's boiling."

Rabbi Josef reaches out and lays his hand on my arm. "I have to admit, I don't envy what you do for a living, Mr. Parisman. You must carry a great deal of pain on your shoulders."

"It's different than what you carry around, Rabbi. But sometimes I get to see what justice looks like. That makes it worth it."

Shayna sets the tea down in front of me—even though I've told her no. There are three heavy glass mugs, each containing a bag of Lipton Decaf—not exactly the "miracle herbal tea" I had envisioned. We talk about the case. I ask her again about the man who went upstairs with her and retrieved the Torah. She has little to add, except to say again that he smelled like an old cigar. Did he say anything to her up there? Not much, she says. He was in a hurry. He pushed her a little bit up the stairs and she thought she might slip and fall, but then he caught her, so she was grateful for that.

They are relieved to have a police presence outside their door. The rabbi has had a long conversation with Officer McCollum, mostly about his religious upbringing, and Shayna's been plying him steadily with jelly doughnuts and coffee. I tell them that Lieutenant Malloy is confident that forensics will turn up some fresh leads from the Buick where they found Marquez. It's amazing what they can do in a lab these days. I don't say a word about Frank Crocker and the connection—if there is one—between an oligarch in Moscow and the lost Torah from Algeria. Sitting here with them in their dowdy clothes in the warm glow of the living room, all that seems like a giant red herring.

The rabbi asks me what *shul* I attend.

"I don't belong anywhere," I say. "My problem is, when it comes right down to it, I don't believe in God."

As soon as I say that, I realize I've opened up a giant can of worms. He's going to be upset, I think, but instead Rabbi Josef nods. "I know just what you mean. There are moments in the day when—I can't help myself—I don't believe in God either. Or at least I question His behavior. He's a strange man, God. Why would He give us that Torah, for example? Are we more deserving than those rich Jews on the west side of town?" A shrug of the shoulders. "And then, out of the blue, why would He come along and snatch it away from us? And really, what kind of God would let someone be murdered in our temple? Where's the compassion? Was it something we did? Something I did?"

"That's where I am too."

Again he nods. "Okay, so I'll let you in on a little secret, Mr. Parisman," he says, almost in a whisper. "This is the good news we don't talk about nearly enough. Nowhere in Judaism is it written that you must believe in God."

"You're kidding," I say.

"No. The Torah asks you to *love* your God with all your heart. Love. That's not the same." He points to his wife. "I love my Shayna with all my heart. Still, we fight occasionally, we argue. Tell me a couple that doesn't. She's a terrific person, a fair cook, too, but she's no Jacques Pepin, she gets it wrong now and then."

Shayna glares at him, sniffs, shakes her head. Her husband, the rabbi.

"So it's not about belief?" I say. "I don't get it. There have to be some requirements. Some hoops you want me to jump through."

"Oh, there are, sure. All sorts of requirements. But God doesn't require you to believe. I mean, for the sake of argument, let's say He exists, whether we believe or not, right? But I think He'd really appreciate it if you just sat down and talked to Him. Argued with Him, even. Wrestled with Him, you know, the way Jacob did in his dream. We make a mistake when we put God far away, up in the sky. In my opinion, God's a lot like you and me: He gets lonely sometimes."

* * *

I phone Harriet Reines, just to let her know I'm still on the case. Her assistant picks up and lets me know that Harriet is busy at the moment, but she'll give her the message, not to worry. I want to tell her "Hey, lady, I'm not worried; it's Harriet's money I'm spending." I want to tell her many things. In the end, though, I just hang up. It just doesn't sound like I'm much of a priority. Whatever, it's fine.

Once upon a time Malloy had given me the name of the dry-cleaner Marquez used on Santa Monica—from the pink slip they found in his wallet. And out of habit, I'd jotted it down in my trusty little notepad. But I didn't think any more about it until this morning, when I spilled some coffee on my shirt. It's a place called Jake's Magnolia, just a stone's throw from the new Gelson's supermarket, and technically it's in West Hollywood, which is a whole different universe, but never mind.

I pull up in their rear parking area and wander in through the back entrance. There's classical guitar being piped through the ceiling; a petite Asian woman in a silk blouse and high heels is waiting on a scruffy customer in shorts, sandals, and a Hawaiian shirt; she has straight shiny black hair and she's making some kind of joke while she processes his credit card. The entrance area is cool, serene; there's a porcelain bowl filled with tiny purple and yellow flowers. But this place is also not far removed from the Industrial Revolution: there is a constant clatter of the rotating coat rack overhead, and thick, unrelenting heat pouring from the machines on the other side of the counter where she's working.

When the guy in the Hawaiian shirt saunters out, I step up. I pull my investigator's license from my wallet and flash it at her. I do it very quickly, so she doesn't get a good look, just sees something official. "I'm interested in this man," I say, matter-of-factly, as I unfold the picture of Marquez and set it down before her. "Goes by Marquez. Jesus Marquez. We believe he brings his laundry in here. What do you think?"

She looks at me, a little disconcerted. This is different. This is not about removing wine stains or altering waistlines, not the kind of chatter she's used to. She studies the photograph intently. "I know him, yes. But his name is Juan, not Jesus. He comes in almost every week. Juan Guerrero. Nice man. Hard-working man. I think he might be a gardener. He's always whistling, happy. I remember telling him I can't do that, I never learned to whistle, and he said he'd teach me someday." Her brow furrows and she fingers the ends of her hair. "Is something wrong? Is he in trouble?"

"We want to talk with him, is all. You don't have any idea where he might live, do you? An address? Any way for us to get in touch?"

She wags her head no. "Customers come and go. We don't have detailed records. Just their name, the date they drop it off, what's involved. We give them a ticket, tell them when they can come back. That's Jake's policy. Keep it simple."

I nod, retrieve the photo, fold it up again nice and neat, and slide it back into my jacket. "Well, thanks for your help." I turn on my heel to go, then remember something else. "This buddy of yours, Juan Guerrero, he's a heavy smoker, yes? That must add up to a lot of extra labor at your end."

"Oh, yes," she says. "Cigarettes and cigars." She makes a sour face to underline her contempt. I'm sure she thinks nicotine belongs in the third circle of hell. "It's just awful. "We have to steam-clean every piece he brings us. And it's the same with his friend, too. Just between you and me, *his* clothes are even worse than Juan's."

"His friend?"

"Yeah, I don't know if they live together or anything, hey, this is Hollywood—it's none of my business—but they come in together sometimes with their bundles and drop them off."

I lean in on the counter. My interest level has suddenly climbed up to ten. "So, tell me," I ask, "does Juan's friend have a name?"

She takes a step back. "You're looking for him, too?"

"Not particularly. But he might be able to tell us how to find Juan."

"Oh, right, I get it." She gives me a conspiratorial wink, like she's familiar with all those cop shows on television. She knows the way we work. "He calls himself Bart. But his Visa card says Bartholomew. Bartholomew Pereira. I can see why he shortened it to Bart. Isn't that from a Dr. Seuss book? I mean, these days you laugh when you meet someone who goes by Bartholomew, don't you?"

"Definitely. You could die laughing."

*   *   *

Omar phones an hour later. His voice sounds weary. "I know I should have called you earlier," he admits. "Lo siento mucho, señor, but it was late when I got home, and then Lourdes wanted to talk with me. Man, she likes to talk. I didn't end with her until almost midnight. I figured you'd be fast asleep by then. So anyway, here I am."

"That's okay, never mind. Did you follow our Mr. Crocker?"

"I did. But he doesn't live anywhere near there. Not only that, he didn't go directly home. I tailed him to a Peruvian restaurant on Vine, a place called Los Balcones. He spent a lot of time there eating."

"Alone?"

"All alone."

"Well, I hope you ate something, too."

"Nope, I just sat at the bar. They make tasty drinks, but I had to keep a lid on it, in case he decided to leave."

"Where'd he go after that?"

"Home," Omar says. "I mean, I guess it's his home. 1843 North Cherokee. A nice set of older apartments. Lots of palm trees and bushes out front. He drove in through the gate. I couldn't follow, but I'm sure we can find out which unit is his if we walk in there."

"What's he drive?"

"It's a Mini Cooper. Blue and white."

"That's terrific, Omar. We're closing in on this."

"Why? Just because we know where he lives? What the hell does that do?"

"Well, I'm sure he didn't send the Torah off to Montreal. It would have shown up in his shipping log as something heavy—twenty, thirty pounds. And it's not still at the warehouse in Inglewood, we've already established that."

"So now you think he's got it stashed away in his apartment?"

"That's a possibility. Something we ought to check into, at least. See, the problem is, right now he's in a bind. He has no way to send it to Moscow without Sokolov's help. Their supply chain is broken. And if it's at his house, it's a hot potato. He's going to need another place to store it, that's for damn sure."

"You want me to keep tagging after him?"

"You could. But I'm going to talk to Lieutenant Malloy in a bit, see if he can't spare some people for that chore. I mean, you and I pay his salary, don't we?"

After I put down the phone, I sit in the kitchen and nurse my second cup of coffee of the morning. Now I'm thoroughly awake.

Loretta, though, has nodded off on the couch, for which I credit the warm pink blanket I've tucked her under and how stupefied she must have finally become, watching today's episode of *The People's Court*. I've sat through a few of these ridiculous cases, and ten minutes in, I swear to God, I'm ready to heave a brick at the TV. Not Loretta. She has a wonderful tolerance for the misery and short-sightedness of human beings; she's attracted to folks who aren't perfect, to the young man who couldn't find the rent money because he lost it accidentally in a poker game, to the woman who forgot her solemn promise to feed a neighbor's pet snake while he was away on vacation. She understands their predicament. I think that's because somewhere inside, even though she's lost a step or two, she doesn't believe she has an illness. She doesn't want to admit she's not the same person she always was, that things have changed irrevocably and it's beyond her control. If she could set her hand on a Bible and testify, she'd probably say that what she has now is no different than the failings of those ordinary plaintiffs and defendants shuffling in and out of court. *I'm not sick, your Honor.* That's what she'd say. *I'm like them. It's just a flaw, an error in judgment. I made a mistake. Everyone makes mistakes, right?*

I call Malloy on his private cell. "I've got a name for you, Bill. You're going to thank me when this is over. You might even want to take me out to lunch."

"Sure, sure," he says, brushing me off, "what do you got?"

I tell him about my morning at Jake's Magnolia. That Jesus Emilio Marquez might very well be the handle he went by at DMV, but down at the West Hollywood dry cleaner, where a man's word is his bond, he's Juan Guerrero.

"In case you forgot," Malloy says, "Marquez isn't the guy we're looking for anymore."

"No," I tell him, "of course not. Marquez, Guerrero, whoever he was, is dead. It's his partner you want."

"And what about his partner?"

"That's what I have, Bill. His name, according to my friend at the dry cleaner, is Bartholomew Pereira." I spell it for him.

He is silent for a minute. Maybe he's scribbling it down on a pad somewhere, or pushing it over to Remo or Jason, who are always hovering over him. But when he comes back, he's all business. "You don't also have an address, do you?"

"Sorry," I say, "that's all I've got."

"That's all right. For now, a name's enough. We'll find him."

I tell him I hope he'll keep me in the loop. He says he'll think about it.

"One more thing, Bill. A small favor you could do for me, maybe."

"You mean, to pay you back for Pereira."

"No, no, not at all. Pereira's a gift. But in fact, you'll see, when you weigh it all out in your mind, you'll really be doing yourself a favor."

"Oh, well, since you put it like that," he says, with a whiff of sarcasm, "how can I refuse? I mean, of course I can refuse. I can't do anything that's not in line with regulations, you understand. I'm just a public servant."

"Exactly. A public servant. And who pays for public servants? Taxpayers like me."

"Okay, Amos," his tone changes. "You've buttered both sides of the bread. Now tell me what you want."

"Francis Crocker. If you could watch over him for the next week or so, I'd be much obliged."

"Surveillance costs money," he says. "It's a big fucking deal. Why would I do that?"

"Because I'm convinced he's part of this *mishegas*. He took that Torah. Or Marquez and Pereira took it on his say-so. That's what it looks like. And as soon as he gets another safe connection back, I know he's going to send it straight on to Russia."

"You're convinced, huh? Based on what? What Zaslow told you?"

"Zaslow's not wrong, Bill. The Russian government is in business to steal our secrets. They rip off anything they can get. That's what they do. That's what the whole society does. My grandmother, my baba, left her village in Ukraine a hundred years ago. You wanna know why?"

"Because they hated Jews?"

"No. Well, yes, they hated Jews, but it wasn't that. It's because they were thieves. Gonifs. Everyone, right down to the milkman, was stealing. And now there's an oligarch named Kuznetsov who collects relics. Italian triptychs. Paintings from the Louvre. Buddhist sculptures. Maybe Torahs and candlesticks. He's got a room full of shit that doesn't belong to him. It's his hobby. He's got people everywhere. And Crocker's his coffee boy in California."

"According to Zaslow."

"Damn right, according to Zaslow. But it's more serious than that, Bill. You know there's a link. Come on, why else would he be shipping hardware off to someone named Armen Sokolov in Canada? Why else would Sokolov be sweating in a jail cell in Montreal?"

"Costello is supposed to be handling all that. You want me to go in there? And blow the FBI's cover?"

"I don't want you to go in there. I just want you to keep an eye on him. You've got the manpower for that kind of operation; I don't. Besides, Crocker already knows Sokolov's been busted. That they're interrogating him, that it's almost time to close up shop. He probably thinks he's next."

"He knows? How the hell does he know?"

"Because I told him," I say. "I want him scared. I want him to lead us to Pereira and the Torah."

"You're a very impulsive guy, Amos. You went out on a limb, though, talking to him."

"What would you have done, Lieutenant?"

"I'm not the gambler you are. I'd have kept my mouth shut. Not tipped him off. What makes you so sure he doesn't already have the Torah?"

"He might, he might. But if he does, he hasn't put it in the mail to Moscow yet. Or maybe Pereira still has it. It's still in town. That much I'm sure of. I'd like to get it back."

I give him Crocker's address on Cherokee. He tells me he'll look into it, see what he can do.

"I have to talk with the captain on this first," he says. "And

Costello, too. No promises, you understand?"

For as long as I've known him, William Malloy has been a cautious soul. It probably dates back to his youth, in Chicago. His father died in the middle of the night from an aneurysm. That left his mother to raise him by herself. Early on, she decided he would become a priest, an example to others. To that end, she watched his diet, bought him fresh clothes every season, and sent him to private Catholic schools, where she made him take Latin. They went to mass together twice a week. The boys he played with on the street had good Irish names, their parents were all Democrats and union members. She wasn't as obsessive about it as it sounds, but with her husband gone, it gave her a purpose: she felt renewed. Each morning, she thanked God for granting her a son. And each morning, in some small, quiet way, she mapped out the next stretch of the road for him. It didn't always come to pass; he staged rebellions as a teenager, but in general he went along with the program. He enjoyed the company of the Jesuits, liked arguing with them, liked the respect and camaraderie they showed one another. Catholicism, with its ethical core and the uniforms the priests and nuns wore, was appealing to a young, gawky, fatherless kid. But then, one day walking home from high school, he watched a police officer make an arrest. A man was beating his wife. She was screaming and she'd run out into the street to escape, where the beating continued. The officer, who was just driving by, stopped his car. He took out his baton and put an end to the problem then and there. "He delivered justice," Malloy told me years later. "I didn't know that was possible. I thought justice only came from God."

My coffee cup is empty. I rinse it out, stick it upside down in the dishwasher. Maybe Bill Malloy's not that hard to understand, I think. He hasn't changed, at least. He still likes to weigh things out. And he's drawn to the LAPD now the same way he once was drawn to the church. So, in a sense, his mother's efforts have borne fruit.

The following night, I make special arrangements for Carmen to sleep over at our apartment to be there in case Loretta should suddenly wake. I haven't heard back from Malloy about the surveillance, which I'm guessing means he hasn't persuaded the captain to authorize it yet. I call Omar and tell him to meet me at 1843 North Cherokee.

"When?"

"How about an hour from now?"

I can tell he's not very keen on this idea. "Aren't you getting just a little bit tired of being a burglar?"

"Maybe we won't have to," I say. "Let's hope he's home watching TV and we can just go in and have another chat."

"I wouldn't think he'd be open to that, not after your last visit. Sounds like you really pissed him off."

"That's why I want you along, Omar. To teach him some manners."

*   *   *

The sun is hanging low in the sky as we meet by the iron gate in front of the apartment house on Cherokee. It's an old two-story plaster building—old, at least, by LA standards: Spanish tile on the roof and a heavy arched front door, well-shaped bushes and plants. It has what realtors in these parts are always calling "charm." Charm is one of those indefinable qualities. If you're buying, it means there's probably a leak in the ceiling you'll never be able to find. If you're a seller, it means you had a ton of sweet memories in this place and you hate to leave it, leak and all. Marilyn Monroe and Cary Grant were thought to have charm, meaning movie audiences couldn't stop gawking at them—and wondering privately what it would be like to be in bed shtupping them. Gore Vidal and Jackie Kennedy had charm, but that had to do with manners and a certain acid wit—and maybe the fact that Jackie Kennedy had studied French as a girl and wasn't afraid to flaunt it in public. Some folks even said Albert Einstein was charming—that is, if you could ever get past his wild, goofy hair and rumpled clothes. He was a bright guy, no doubt about that—he could sit there, puffing on a pipe, and talk about a serious topic the rest of us knew zip about. The Bomb. The end of civilization. A sweet old man with the power to scare the shit out of you. That alone made him great; and greatness, too, I think, gives off a kind of charm.

Omar is dressed for action, like he was the other night in Inglewood. "So, how is this gonna work?" he says. "You brought your little tool?"

"I did, but let's see if he's around. If he is, I think you're right, he's not gonna be happy to see me. But we don't have to stay long. I just wanna do a quick walk-through of the rooms. It's not that easy to hide a Torah. He won't be expecting us, and he doesn't know what we're after."

"No," Omar says sarcastically, "he thinks you're on his case because he's a Russian agent."

"He *is* a Russian agent but if we find the Torah in his living room, I'll take it home and call it even. That's all I care about right now."

Omar shakes his head. "I don't like this, Amos. It's making me nervous."

"What's the matter, you scared?"

"Nervous," he says again, as if to clarify. "This guy has a lot on the line. If he's the one behind that security guard getting shot and stealing stuff from the Navy and sending it to Russia, he's gotta be pretty cold. I just wonder, you know, whether we're getting in over our heads."

I swing open the iron gate and we walk toward the door. "I've always been in over my head, Omar. It's the story of my life. I ever tell you how my cousin Shelly talked me into joining the Marines and going to Vietnam?"

"You did. Several times."

"I was seventeen years old. Stupid. I got decent grades in high school, but it didn't matter. I just needed to believe in something. I was really, really stupid. And that was a stupid fucking move. Seventeen. I lied about my age. That's how much I wanted it. Damn near got myself killed."

"I remember what it was like to be seventeen," Omar says soberly.

"It wasn't so long ago. You saved my life back then."

There's a simple, animal purity about Omar. I felt it the first day we met. I can still see him glaring at me that afternoon, when they brought him in from the holding cell. At the time, he spoke no English—he'd just arrived a few weeks before—and the public defender needed a translator in the room. When I relayed—in my clumsy high school Spanish—that I believed he was innocent and I'd help get him out, well, that's all he needed to hear. He started sobbing. He gave me a huge bear hug and almost wouldn't let go.

There's an elaborate silver mailbox with small slots for all eight tenants' names and a large one underneath for packages. Crocker is in 4B. I try the main front door. It's locked, naturally, so I whip out my metal tool, the one my friend Jerry Vournas gave me years ago when he decided to go straight and stop breaking into houses.

It takes a few tries, patience is key, but eventually I feel something shift and it gives way. When the door opens, we're staring at a dimly lit pale green hallway. Black and white linoleum squares on the floor. Two apartments on either side, and a broad staircase with smooth wooden handrails to the left. We take the stairs, which creak a little with age, as I thought they might.

At the top of the landing there's a round wrought-iron table with a glass top and a vase full of fresh flowers. "Now, *this* is a neighborhood," I whisper to Omar. "Look at these flowers. These people know each other. They've been here a long time." I hear canned laughter and a television playing in 2B, and in 3B a real live married couple appears to be arguing. About what, I couldn't tell you. 4B is toward the rear. A warm light is seeping out from under the threshold, but there's no noise of any kind to go along with it.

We take turns putting our ear to the door. Nothing.

"Maybe you should knock," Omar says. Which seems reasonable.

I tap. Not too hard or insistent. You know, just a friendly well-intentioned knock, the kind that could net you a cup of sugar, say, if you'd decided to bake a peach pie and it was too late to run down to the market.

Still nothing.

"Maybe he went out for tacos and forgot to kill the lights," I say.

"Yeah, or maybe he's worried about guys like us."

"You think?"

"I dunno. But that's what people do in LA. They worry a lot. They go away and leave the lights on."

I slip my Glock from the shoulder holster and hand it to Omar. "Here," I tell him, "you hang on to this. And keep it pointed in the right direction, okay, just in case he's in there and decides to defend his castle. I'm gonna force the lock."

I take out my tool, bend over, and go to work.

"You want me to shoot him?" Omar whispers right behind me.

"Only if you have to," I say.

CHAPTER 11

W hen Crocker's door finally opens, well, it's not what I expected. I mean, to be honest, I didn't know what I expected. I'd hoped to hell he wasn't there. I was scared as hell he would be, and anxious that if he was, all hell would break loose and at least one of us would wind up in the hospital. But I wasn't expecting to see him splayed out on the living-room couch, a hand clutching his gut, dead. Someone had pumped four or five rounds into him. They only needed one or two to do the job, but I guess they wanted some insurance. Like they'd come so far, gone to all this trouble, no point now in fucking it up. Four will almost always do the trick. Although I knew a guy once—a doctor who cheated on his wife—took five slugs in the stomach and he's still walking around on this earth.

"Jesus," Omar says, under his breath, when he sees the body. Blood has stained Crocker's white T-shirt and pressed tan pants and pooled onto the Turkish carpet. "Somebody really had it in for this guy." Crocker's face is already going gray. His right eye is half shut. The left eye seems like it's wandering, gazing out at us. His lips are parted. He looks surprised. Or maybe not surprised. Puzzled, perhaps. Embarrassed. A few feet away, against the opposite wall, there's a TV still on, tuned to Channel 4. The sound is low. Droplets of blood have stuck to the screen where a pleasant Armenian woman is doling out the nightly news. He would have been looking at it about now. There's an open can of Coors and a Styrofoam box full of Chinese takeout on the coffee table in front of him. Apparently, the door wasn't locked at the time. He'd evidently just sat down. He'd been about to dig into his food when the killer walked into his apartment and opened fire.

"Don't touch anything," I warn Omar. "We'll just do a quick little visual tour, then let's get the hell out."

Omar nods and makes his way into the kitchen; I head for Crocker's bedroom, which isn't much to write home about. There's a queen-size, with a few pink and lilac throw pillows and an extra blanket in case it gets cold. A small throw rug. A couple of side tables with gooseneck lamps and a stack of magazines. A clock radio. The magazines are well thumbed over and almost all in Spanish.

I poke my head cautiously into his clothes closet, which is surprisingly large. I check out the bathroom. Nothing unusual in the medicine cabinet. An old toothbrush and an empty water glass beside the basin.

There's no Torah to be found.

Omar meets me out in the living room. I retrieve a clean handkerchief from my back pocket and use it to close the front door tight and wipe it clean. Then we retreat down the creaky stairs as fast and as quietly as we can.

Outside, the sun has set, and the night air is cool, liberating. "Okay," I tell him, "you go on home. I'm gonna call Malloy, make up some reason to send a squad car over here so they can start to work."

"Just please keep me the hell out of it," he says.

"Don't worry," I say. "You were never here."

After he drives off, I hike around to the rear of the building. The Mini Cooper is sitting in the carport, along with four other vehicles. A motion detector goes off and a garish yellow lamp goes on as I approach, which lets me peer inside the windows. Clean leather interior. No Torah. I go back to the sidewalk, look around in all directions. The street is silent. Then I phone Malloy. "Listen," I say. "You better get someone over to Crocker's place on Cherokee right away. I was set to meet him tonight. He said he'd be home, waiting. But he didn't come to the door when I rang the bell."

"Gee, maybe he changed his mind," Malloy says. "Maybe he realized how much he hates you and decided to go to the movies instead."

"No, no," I say, "you don't get it. It wasn't like that. He *wanted* to talk to me. He was starting to come around. I had a feeling he knew where I could put my hands on that Torah and he was gonna tell me."

"You had a feeling. That's nice, Amos. That's terrific. I'm a big fan. But it's still no reason for me to send someone over. I'm not familiar with any law that says you have to open the door just because someone knocks."

"I checked the carport out back, Bill. He said he'd be home, and his car is parked there. And all the lights are on in his apartment upstairs. Something's wrong, I'm telling you. This is no joke."

"Okay, okay," he sighs. I can see him shaking his head in bewilderment. *Why do I put up with this guy?* "I'll send a squad car. But you stay where you are. They may want to talk with you."

"Sure," I say. "I'm not going anywhere."

*   *   *

An hour or so later, there are half a dozen squad cars on North Cherokee, their red and blue lights illuminating the block like an eerie, otherworldly carnival. Neighbors from both sides of the street are clustered together, talking, gesturing.

The two officers who first arrived were clever, they got in by ringing the buzzer for one of the downstairs apartments. A young, skinny, bearded kid in shorts and flip-flops opened the main door. He was maybe twenty years old. His eyes were dilated, and he seemed clearly wasted to me. When the cops told him who they wanted, he pointed his finger immediately to the staircase. "I think he's 4B. All the way to the rear. Nice guy." Then he looked over at me, shrugged like it's none of his affair, and ambled back inside where he came from. A hint of sandalwood incense trailed after him, and from within the apartment there was some kind of soft, rhythmic music playing. Ravi Shankar? I followed the police up the stairs.

Now I'm outside again with Malloy. Remo and Jason have talked at length to the other residents, who, including the stoned young fellow with the beard, haven't heard a peep.

"It's so weird," I tell the lieutenant. "How do you shoot a man four times in a tight space like that, people upstairs and downstairs, and still no one hears? Think about it. I mean, the walls in these apartments aren't even insulated, I'd bet."

"What are you saying, Amos?" Malloy is annoyed. His tolerance for riddles is limited, even on the best of days. Now it's late: he wants to go home. He probably had other plans this evening, and I've ruined them by dragging him out here.

"I didn't notice anyone wearing hearing aids, did you?"

"No."

"No. Me neither. Which might mean our killer used a silencer. That would explain it. Of course, to me, that elevates it to another level. That says he wasn't just your ordinary killer."

"How many ordinary killers do you know, Amos?"

"Point taken, Bill. No ordinary killers. They're all psychopaths. Still, if you ask me, this looks like a professional hit. In and out in seconds. Quiet. No muss, no fuss. What do you think?"

"I agree," he says. "He knew his business. But I'm not willing to crawl into bed with Zaslow and his global conspiracies. Crocker was working the wrong side of the street, okay, fine, but this isn't James Bond. In the end, he was nothing, a pissant."

"And you don't think they'd have wanted him gone, just to cover their tracks?"

"They? Who is they? The Illuminati? The KGB? Listen to me, Amos, this was an LA murder, a local job. I'd stake my career on it. It wasn't authorized by some colonel in Moscow. Give it a rest."

"You know that for a fact? Did you check with Costello? What's the FBI have to say?"

He seems ready for this question. "We've been talking off and on all night. Costello's people picked up Richard Sykes at his apartment half an hour ago. They brought a search warrant, and he's being interviewed as we speak." There's a satisfied expression on Bill Malloy's face: he's put it all together, the wheels of justice are slowly rolling.

"Okay. And why would Sykes kill him?"

"Because he's terrified. Hell, he's got a lot more incentive than the Russians. It's a good bet Crocker told him about the bust in Montreal. That their game was over, that their man in Canada was giving away the store. Sokolov knew Crocker. He probably didn't know Sykes; but once they rounded up Crocker, well, it was just a matter of time."

I nod. "That's plausible, I suppose. Sykes doesn't live all that far away."

"And the other thing is, Crocker was comfortable with his murderer, comfortable enough, anyway. Letting him come upstairs and leaving the door unlocked. A professional killer, a stranger, wouldn't have that kind of easy access."

"Maybe," I reply. "Unless he picked the lock."

Malloy rolls his eyes. "There you go again."

The coroner's team is just emerging from the entrance with a gurney: three strong, no-nonsense guys, two of them with their heads shaved, followed by an older, frail gentleman in a rumpled suit. Crocker's corpse is wrapped in blue plastic and strapped down. We stand aside, watch as they load him gently into a waiting coroner's van.

"So maybe that's it, then," I say.

"Yeah, maybe," he says. "We'll see what happens with Sykes. Costello promised he'd keep me in the loop."

"Right." I fold my arms in front of me. "But you know what? There is still a hole in this case. We don't know who killed Marquez or Guerrero or whatever his name is, and we haven't accounted for the Torah. You don't have any more on Pereira, do you? I mean, that's the whole reason we're here now, right? Because of the Torah?"

"That's how it started out," Malloy admits. "I only wish it had stayed as simple as that." Then he mumbles that they came up with an address for him on Bonnie Brae.

"Really? When was that? You coulda let me know."

"I could have, yeah. But I didn't. It was nothing, a dead end. Just a small mother-in-law unit in the Westlake District. The woman who answered the door told us he vanished a week ago. Said he trashed the place. Left in the middle of the night. Skipped out on the rent, too. She was glad to see him gone."

Sometimes nothing is something. I ask him if he still has the address handy.

"Remo does," he says. "He and Jason did the interview. They're still wandering around here looking for witnesses. He won't remember it, but I'm sure it's in his notes back at headquarters. Why don't I have him give you a call first thing in the morning?"

"That'd be great, Bill. Thanks."

"Don't mention it. Like I say, it probably won't do you any good, but what the hell."

*   *   *

Sergeant Remo is an unreliable SOB, which is the nicest thing you can say about him. Well, actually, that's not entirely right. He's reliable when it comes to constabulary matters. He jumped through all the hoops at the Academy and has done his fair share of time on the street. He's also tough and surly in the way a lot of cops are, but from day one we've never really hit it off. On top of that, he has a serious problem with jealousy. He's a control freak. I'm no psychiatrist, I just see how he acts whenever I'm in the room with Malloy. He wants the lieutenant all to himself.

He calls the following morning and reluctantly gives me the address on Bonnie Brae. Then, before he hangs up, he adds, "The landlady's name is Dorothy Liebowitz. People call her Dot, that's what she'll tell you once you get her going. Or Dottie, if they have it in for her. She likes to be called Dorothy."

"People have it in for her?"

"I wouldn't know," Remo says. "I made the mistake of calling her Dottie. It didn't go so well after that."

"Thanks for the tip. I'll try not to muck things up."

"That's all you know how to do, Parisman. Muck things up."

Afterward, I sit around my kitchen table and wonder how a cretin like Remo manages to fit into that world—or any world, really. More to the point, how Malloy can stomach working with him eight, ten, twelve hours a day. Jason's not so bad. He and I don't talk much, and all I know about him is he's married, has a young kid, and that his wife belongs to some fundamentalist Christian church in Burbank. So, I assume he's part of that scene. What he actually believes is anyone's guess. The truth is, Jason and I live on different planets. And that's okay.

I find myself folding and unfolding the slip of paper with the address on Bonnie Brae.

Jason and Remo probably didn't make much headway with the landlady. And Malloy might also be right: it could be a gigantic waste of time talking to her. On the other hand, she's the only person in this town who has a sense of who Pereira is and what makes him tick. The only living person, that is.

If this was a normal Tuesday, I'd be leaving about now to look for him, but I can't. Carmen's not here. She had to take Antonio, her husband, to the doctor. He tweaked something in his back—he was tossing and turning, couldn't sleep all night, and now he's not fit to drive a truck up Highway 5. Carmen promises this won't take too long; the free clinic they go to in Pasadena is very efficient. What she means is that the doctor there is under a lot of pressure; he goes from room to room and only spends about five perfunctory minutes on each patient. He'll look at Antonio, ask him what happened, maybe check his blood pressure, lean in and listen to his heart with his stethoscope, then write out a prescription and show him the door. Carmen and Antonio both know this isn't exactly the kind of care Anglos receive, but everyone in the clinic is kind. And they all speak Spanish, she says. That counts.

Forty minutes later, Carmen shows up. She apologizes as she peels off her orange sweater and hangs her purse on the hook by the door. When I ask her how Antonio is doing, she shakes her head, says he was given a muscle relaxant for the spasms in his back. He just needs to rest a few days. He'll be okay. Then, as I'm heading out the door, she adds, "The doctor also told him not to drink anything when he is taking these pills. No alcohol. No cerveza. Nada. Antonio was not happy."

It's a short drive to 1501 Bonnie Brae. That's the number Remo gave me. I park across the street. Westlake is not so different from many other ephemeral areas in LA—its popularity comes and goes. Right now it's gone. Back in the 1920s, everyone thought it was a good idea, it had a brief glittering moment in the sun and then, like silent movie stars and hula-hoops, well, what can I say?

Young, determined, dark-eyed men on bicycles stream by, and there's a cluster of women on the corner with small children and shopping bags; everyone's waiting patiently for the bus. Westlake is close to downtown, the rents are lower than where I live, and it's become a home now to new arrivals from Mexico, El Salvador, and Guatemala. What it lacks in natural beauty it makes up for in vibrancy. There's an old toothless man selling tacos and burritos out of a cart. This sidewalk is his beat.

Dorothy Liebowitz lives in a rambling three-story Victorian. There are steel bars on all the windows. In its heyday, the front yard might have been something to behold; now, except for a pair of sturdy lemon trees, it's rocks and weeds. Behind the freshly installed cyclone fence, there's an old, ornate wooden porch that extends halfway around the house. Charming, but okay—it could use a paint job. If you asked a licensed contractor, he'd probably tell you it needs a helluva lot more than that.

I cross over and navigate the path to the stained glass door. It's a delicate floral pattern, part of the original residence—plump red roses creeping ever upward to heaven. I ring the bell. While I wait for someone to answer, it occurs to me that these roses are aspirations from another era; there's not much spiritual about this neighborhood now.

A woman shouts at me through the thick oak door. "What do you want?"

I smile at her. It's hard to tell just who I'm looking at—we're separated by sheer curtains and glass roses, after all. "My name's Parisman, Mrs. Liebowitz. Amos Parisman. I've come from the police." For a moment I consider flashing my investigator's license at her, like I did with those Latinas in Inglewood.

"The police?"

"Yeah, I understand you had a conversation with Sergeant Remo. That it was difficult. That he rubbed you the wrong way. Part of the reason I'm here is to apologize."

The door cracks open an inch. Then six inches more. A slim, attractive, dark-haired woman in her mid-forties pokes her head out. She's got on blue jeans and a frilly top. No makeup, but nice European-looking sneakers. Maybe she was just about to head out somewhere. "Well, now, that's refreshing," she says. "I haven't heard that in some time. An apology. And from the police, no less."

"May I come in?" I ask. "Remo probably wasn't the best person they could have chosen. He's a little brusque sometimes. Shoots from the hip, you know."

"You're telling me," she says, showing me into the living room, which is off to the right. There are a number of half empty bookcases along the walls, some of which she has filled with ceramic animals and clay pots and old cooking utensils. The space has a sad, unloved feeling about it; it's as if she just threw a handful of random objects together, things she'd salvaged from going around to yard sales, maybe, and labeled it a living room. We settle onto an antique sofa, and she clasps her hands earnestly together in her lap. I was hoping to draw things out a little; but instead, her gray-green eyes drill straight through me; she isn't being impolite, but she's one of those women who doesn't dance around the edge of the carpet: she's got things to do and she's not about to offer me tea. "So, now that you've apologized, Mr. Parisman, what's this really all about?"

"It's about your tenant. Bart Pereira."

This doesn't sit well. "I told Sergeant Remo everything I know about him."

"I'm sorry," I say. "Again, you'll have to excuse Remo. He doesn't take notes. Not good ones, I mean. Nobody could decipher what he came back with. And I know he offended you. That's how I came to be here."

"I see," she says. "All right, it's like this: Bart Pereira rented my spare unit out back. Up until last month, he always paid on time, and I never heard him complain. It's hard to get tenants like that."

"Do you know what he did for a living?"

"I know what he told me," she says. "He told me he was testing the water, trying to see if he had what it takes to be a detective."

"No kidding."

"He'd finished his time in the army," she continued. "It just seemed like the natural thing to do."

I had to fight the urge to grin. I've never looked for a private detective before, if that's what he actually was. Somebody like that, somebody like me, could be tough to find. At least he'd know how to disappear.

"He ever tell you about his cases?"

"No. Not a word. But he was often out late at night. Sometimes he'd be gone for days. He'd come rolling in at two or three or four in the morning. I assumed it was some kind of surveillance he was doing."

"Did he have a bank account? Did he write you a check every month?"

"No," she says. "Funny you should mention it. He always paid cash."

"And you never said anything? That didn't bother you?"

"Tell you the truth, I was relieved he paid cash. One less thing for me to report to the IRS."

I nod. I feel like I'm beginning to fill in the blanks about her. "How long have you lived here, Mrs. Liebowitz, if you don't mind my asking?"

"No," she says, "I don't mind. My husband was a carpenter. He and I bought this place eighteen years ago. It was supposed to be temporary. Paul was going to fix it up in his spare time and flip it. We weren't going to stay. Even then we didn't care for it; we planned to move somewhere better. Santa Monica, maybe. Or Venice. Paul was good with his hands."

"So what happened?"

"What happened? He came home and had a stroke after work one night. Collapsed in the shower. I didn't know what else to do, so I stayed on. Rented out rooms to make ends meet."

"And that's how Pereira came along."

"Pereira," she nods, "and a lot of other folks. I have three families upstairs right now. One's from Mexico, the others are Nicaraguan. I don't charge them much. It's a little global village. We get along."

I take out my notepad, just in case she says something I won't remember. "Getting back to Pereira," I say, "in the time he lived here, you must have had some conversations, right? I mean, you were neighbors."

"We talked now and then, yeah."

"What about?"

"Hell, I don't know," she says. "I remember once him saying how he wished he'd learned how to cook."

"He didn't cook?"

"No, he was lazy that way, he bought takeout. Chinese. Thai. Whatever. But he said he missed eating things his mother used to make, you know—shakshuka, hummus, falafel—dishes from his homeland."

"Did he tell you where he came from?"

"Israel, of course. Didn't you know that?"

"No. No, I didn't. Pereira's not an Israeli name. Sounds Spanish or Portuguese."

"Maybe so. I never asked more than that. It was the rent I cared about."

Every once in a blue moon, a person like me knows when he's being lied to. This is one of those occasions. Something about the casual response, the way it flicked off her tongue. *I never asked. It was the rent I cared about.* Makes me wonder about the inner life of Dorothy Liebowitz, whether she ever had any yearnings, living all by herself, or practically all by herself, in a big rattletrap house like this, listening to her tenants creaking around upstairs, the flushing of toilets, the din of radios, the endless calling out to each other in Spanish at night. Was she lonely? Maybe he stiffed her for the rent, but was Bart Pereira a breath of fresh air? He was different, at least, compared to her other lodgers.

I ask her if I could maybe see the rooms he lived in out back. She shrugs, leads me through the house to the rear door and down another short set of rickety stairs. "Be careful," she says, "I'm going to replace them one of these days."

The mother-in-law unit is a small cinderblock structure attached to the garage. It might have been used as a utility closet or a work-shop at one time. She takes out a set of keys from her jeans and fiddles around until she finds the right one. The door pops open. She reaches in and flips the light switch. Right away, I can see this is a dead end. The entire room—that's basically all it is, one large space plus a modest bath and shower—has been repainted a stark white. She has left all the sliding windows open for air, but you can still smell the fumes. A painter's tarp is folded up in the corner. Someone has scrubbed and cleaned the gunk off the four burners on the stovetop. It'll never look new, but it's serviceable. In the center of the room there's a round Formica table and four matching chairs. An empty bookshelf. A single bed that maybe doubles as a couch.

"I'm going to change out the silverware and plates," she says, as if making a vow to herself. "Throw in a couple of non-stick fry pans, make it more livable. Everything that man touched turned to crap."

"Just out of curiosity," I ask, "what does something like this rent for?"

"These days? You don't want to know." She smiles then, ruefully. "But I'm not traipsing off to the Bahamas, if that's what you're getting at."

We turn around and return to the living room in the main house. I comment that Bartholomew Pereira was a heavy smoker, and she nods and says that's the reason she ended up repainting the paneling inside, just to help get rid of the smoke. "I don't know how often I told him he was killing himself with those goddamn cigarettes. Probably every time I saw him, I guess. But he was such a stubborn man. Wouldn't listen."

"You say he skipped out without paying the rent. That must have pulled your chain."

"I made him give me a security deposit," she says. "It wasn't a total loss. Also, when I went in to clean the place up, he'd left me a pile of junk, naturally."

"Junk?"

"Well, treasures. Ashtrays. Clothes. Books. Other stuff."

"And what'd you do with it? I hope you didn't throw it out."

"Oh, I will, believe me. What I can't get rid of. I put it in the hall closet with everything else I've been collecting all year long. In September I have my annual yard sale. Right now, his is sitting in a garbage bag."

"You think I might be able to look it over?"

"Sure," she says. "No problem. Anything you find in there is yours." Then she raises an eyebrow, a mischievous look, and I find myself thinking again how attractive she is. Living here alone, all these years, managing these families rotating in and out, can't have been easy for her. "Of course, you'll have to pay me, you realize. I'm still in the red with that guy."

"Understood," I tell her.

We both get up and I follow her into the hall. She roots around in the closet for a minute. At last, she drags out a dark-green plastic garbage bag. PEREIRA is duct-taped to the outside. "Knock yourself out," she says, standing aside.

I squat down, untwist the plastic bag, and peek inside. A very faint rank odor seeps out. Smoke, which must still be embedded somehow in a dozen glass ashtrays, many of them with the logos of hotels and other fine establishments he probably stayed at over the years. There are also several books—a Bible, some well-read and dog-eared paperback mysteries, a street guide to Los Angeles, three different maps of Southern California, and a bulky reddish copy of something called *The Jews in America: Four Centuries of an Uneasy Encounter.* The author is Arthur Hertzberg, who I've never heard of, but I guess he's famous in certain circles, so the fault is likely my own. There's a small pile of wrinkled polo shirts, a straw hat, a pair of sunglasses, and a blue sport coat that's too long for me in the arms. A couple of pairs of loafers have seen better days. I'm about to close the bag and forget about it, when I see something shiny off in a corner. I reach down, pick it up. Turns out it's an old knife. A switchblade. I choose the knife, and, on a whim, the Jewish history book.

Dorothy Liebowitz charges me ten bucks for the pair. I fish out two fives from my wallet. "There you go," I tell her. Then, as I'm about to leave, I give her my business card. "In case he ever comes back, I'd appreciate hearing about it."

She glances at the card, then up at me. "You lied," she says. "You're not a cop." She's surprised, but not dismayed, not really. Maybe in the tawdry universe she lives in, people lie to her all the time. Maybe everything's a lie, so what difference does it make? "Somehow I didn't think you were." She scratches her head. "Even though you said so. Guess I ought to learn to trust my intuition more."

"No," I say, "I'm not a cop. But don't get me wrong: I didn't lie to you. I wouldn't. I said I came from the police. Which is true. They gave me your address. I also know that Sergeant Remo was out of line with you. And for that, I really do apologize."

CHAPTER 12

Switchblades aren't usually part of a nice Jewish boy's upbringing, but I figured Omar, since he'd lived much of his life on the street, must have seen them before. We're having French dip sandwiches and coffee at Philippe's, on Alameda. I wait until the waiter serves us, then I pull out the one I bought from Dorothy Liebowitz and slide it gently across the table.

"What do you think of this?"

"You mean, as a weapon?" He turns it over a couple of times, weighs it, lets it warm in his hand, pops open the blade, then tucks it all back together, neat and tidy. "I wouldn't use it," he says, "not me, not unless I had to."

"Por qué?"

"Because the blade's too goddamn short, for one thing. A knife's not like a gun. You know how many chances you get with a knife? Just one. If you're going to stick somebody, you want it to penetrate. Get deep inside so you can twist it, do some damage."

Philippe's is crowded. Every table is full, and there are more people at the door, waiting for a table. I turn around in both directions, realize what we're talking about is maybe not the greatest lunchtime conversation. Still, a man's gotta eat, right? I dip my sandwich in the warm sauce, take a bite. I have several paper napkins at the ready. You can't eat French dip without consequences. "And this wouldn't do that, huh?"

"Oh, it would do damage, sure. Plenty, but not right away."

I tell him where I found it, remind him that Marquez, Pereira's partner, had been jabbed five or six times with something closely resembling that knife. That it probably took Marquez a long time to die.

"Yeah, but why would Pereira go after Marquez?" Omar wants to know. "I don't get it. How does that make sense?"

"I can think of lots of scenarios," I tell him. "Maybe they had a falling-out over something. Maybe they didn't like each other to begin with."

"I don't know," Omar says. "They both sound a little bit loco the way they act. They're like . . . they're like a couple of grenades rolling around in a pail, you know, just waiting for someone to kick it or pull the pin. Look at how they shot that security guard, right? Look how they treated the rabbi and his wife."

"What are you saying, Omar?"

"There was no fucking need for it, man. None. No thought behind it. Just sprang out of nowhere. That tells you who you're dealing with."

"So you don't think he stabbed Marquez?"

"Maybe he did, maybe he didn't. I'm saying that kind of violence, it makes no sense."

It has taken me a few years to realize, but when Omar gets all hot under the collar and talks this way, he's thinking more with his heart than his head. Sometimes I imagine the words out of his mouth jump straight from his heart; that's how sure he is. But being so sure doesn't always make you right. It just makes you young.

I sip my coffee, take a deep breath, remind myself once again to focus. That's the key. To solve a crime, any crime, you've got to be patient, think things through. Give it time. Emotions only get you in trouble. This business is about asking the right questions. About moving people around to different rooms, shifting them gently here and there like a jigsaw puzzle until all at once they fit. I say, "If you had some idea about what you could do with that Torah—other than hand it over to Frank Crocker—it makes perfect sense."

"You think Pereira was freelancing?"

"Could be," I say. "Somebody stuck Marquez with a knife, that's for sure. And Frank Crocker was waiting to have a Torah delivered to his door. It didn't happen. Now Crocker's dead and there's only one person I know of who connects to those two things."

Omar polishes off the last of his French dip sandwich, washes it down with coffee. He looks slightly calmer than before. Probably the food, but who knows? Maybe something I said made sense to him. "Pereira might not be done with Dorothy Liebowitz," he offers. "You ever consider that? He moved out in a rush, yeah, like he does everything, but what if he suddenly remembers his knife? Don't you think he's gonna want it back? Nobody leaves a murder weapon behind for the landlady to find, do they? She could be in trouble."

"That's a point, Omar. But I've still gotta turn it over to Malloy first, let his people put it under the microscope. They may be able to turn something."

"You're not going to at least warn her about Pereira?"

"What? That he might be back?"

"No, man—that he's a killer. That she was renting to a stone-cold killer all that time."

"She doesn't know that, Omar. And frankly, I'm not willing to call him a killer. Not yet. Not on the strength of this." I hold up the knife. "I certainly didn't tip her off, and I'm sure Remo and Jason didn't either."

"So you think she's safe? *De veras*? Really? Like the rabbi's safe?" He frowns, shakes his head, and throws up his hands. He's back to thinking with his heart again.

*   *   *

After lunch, in part because Omar is still antsy about the rabbi's situation, we swing around to Formosa Avenue and drop in on him. Officer McCollum waves us through. The old man lumbers to the door, rubbing the stars out of his eyes. He was alone, just taking a nap on the couch, he explains. His wife went off to the market.

She'll be back shortly. You should excuse her.

We go into the living room. The heat seems to be on in the house, which is odd for June, but then I remember my parents' place was always overheated, that was how they liked it. I introduce Omar, and they shake hands. Rabbi Josef can't get over how tall he is. "You should be a basketball star," he says. I don't know if he says that to everyone who's taller than he is, or whether meeting someone like Omar unexpectedly in his living room just makes him nervous. Rabbis aren't ordinarily awkward around strangers; maybe he's the exception. Then he points to the sofa, which is still warm from where he was fast asleep. "Sit, gentlemen," he tells us, "please."

He seems perfectly fine to me, but now that we've established that, I can't just get up and walk out the door. So, I say, "I have good news: the case seems to be opening up; there are some fresh leads."

"Oh, so you've located the Torah?" There's a modicum of hope in his voice, though, after all he's been through, he's not letting himself get too excited.

"No," I say, "but I'm pretty sure who took it. We've identified the two men. You already know about the fellow who hit you with the pistol, the one named Marquez."

"The one who died." He shakes his head, frowns, chews on his lip. I'm a reliable source of sorrow for him, I can see that. Every time we meet, we seem to rekindle the pain of the recent past. The weight has become oppressive; now maybe in the back of his mind he's regretting this ancient Torah that turned up at his door. He never asked God for such a privilege, after all. It's given him a lot to think about. "The one who died," he says again.

"Who was stabbed, yes. Well, now we're after his partner, the taller gentleman, the guy your wife said smelled like a cigar."

"Yes, yes, he seemed to be in charge."

"His name is Bartholomew Pereira. Calls himself Bart. Tell me, Rabbi, does that ring any kind of bell?"

"Pereira?" he says. "No, maybe, I can't be sure. Bartholomew Pereira. I'm not . . . I'm not familiar."

Omar leans in then. "He sounds Latino to me. But his landlady, you know, she swears he's from Israel."

A memory from the far side of the moon jogs Rabbi Josef's brain just then; he blinks several times, his soft brown eyes light up. Ever since he opened the door he'd been settled on the sofa. Now he pushes himself off with difficulty and approaches the bookcase. It's about seven feet high and filled with a hodgepodge of manuscripts and paperbacks and leather-bound works with Hebrew lettering on the spine. He reaches for the tallest shelf. His index finger slides from one dog-eared volume to the next until he finds what he's searching for. "Pereira," he mumbles, licking his thumb as he flips the pages, "Pereira, Pereira, Pereira. Ah. Ah, here it is. Yes."

He lays it down triumphantly on the coffee table for both of us to see. It's a tattered book of Jewish surnames and looks as though it was printed some time in the thirties or forties. The tan jacket with the faded blue Star of David on the cover is chipped and torn; someone has mended it meticulously with Scotch tape.

"Pereira is an old Sephardic name. I haven't opened this book in years. Pereira. From Spain or Portugal," he says. "Or maybe Galicia, in Poland. Means 'pear tree.' Pereira." He settles down again into the sofa, a satisfied smile on his face, his memory, at least for now, redeemed.

*　　*　　*

That day it's another scorcher down at LAPD headquarters on 1st Street. Some of the staff have come up with a reasonable excuse to be gone; half the desks are empty. The fans are rotating at high speed, and the poor folks still wearing a tie and carrying a weapon now at three o'clock are all drinking Diet Coke and iced tea, trying to keep cool.

Malloy is delighted to see the switchblade on his desk, which I've placed in a clear plastic bag. He hands it to Jason and dispatches him off to the lab for analysis, wants to know what else I've dug up.

"Not so much," I say. "His landlady was pretty forthcoming, as soon as I apologized for Remo's missteps. Dorothy's actually not a bad sort, once you realize what she's been through. Beautiful, in a salt-of-the-earth kind of way."

"Beautiful?" He throws me a disapproving glance—Father Malloy—as though a wizened old guy like me, a happily married man, ought not to be entertaining such sinful thoughts.

"'Noble' would maybe be a better word. She's been stranded in that house on Bonnie Brae for decades. Husband dropped dead. She's rented it out piecemeal to less fortunate people ever since."

"She sounds Irish," he says.

"Jewish," I correct him. "Speaking of which, did you know that Bart Pereira moved here from Israel?"

He raises an eyebrow. "What?"

"That's what she told me. Said he misses his mama's cooking. Shakshuka. Falafel."

Malloy frowns. In his mind I'm guessing he's already had this mapped out. Nothing too fancy, just your simple ordinary dishonor among thieves. And now here I am, being a *nudnik* again, dragging him out into deeper international water. "So? What's that got to do with anything?"

"Maybe nothing. But I think it's kinda interesting—well, odd at least. That a Jewish boy from Israel with a name like Bartholomew Pereira would end up renting an apartment in a rundown part of LA. It's like he was trying deliberately to fade into the wallpaper. Doesn't fit, exactly. I mean, all the young Israelis I ever met want to live on the west side of town, where the action is. Oh, by the way, did you know he was a private eye? That's another thing he told the landlady."

Malloy rubs an errant speck of dirt out of his eyes. "You know something, Amos? For a guy who said he didn't learn much, you're full of surprises."

I get up to leave. Omar's waiting for me out in the parking lot. This has already taken me longer than I told him it would. I really just came by to give Bill the knife, see if he could tie it to Guerrero's killing. I don't have much hope he'll take my impressions of Pereira and run with them. That's not how the good lieutenant works.

"Omar and I went out to see the rabbi earlier, Bill. I almost forgot. He'd never heard of Pereira, naturally, no reason why he should, but I thought there might be a slight chance Pereira had dropped by his *shul* before. That he might have showed up on a Friday night, say—not for the service, but maybe to case the joint."

"So this could have been in the works for a while. Is that what you're saying?"

"Maybe there's something else going on. When he moved out, Pereira left some other things behind, besides the knife. There was a Bible and a collection of Judaica. Just a few books, but he'd clearly read them all, and, you know what, it got me thinking."

"About what?"

"He's not an idiot, Bill, not like Guerrero. I can't get inside his head, but I'd be willing to bet there's a flash of brilliance, every now and again."

"Because he's read the Bible? Charles Manson read the Bible. You're going to give him a pass because of that?"

"No. But I'd like to get to know him better before you sentence him to death."

"I'm not sentencing him to death," Malloy insists. Something in his tone suggests I'm being harsh; at the very least I've crossed a delicate line. I know how he regards himself: he's a police officer, first, last, and always—sworn to serve and protect. "Nobody's sentencing him, not until he's had a fair trial." Then his jaw relaxes and we're friends again. "Oh, and Amos, thanks for the knife."

*   *   *

The following day, after Loretta and Carmen have finished mixing up a batch of brownies and the two of them are hard at work slamming dominoes down on the kitchen table, I get in my Civic and follow the Arroyo Seco out to Pasadena to see Pete Zaslow. The neighborhood on South El Molino is as calm and leafy as ever. Four bronze exuberant young men in shorts are playing touch football in the front yard across the street. They're laughing and shouting back and forth; they act like they've known each other forever. I can read what's going on immediately. I mean, it doesn't take a genius to see that they've just come back from their assorted colleges. That they grew up together right down the block, the closest of pals, and this is the first time they've managed to see each other since grad night when they all got drunk and did things they'd be ashamed of now, if only they could recall what happened. They are the same sincere, brilliant, good-natured boys they always were, the shiny red apples of their high school, at least that's what they want to believe. Nothing's changed. But now a private truth is tugging at their hearts. The truth cannot be denied. They're flying back to Yale or MIT or Duke next week, or next month. They have interviews lined up with law firms and computer startups, and they know their old lives will be a dream after that. That you can't go home again, not really. Now, the future? That's another matter. The future's all laid out. It's a New Year's Day parade. Any fool can predict the future. They'll meet some fabulous someone and fall in love; there'll be romantic dinners, weddings in far-off places, children, job promotions. They know that in their bones. They'll rise like kites in their fields. They'll be transferred by their company to God knows where—Cleveland, Dallas, Tokyo. It'll be glorious. But right now, they're not dwelling on that. Right now, it's a sweet summer morning in Pasadena, and they're holding on fiercely; time slips away, they know that, and all they want is to run through the grass like they used to do, run through the freshly mown grass and score.

Pete Zaslow gives me half of his toasted sesame bagel with cream cheese. He can't bear to see me go hungry, he insists. The truth is, he's on a diet, so I'm doing him a big favor by eating. We sit in the dining room, the sun glinting off the glass doors that lead to the back deck. Muriel is rummaging around in the kitchen, singing show tunes from Broadway musicals. I could listen to her all day, but I shut her out because I need some answers from Pete.

"I have a couple of names for you, Pete."

"Is this a guessing game?" he asks. "I love guessing games."

"Not a game," I say. "You ever hear of a Juan Guerrero? Or Jesus

Emilio Marquez?"

"No."

"No reason why you should. Jesus Marquez and Juan Guerrero are the same person. How about Bartholomew Pereira? Also known as Bart?"

He rolls his eyes. "Bartholomew? Who are these people?"

"They're the two we think stole the Torah. Guerrero is no longer with us. Him we can forget about."

"What happened?"

"Stabbed to death in his car. A meter maid found him. And not long after that, someone—I figure it was the same fellow—paid a visit to Francis Crocker and shot him, too. Only whoever shot him must have used a silencer there. It's a small apartment building, and nobody heard anything."

"My," Zaslow says, "you've had yourself a busy few nights." He puts down the bagel he was about to eat. "I can't speculate about Guerrero, but Crocker was probably a marked man the minute they picked up Sokolov in Montreal. I told you I thought he was likely to disappear before too long."

"No, Pete, you said he'd be hard to locate once he heard about Sokolov. That he was gonna shut down his shop."

"Well?"

"Well, he knew about the bust and still he didn't go anywhere. He was just sitting in his apartment in Hollywood. Someone just walked in and shot him."

"And you think it was Bartholomew Pereira? Why?"

I play with the knuckles on my left hand. They feel okay now, but whenever it rains in LA they seem to require a lot of attention. Fortunately, it almost never rains in LA. "There's no evidence that Crocker ever took delivery on that Torah. It wasn't anywhere in his warehouse, which would have been the obvious drop-off. It wasn't in his apartment, either. I know, we checked."

"What do you mean, you checked?"

"We visited. Before the cops showed up."

His brow furrows. "You walked in on him? And he was dead?"

"We were careful, Pete. Didn't touch a thing, except for the door-knob, and I wiped that down."

"Just when did you show up?"

"Early evening. It couldn't have been more than an hour after it happened. He was just sitting there on the couch. Like he was wait-ing, you know. Had a carton of Chinese food set up in front of him, all cool and collected. I'm telling you, Pete, he was expecting Pereira to bring the Torah to him the night he was killed."

Zaslow scratches his head. "And why wouldn't Pereira do just that? Deliver it and be gone? Why knock him off? What's in it for him?"

"That's the thing. Guerrero was just a common thug, from what I'm gathering. He wouldn't know which end of a Torah was up. And he wouldn't care as long as he got paid. But there's a lot more to Pereira. His landlady told me he said he worked as a private investi-gator. Also, he was raised in Israel."

"Where are you headed with this, Amos? I'm not sure I follow."

"Pereira stiffed her for the rent and vanished a week or so back. Right after the robbery. But he left a few things behind. Some books on Judaica. And a switchblade. I'm guessing that's what did in Guer-rero. Or Marquez. Or whatever he called himself."

"But you don't know."

"No. Not yet. I turned the blade over to the LAPD. Their scien-tists are having a go at it. It's sharp enough, and he might not have cleaned it entirely. They do wonderful things with DNA these days. So, we'll see."

"But, again: Why would he kill Crocker? What's that about? Weren't they on the same side?"

"Maybe not. I have questions about Pereira. Number one, he's Jewish. The name is even Sephardic, the rabbi checked. And he grew up in Israel. Which means he was likely in the military. Unless you're missing an arm or a leg, everyone there serves in the military. Number two, he told his landlady he was a private investigator. That has to be some kind of cover story."

Zaslow stares out the window into the back yard while he nurses his coffee. He's taken in every syllable I have to offer. It's a glorious green summer morning. Way off in the distance, I can hear the sounds of impassioned young men shouting. Zaslow's silent, but I can see he's trying to work through the maze in his mind.

"I'm hoping you might be able to help me, Pete. You know people in D.C. And even if they can't give you anything, they know people in Israel who could. You see what I'm saying?"

Zaslow nods. He pushes his chair deliberately away from the table, folds his yellow napkin into a neat triangle. "Let's take a little walk," he suggests.

We do a slow circle of the neighborhood. He points out the splendid old oaks, the jacaranda, the bougainvillea, the trimmed lawns, the silent, well-appointed houses, all with signs in the ground pointing out to would-be thieves that they are protected around the clock by this or that agency. "The folks around here love where they live," he says. "They've paid a ton of money for the privilege, and, as you can see, they're willing to shell out even more to protect it. Obviously, I don't know your man Pereira. But it's plausible he has roots in Israel. That might mean something. Maybe he's operating on his own in this. Maybe there's some connection to the government. Whatever. I'll fish around, get back to you."

"Thanks, Pete."

"In the meantime, though, do me a big favor."

"What's that?"

"Don't go breaking into any more houses, okay? You're too fucking old to be in jail. The food's terrible, and orange is not your color. I'll grant you, the cops are slow, but don't underestimate them."

CHAPTER 13

That evening, as the sunlight slips away, I climb into the back seat of Harriet Reines's big shiny black Lincoln to tell her what I know. There's something intimate about these meetings that I can't quite put my finger on. I dunno, maybe it reminds me of other back seats I used to climb in long ago when I was a teenager and my hormones were bouncing all over the place. Geoffrey is seated behind the steering wheel, staring straight ahead. The interior smells of newly polished leather. There's also some kind of wonderful spicy perfume she's wearing that speaks to me of Vietnam—warm and sweet like certain streets I still remember from the few precious nights I spent in Saigon. Harriet herself is all dolled up, she's paid a lot of attention to her face and nails, as though after this meeting she's going on to a fancy restaurant or a party somewhere. Next to her I'm not much to look at.

"It's been a few days, Mr. Parisman. I've installed all those cameras and safety measures as you suggested. Now, where are we with the Torah?"

"We've made progress, Mrs. Reines, I can tell you that. The two men responsible—the ones who attacked the rabbi and his wife, anyway—we know who they are. One's dead, the other is on the run. We think he's in possession of the Torah, but that's still unclear."

"I assume the police know these individuals?"

"Oh, sure. We're working hand in glove with the police."

She presses her palm against her skirt to straighten it out. You wouldn't call her beautiful, I think, although twenty years ago she was. Things fade. Gravity takes over. Now she puts in time and money at the salon to achieve whatever she can. Now she's elegant, which ain't too shabby.

"Do we know what they—or rather, what this remaining gentleman—planned to do with the Torah? Sell it? Ransom it? Destroy it?"

I hesitate. I'd like to tell her about Kuznetsov and the gravy train to Russia, but that's going pretty far out on a limb. Hell, I'm having a hard enough time convincing Malloy, who has insight into this; who knows how she'll react? My impression is, she's never been to a James Bond film in her life. No, I think, let's keep it simple. "That's a tougher question. In some universe, there may well be a buyer, we just don't know. No one's tried to contact us about a ransom, not yet. Personally, I'd be pleased if they did."

"And why on earth would that be?"

Now she's baiting me. Maybe this is how she talks to all the servants, I don't know; maybe, from the way she looks at things, everyone is her servant. Most of the time she's content to run around playing Santa Claus with her husband's fortune, but I have to guess this business with the Torah has unnerved her. It's serious. People have died, and now she wants her money's worth. Okay, fine, Parisman, the meter's ticking. Give her your professional spiel.

"Once they make contact," I offer, "once there's negotiations going on, well, that opens the door, doesn't it? Then it's a two-way street. How do you think we found these *mamzers* to begin with?"

"How, indeed?"

"Because they're human," I reply. "Because they talk too long on the phone. Because they leave their spit or their fingerprints or their DNA or some other calling card behind. In this case, it was a ticket from a dry cleaner in West Hollywood. Sometimes it's as simple as that."

"The Torah still exists, then, in your opinion?"

"Oh, without a doubt. They went to a lot of trouble to get it.

They could have destroyed it when they invaded the rabbi's home, but that didn't happen. No, it's still around. I'd bet my last dollar."

She seems reassured by this. She leans back in her seat, her expression of concern easing into a more neutral state. I let my eyes travel up to the front where Geoffrey, who's heard every word, is staring intently into the rearview mirror, waiting for her signal to start the engine. I wonder where Geoffrey fits into the puzzle of her life. Do they ever speak? Does she care what he has to say? She gestures with her right hand, the one with the diamond ring on it, a slight imperial movement that waves me off like yesterday's weather report. The queen has spoken, I'm no longer needed. Ironically, this doesn't squash my feelings; in fact, I'm kinda relieved. As long as she's still footing the bill, being a servant has its perks. "We'll talk another time," she says. "Thank you; you've been very helpful."

"Hey, you bet." I give them a mock military salute as they pull away from the curb and head for the main gate. When the crossbar goes up, they turn left toward the high-rises on Wilshire and vanish.

*   *   *

"You might want to have another talk with that landlady down on Bonnie Brae," Omar says the following morning. Carmen is getting Loretta ready for a trip to the LA County Art Museum, helping her lace up her tennis shoes. It's just a few blocks away, and Loretta's been there many times. She loves it, but she never remembers what she sees and which artist is which, so it's an endless goldmine in that respect.

"Why?"

"I don't think she's being straight with you, that's why. Didn't she tell you Pereira left suddenly without paying the rent? That she hates his guts?"

"I don't believe she put it like that. He did leave her high and dry, however."

"Yeah, well, according to her he showed up again last night around supper time. Knocked on her door, said he left a few items behind. Wanted them back."

"How do you know all this, Omar?"

"You know how you keep paying me to keep tabs on people? How you keep giving me too much money? So I made a friend down there. His name's Eduardo, he's from Managua. He used to be a farmer but now he does construction. Nice guy. I told him I was working this stakeout and I'm all alone and I can't be here twenty-four hours a day and would he tell me if Pereira shows his ugly face again? I gave him fifty bucks and left him my phone number just in case."

"And Eduardo called you? When?"

"About an hour ago. Just before he left for the construction site. I drove right over, of course, told Mrs. Liebowitz I work with you, and I heard a little rumor that Bart's back."

"What'd she say?"

"She said he dropped by yesterday, yeah. They talked. It wasn't pleasant. She asked him for the rent, and he said he was sorry, promised her he'd bring by what he owed soon. Maybe by the weekend. Something came up, he said. He had to leave in a hurry."

"And she bought that line?"

"I don't know, man. But I don't think she hates him nearly as much as she told you. She let him go through the garbage bag with his stuff, anyway. What does that tell you?"

"That you're right, Omar. She doesn't hate him."

"Also, she lied to you, man."

"Yeah, well." Loretta gives me a perfunctory hug as she shuffles toward the door. Her hair smells sweet and damp from her morning shower. I hand Carmen my wallet so she can take out what she'll need for the museum and their lunch afterward. Two twenties slip into her purse. "What else happened, Omar?"

"He was looking for the knife in that bag. She said he got mad when he didn't see it."

"He told her that?"

"No, he told her something's missing. He wanted to go back to his old apartment, look around."

"And she took him there?"

"She did, yeah. Eduardo was upstairs in the bathroom. He'd just come out of the shower. It was a hot night. The window was open. He heard them talking in the yard."

"Thanks, Omar. I'll take a spin out there later this morning."

"You want me to be there, too? I'm free. We could meet if you need some muscle."

"No, that won't be necessary. This'll be a friendly chat. Just the two of us."

"What if Bart shows up?"

"He won't. But if he does, hey, that'll be a bridge when I cross it."

There's a touch of petulance in his voice when he comes back on the line, and I remind myself that he's still green and needy. Like he deserves more credit for finding this out. Like I should pat him on the back for his creativity, enlisting Eduardo. "She's not being straight with you, man."

"I know, Omar. You mentioned that."

*   *   *

Around noon, I make a quick pit stop on 7th at Mama's International Tamales across from MacArthur Park and chow down on a plate of their tamales. It's a lucky accident that I'm eating here at all. Years ago, I was trying to go to Langer's Deli, which isn't that far away, and there was no parking. I went around the block three times; my stomach was growling and I was getting a little frantic. Then I saw this place. Mama's is Salvadoran cooking. It's just a joint with some art on the wall, but the people are welcoming, and the food, I guess, is authentic. Different. Hell, what do I know? I've never been south of Ensenada.

Afterward, I drive over to Dorothy Liebowitz's boarding house. I've been thinking long and hard at lunch, putting too many chips and too much salsa into my mouth, and even though I'm full now and my blood sugar is where it's supposed to be, I still don't know what I'll say to her. Omar's right. She wasn't being straight when she talked about Bart Pereira. On the other hand, I wasn't being totally straight with her either the other night, so maybe that makes us even. I stand on the old rickety wooden porch and press the bell. It has a hollow sound. The house seems empty. I ring again, then knock gently on the glass. A voice from within shouts, "Hang on, hang on, I'm coming!" A few seconds later she flips a couple of deadbolts from the other side and throws it open.

Dorothy Liebowitz seems utterly transformed from our previous evening. She's wearing a beige blouse and dark slacks. Her hair is pulled up in some kind of complicated bun, she's put on fresh lipstick, and there's a pair of opal earrings as well. She has a smile on her face, but somehow I don't think it's meant for me.

"Sorry to bother you again," I say.

"Oh," she says, "oh, it's you." The smile fades. Still, she invites me in. This time she leads me into the dining room. It has a long plain cherry table with eight simple chairs that look like they were lovingly fashioned by the Amish. There are woven placemats in front of the chairs, and white cloth napkins, and old chipped china plates, glasses, and silverware. A shallow bowl filled with water and pink camellias. We take seats opposite each other.

"What can I do for you, Mr. Parisman?"

"Well, I was hoping we could talk some more about Bart. But maybe you're busy getting ready for guests tonight. I could come back tomorrow."

She sees me staring at the table. "Oh, you mean this? I invite my tenants over for dinner one night a week. It's a tradition we've had for years. I bring food, they bring food. It started not long after my husband died. I was lonely. It's helped me get through some pretty dark times."

"You ever invite Bart Pereira?"

"Sure," she says. "He didn't always show up, and he didn't usually bring food. Like I told you, he wasn't a cook. But wine or beer? He was good for that."

I nod. She drops her hands in her lap and rubs them together as if she's cold. It strikes me again how she stands out, how quietly captivating she is, the way a single line from a poem can stay with you sometimes, even after you've forgotten everything else. I wonder if Bart saw that same quality in her, whether she saw something in him.

"He sounds like he didn't really mean to ditch you like he did. I mean, he came back, right?"

Her face is dismissive. "He came looking for his knife. The one I sold you."

"Did you tell him I had it? Maybe I'd sell it back to him."

"Let's not kid each other, shall we?" Her eyes narrow. "The cops have been here, your Mexican friend was just here, and now you've been here twice. You're after Bart because you think he did something awful. It's not true."

"And how do you know that, Dorothy?"

She brushes a stray hair away from her face before she speaks. She's choosing her words carefully. "The Bart Pereira I know, the guy who lived in that tool shed for the last six months, he was a kind man, a thoughtful man. Heroic, that's how I saw him. He brought me flowers once, for no reason. He'd had a difficult life, he could be rough around the edges sometimes, but he never forgot his roots, his purpose."

This little speech of hers catches me off guard, and for a moment I'm thrown inexplicably back into my teens. I wasn't the sharpest kid in the classroom. I never raised my hand, my book reports were as short as I could get away with, my science projects were sloppy last-minute affairs—a square of cardboard with a chart of high and low temperatures in red and blue markers. Which isn't science, really, it's plagiarism. The truth is, I slept through high school, I didn't care; what I learned was how to pass. But one skill I've worked on a lot since then is listening. And what I hear about Pereira from Dorothy Liebowitz now doesn't jive with that body slumped over in the parked car. It doesn't jive with the portrait of Francis Crocker on the couch, either.

"You know, the last time I was here, the impression I got was that you and Bart didn't have much in common. He was this loner, and all you cared about was the rent, I think you said."

"The rent *is* important to me. I still have a mortgage."

"Yeah," I reply. "But he was living just a few yards away. I get how you need the rent, but when we talked the first time, it was like you hardly knew him. He was a stranger. Now you're telling me he wasn't quite so feral."

"I never said that."

"No. No, you didn't. I was just interpreting. I do that a lot, read between the lines. Guess I misunderstood."

"Yeah, well."

"Still, you guys talked every so often, right?"

"I suppose."

"And now, over time, it sounds to me at least like there's more. He brings you flowers, for example."

"We're friends, okay," she admits under her breath. "We've become friends."

"And you don't think a kind, generous fellow like that—a friend—would ever be capable of violence? Is that it?"

She doesn't live in the same *farkakte* world I do, and it's not fair to speculate. But the question is abrupt, a bridge too far. I can see by the startled reaction on her face that I've crossed a line.

"He's never been that way with me," she insists. "I know he served once in the Israeli army, that he fought somewhere, Lebanon or Syria, but that was different. War always pushes men into corners. He had to; he had no choice."

I let the silence take over. A minute passes. She seems to relax. Or maybe she's mulling over all the discrepancies she's noticed about Bart in the short time they've known each other. Maybe she's questioning herself, wondering what it means to really know somebody, whether she's misunderstood his flowers, his penchant for solitude, how he could vanish for days on end with no explanation.

"Tell me something," she says. "What's he done? Don't I deserve to know that? Why are you looking for him?"

A voice in my head tells me to shut this down. She's not to be trusted, she has a weakness for Bart and he'll be hearing about this conversation before long. But then I wonder whether that's not a good thing. Dorothy Liebowitz isn't running away. And you can bet on the power of love. "It's complicated," I say. "We think he was involved in a theft. The man he worked with, his partner, was found dead not long ago. Somebody stabbed him."

"And that's why you took his knife?"

I nod.

"He wouldn't do that," she says reflexively. Her lips tighten. "No, that's not who he is. It makes no sense."

"Maybe not. Maybe he didn't murder anyone. But his buddy's dead, and the Torah's gone."

"Torah? They took a Torah? Why?"

"It wasn't just any Torah. More like a relic, a piece of fine art. Two hundred years old, you know what I'm saying? From Algeria. Apparently, there are people in Israel, in Russia, other places, who'd pay big bucks for something like that."

This only seems to shore up her opinions. "He's not religious, Bart. He doesn't believe in God, I can tell you that. And you've seen most of his possessions, what's in that garbage bag. The man lives like a hermit. Money means nothing to him."

"You may be right," I tell her. "This could all be a gigantic mistake. But right now the wheels are turning down at the DA's office, and the only way I can put on the brakes is if I talk with Bart. You already know I'm not a cop. I don't care about busting him and I'm not looking for publicity. Just the Torah." With that, I get up to go. She sits there, numbed by everything, her hands still in her lap. She doesn't bother to walk me to the door.

*   *   *

Florence, who's in charge of the front desk when I walk in, tells me Malloy is having a late lunch at the HomeBoy Cafe in City Hall. I wander over and see him sitting there, making small talk with a pair of earnest, young Black men. They both have pencil-thin mustaches and shaved heads. Beneath their long dark canvas aprons, they're wearing white T-shirts and blue jeans. When they see me approach, they turn and disappear into the kitchen.

"Hey," I say, pulling up a chair next to him. "Is this taken?"

"No," he says, "I was just shooting the breeze with a couple of old pals."

"They don't look too old to me."

"They're fine men, actually. We've become friends. Marlon's a natural-born comedian. I sent them both to prison six years ago. Burglary. Now they're cleaning up their act, working here. The food business suits them, I guess. Chopping, dicing? Beats breaking and entering, anyway." He lowers his half-eaten sandwich, puts on his cop face again. "How'd you find me, Amos?"

"Florence."

"She knows everything, that Florence."

The two born-again burglars are leaning on the counter, smiling and staring at us from a safe distance, whispering back and forth. Bill calls them his friends, but I doubt that somehow. More like former enemies, maybe. I grab a few packets of salt and pepper and lay them out in a nice, precise, alternating row. Pepper, salt, pepper, salt. "I came by because, well, I'm still on the trail, and I'm wondering what your geniuses in the lab ever did with the switchblade. They must be finished by now."

"Oh, yeah."

"So? Don't keep me in suspense. Is that our murder weapon?"

He shakes his head. "I'm afraid not. The blade itself was pretty clean, we couldn't get any useful material off it, but that wasn't the problem. Whatever stabbed Marquez was at least half an inch longer than what you gave me."

"Really?" I say. "It was too short?"

"Too short to do him in. Pereira might have killed him, don't get me wrong, but if he did, he used something else. Also, why would he kill him? They're both probably salaried employees. It's not like he could fence the Torah on his own and make a fortune."

"So he's off your radar, then?"

"For the time being. As far as murder goes, anyway."

"What about Crocker?"

He frowns. "What about him? There's no connection. Maybe you can show me something that says Crocker even knew Pereira or Marquez. I wouldn't need much, Amos. Hell, if Pereira just left his prints on Crocker's doorknob, that'd be more than enough. But guess what? He didn't. Nobody did."

One by one, I pick up the salt and pepper packets and set them back where they belong. "In my book, he's still suspicious," I say. "At the very least, you need to bring him in about the Torah."

"We need to find him first. And then what?" He lifts his hands in consternation. "You really think the rabbi and his wife could pick him out of a lineup? I wouldn't bet on that."

I glance over at the strapping young men from HomeBoy. They've stopped watching us and gone back to the menial comfort of stacking plates and polishing silverware. "So, where does the LAPD reckon we are with this?"

"I can only speak for myself," he says. "In the beginning we had just one small case—the Torah theft."

"Hey, c'mon, it wasn't small, Bill. They shot a security guard, for Christ's sake."

"Okay, granted. A security guard was killed. That was bad. Tragic. But to me it was manageable. Now, by coincidence maybe, or because of your friend Zaslow, we're in the middle of a whole international spy ring. Which, as I think I've mentioned previously, is way above my pay grade. It's Costello's job from here on out. He's working on Richard Sykes right now."

"You think he knocked off Crocker? Do they have a weapon?"

"No, not yet. But they're going through his apartment with a fine-tooth comb. They're looking at his car. Cracked open his phone. Computer, bank records, credit cards, the whole shebang."

"And?"

"It's early. These things can take time. Turns out, those four slugs in Francis Crocker come from the same kind of handgun the SEALs use. That's something."

"Yeah, maybe."

"Also, since Crocker was his delivery boy, they obviously knew each other. And if he learned somehow that Sokolov was in custody in Montreal, well, let's just say Sykes would be very motivated to stay out of prison. Crocker would have ratted him out, no question."

I start to cough. At my stage of the game, I'm on pills for all kinds of things. Blood pressure. Cholesterol. Heart. Now all at once I realize I forgot the yellow one I'm supposed to take at lunch, and my mouth is dry as the Negev. I roll my tongue around inside. The cough comes back. This is an emergency. Bill's icy water glass is sitting there in front of him, untouched. "You mind?" I say, reaching for it before he can decide yes or no. Aah.

He looks at me, uncomprehending, rolls his eyes. The things he puts up with.

"So, where does that leave us with the Marquez killing?"

"Good question," Malloy says. "At the moment, nowhere."

CHAPTER 14

It's Loretta and my anniversary tonight. Forty-three years? For-ty-four? Something like that. We gave up celebrating a while ago—around the same time she got sick. It hits me just as I pull off the Hollywood. Then I climb the little grade at the Vermont exit and catch a green light, which means I can't stop to give a buck to the Vietnam vet who's always there waiting with the cardboard sign. I swing left, heading for 3rd. Traffic is thick. Another gray LA after-noon. People are in a desperate hurry to get home, they're driving faster than they should, the music is pumping out of their car radios, but I see a small florist shop in a corner strip mall and zip in. Flowers by Chang. Right next to Van's Doughnuts and Wifi World. I run inside, where it's cool and misty, come out five minutes later with a dozen red roses wrapped in paper and cellophane.

When I get home, my cousin Shelly is standing there, gabbing with Carmen in the kitchen. I haven't seen him in at least a week. First thing I notice is how nice he smells. He's all dressed up, too, a blue suit and tie, and not only that, he's brought his new paramour, Nicole, with him. She's in her late twenties or early thirties, and she's wearing a black silk dress that does wonders for her legs. I've met Nicole once before; we smile gamely at each other. I'm also sure that Nicole is aware of Ruth. She knows Shelly's still technically married to her, that there are children involved, that they've gone back and forth for a few years now. Shelly would never keep something like that a secret, not like some men; but how he explained it to her, smoothed it over, I have no idea.

Loretta's in the bathroom. Shelly looks down at his watch, says they can't stay, they're going out to dinner, but he's brought us a bottle of champagne and box of macarons from the La Brea Bakery.

"Hey, it's your anniversary, am I right?"

"That's true, Shel. We don't do much about it anymore. I'm glad, though, that one of us hasn't forgotten."

He spots my paper bouquet. "What do you mean 'one of us'? You didn't forget either, I see."

"Oh, this?" I say, handing it off to Carmen so she can look for a suitable vase. "This is just a last-minute idea. We really don't celebrate. You know how it is. After forty years, what's the difference, huh? We've been at it too long."

Shelly gives Nicole a hopeful squeeze. "Well, *we* haven't, right, honey?"

She tilts her head, laughs politely. What I know about Nicole you could write on a postcard and still have room for a Dear John letter. Nicole is fairly new to LA. She just landed a job at an insurance agency in Westwood. She grew up in a two-bit town in Minnesota or Wisconsin—someplace cold and frozen, anyway—and she was raised Catholic, Shelly said. This is her first time in a big city. I'm comfortable with Nicole, but it's a little hard to know where this relationship is going. I mean, I know exactly where Shelly would like it to go; my cousin has always been painfully obvious about his needs. He falls in love quickly and frequently these days, especially since the trouble started with Ruth. Shelly doesn't call it trouble. Or, rather, he uses the Yiddish word *tsuris*, which means trouble technically, but to hear him say it, it's so much more than that.

Loretta emerges, and when she sees Shelly she grins and goes right up to him and gives him a bear hug. "Hey, sugar," Shelly says. "I want you to meet my friend Nicole."

Nicole offers her hand. She's dubious, or at least confused. "Didn't we meet . . . before?" she asks Shelly, as well as my wife.

"Do I know you?" Loretta asks. This question comes up often

these days. I know it sounds strange, and to some who've known her it probably seems rude, but it's how she's learned to break the ice whenever she feels nervous.

"You do now," Shelly says. He gives a conspiratorial wink to everyone.

Loretta starts speaking about making dinner then, something she hasn't done in months or years and probably wouldn't know where to begin even if she tried. Shelly hugs her again, says thanks for the offer but another time, he and Nicole have to be shoving off. As soon as they're gone, Loretta turns to me, perplexed. "Did they think I was asking them to eat with us? That's crazy, Amos."

"You're right, honey. Craziest thing I ever heard. Why would we ever wanna eat with them? Hell, not on our anniversary." I point out the roses, which, thanks to Carmen, are now sitting in a glorious crystal vase on the dining-room table, along with the champagne and the box of cookies.

Loretta plants a kiss on my cheek. "Not on our anniversary," she repeats.

*   *   *

Later that evening, after she's smelled the roses and eaten far too many macarons and finally gone off to bed, I retreat to my office and call Pete Zaslow.

"You still up?" I ask.

"What time is it?"

"I dunno," I say. "Ten, ten-thirty."

"I'm still up, then. What's on your mind?"

"I'm wondering what you managed to find out about our man Pereira. You said you'd fish around."

"Yeah, I know."

"So, did you catch anything?"

He goes quiet. Then he hems and haws, talks at first about the time difference between Los Angeles and Tel Aviv, how the people he's friendly with there have certain limitations. There are things they prefer not to discuss over the phone, they say—or not so much that, as things they can't always reveal. Political considerations. Israel is a fractured state, politically. So many parties, you understand. All those competing interests. Everyone deserves respect.

"That's fine, Pete. I don't need the whole college course. Let's cut to the chase, why don't we? Who is Bart Pereira?"

"Bartholomew Pereira," he begins. "That's his real name, by the way. Bartholomew Pereira was born on a kibbutz in Galilee. A place called Kfar Hanassi, one click away from the Jordan River and not that far from the Golan Heights. His parents came from Argentina, although the kibbutz was mostly Jews from the UK and Rhodesia and South Africa. They used to stop everything for tea at four o'clock, my friends tell me. Anyway, he grew up there, drove a tractor, picked apples, shoveled chicken shit."

"Sounds lovely," I say. "Too bad he didn't stay there."

"And when he was eighteen, he went into the army. Did quite well, apparently. From there he joined Shin Bet, the Israeli internal security service."

"He wasn't shoveling after chickens with them, I don't suppose."

"Chasing Arabs, actually. Did that for five years. Then he moved on to Mossad."

"So you're saying he's a spy."

"No. I'm telling you he worked for Mossad. My friends didn't have much clarity on that; one of them thought he might have been an analyst, but who knows? Just because he was with Mossad doesn't mean anything *per se*."

"Yeah, but Mossad, Pete—don't they have an agenda?"

"They gather intelligence. They're a giant think tank, for the most part, same as the CIA or MI5. Don't pay attention to all those Hollywood thrillers. The vast majority have desk jobs, they're not hit men out in the field. Most of them look at screens and reports all day long, they sit around in meetings. They go home to their families at night."

"And some of them are assassins."

"A few, sure. There's that capacity if they need it."

"Okay, fine. Then what?"

"Then, six or eight months ago, he left Israel and came here."

"Still working for Mossad? Or did he quit? Or is he here as a mole? That would seem like a pretty important question to ask. Wouldn't you need to know that, Pete?"

"Naturally," he says. "Only I never heard the answer. I asked them several times, in fact, but you know how it goes. They told me what they wanted me to hear."

"You said they were your friends."

"They are. When we see each other, we go out to dinner. We laugh, reminisce, tell jokes. Naftali and his wife were in town last March on business. They stayed overnight with us. He still plays a mean game of chess. They're like family to me."

"But they stop short at Pereira."

"What's that poem?" he asks, and I can picture him sitting back on his plush living-room couch, growing wistful. "'The fog came in on little cat's feet'? Isn't that what Sandburg wrote? Something like that. It came and went. The fog, that is. So, my friends changed the subject. It was all very polite. They just wouldn't say."

"He told his landlady he was a private investigator."

"Could be. I mean, it sounds plausible. Shin Bet has plenty of investigators. Those guys are always skulking around, looking for something."

"Right." We are silent for a moment. Pete's read a lot of books, and I know he has certain fixed ideas about the world, about how it works, the nuts and bolts, about the arc of history, about the existence of good and evil, red lines drawn in the sand; all that stuff means something to him. He'd be scared to step out of his own front door, he told me once, if he couldn't rely on a moral, orderly universe.

I realize all at once that I now have to meet Pereira face-to-face. That's the only way I'll ever be able to take the measure of the man. There's too much contradictory stuff swirling around him. Mrs. Liebowitz has feelings for him; Zaslow's informants clam up when his name is mentioned; and he goes around with lowlifes, roughing up old people, ripping off Torahs. "I should let you go to bed, Pete. But one last thing: Your friends in Tel Aviv, you said they went silent when you pressed them about Pereira."

"That's true. It ended up putting a damper on our conversation."

"But that's not the end of it. Not in my business. Silence can speak volumes sometimes, know what I mean?"

"I do."

"So okay. You're a smart guy. I guess what I'm digging for is an inference."

"About what?"

"They weren't just being polite. For whatever reason, they were privy to something they couldn't reveal. Help me out, Pete. What's your best guess?"

He pauses, and here is where I expect him to act incredulous. I'm going out on a limb, after all. "Are we talking state secrets, old man?" His voice softens. He sounds kind, solicitous.

"That's not what I'm asking. You said Mossad is a think tank. And we know they have a few contract killers. Could one of them be Pereira?"

"No," he replies evenly. "I didn't get that impression from what they said. But I'd be very careful going up against him. Think about his background. All those years. He's trained. He knows what to do."

*   *   *

The next morning, because it's another sweltering day in paradise and I have nothing better on my plate, I get in my Honda and take a solitary drive out to Inglewood. I figure there's a three-to-one chance the warehouse might be permanently closed now that Crocker's gone to heaven, but maybe not. He was on the road in South America an awful lot. He wasn't planning on dying, and the young ladies working there might not know yet. Why should they? Who would tell them? Also, it goes without saying that they still need the work.

I pull into the parking lot. There are a dozen muscle cars and pickup trucks alongside me. They seem to favor Gramercy Appliances, although there's an older Volvo station wagon from the last century with bumper stickers promoting world peace and literacy, which I'm sure belongs to Ortega Office Supply. There are no vehicles in front of Crocker's establishment, but I can see a glint of neon through the bank of high windows. Maybe the two women I met before don't make enough to own a car; maybe they take the bus.

I tap gently on the door, then pull on the knob and it opens. In a recess overhead, a portable radio is playing soft norteño music. The same two Latinas are leaning over the long counter. The older one is pouring a gallon jug of bluish liquid into a series of small plastic bottles, using a funnel. The younger woman is unpacking a cardboard box. I spot the words PERU and FRAGILE stamped on one of the many green stickers. They both stop what they're doing when they see me.

"You want Señor Crocker?" the younger one asks. "He's not here. Out of town."

"No," I say, "I realize that. I actually came by to speak with you."

Startled, they look at each other, then back at me, but this time it's like I'm suddenly an extraterrestrial. No one's ever wanted to speak with these ladies.

I take out my wallet, which contains my investigator's license, and flip it casually in their direction, then slide it back in my jacket. This is all for show, of course, a little magic act. I hope they also get a glimpse of the leather shoulder holster and the deadly weapon tucked inside. "My name's Amos Parisman. I work with the Los Angeles Police. I need your cooperation."

"We don't know nothing," the older one stammers. There's a tinge of fear in her voice. "We just come here every day. Do our job."

"What's your name?" I ask. "¿Cómo se llama?" I pull out my notepad and a pen to write it down. The more official you make it, the better.

"Gutierez," she mumbles. "Emilia." She indicates the younger one. "This is my daughter, mi hija, Karina."

I dutifully scribble their names onto my notepad. "Gracias. Now, let's talk about Francis Crocker. He's been involved in some suspicious shipments of goods to foreign countries."

"The police were here yesterday," Karina offers, as if this will clear everything up.

"Did they tell you why?"

"No, no, they don't tell us nothing. They just looked around. Two guys from the Inglewood Police Department. They asked when was the last time we saw Señor Crocker."

"And what'd you tell them?"

"Four days, maybe a week. He doesn't care about this," she waves vaguely at the warehouse and all its contents, "as long as the orders get filled."

"Well, I'm here to follow up. I'll be needing to check his files, if you don't mind."

"The files are in his office," Karina announces. She wraps her bare arms around her waist defensively. "It's locked."

"Okay. Do you have a key? Or shall I break it open? This is serious."

Karina doesn't respond.

"Señor Crocker has a key," Emelia jumps in suddenly. "But there's an extra one we keep in a jar. For emergencies. Or sometimes, you know, when he's on a trip he calls and asks us to clean it up before he comes."

Karina cuts her mother an angry look out of the corner of her dark eyes, like *why'd you have to say that?*

"Fine," I tell Emilia. "Will you go get that for me, please?"

She glances again at her daughter and glides hesitantly away from the counter. At the rear of the second aisle, she pulls what looks like an empty glass jelly jar off the shelf and extracts a gold key with a rabbit's foot attached. Then she returns and hands it over.

"What do you mean, 'suspicious shipments'?" Karina says. "It's just legal medicine we send out: herbs, roots, native plants. No narcotics."

She's more savvy than her mother, or at least a little more at home in LA. Maybe someone has told her she has rights. Maybe she's seen a lot of crime shows on television. Or I dunno, maybe she didn't find my quick impersonation of a cop so convincing.

"I'm not after narcotics," I tell her as I unlock the office door. "I'm looking for names and addresses."

The two women stand there watching at a safe distance. They're not about to confront me; how America works is still a mystery to them. They've learned to survive so far by following their instincts, and by staying in the shadows. I pull open the metal filing cabinet and start thumbing through it. It's just invoices from pharmaceutical firms in Brazil, Peru, and Colombia. Also, files with several different banks where Crocker kept accounts. Chase, Wells Fargo, Union. Why would he spread his money all over the place?

I yank on his desk drawer. I thought it would be locked, and I'd have to go through the same song and dance again, but it slides right open. It's got the usual tchotchkes—pens, paper clips, staples, Post-it notes. There's also a little brown leather notebook. Back in my father's day, it was the kind of thing men used to jot down names and numbers of their girlfriends. Or if they didn't have any girlfriends, drinking buddies. Or sometimes it had the number of a lawyer who'd come down at midnight to spring you from the drunk tank. My Uncle Al had such a book. He called it his *Influencer*. I gotta consult my Influencer, he'd say. Which usually meant he had to call his bookie. "This needs to be examined more carefully," I tell the women, as I slip it into my jacket pocket. They're like crows on a wire, watching my every move. "This is evidence."

Then I go back into the shipping area and start poring through the register. Sokolov's name comes up regularly on the fourth or fifth of every month for the past year. The weights of the packets vary, but they're always heavier than ones they send out to the holistic food places in Arkansas and Tennessee.

"You have any other boxes going to this fellow in Canada?"

"Not so far this month," Emilia says. "The boss brings those. He packs them himself."

"So you've never seen what's inside?"

Emilia shakes her head. "We do our job."

"I'm sure you do," I say. I take a step toward the door. They stand there, both with their arms crossed. I think about telling them the truth, that they should go home early, that Frank Crocker is never coming back from the trip he's on, that these insignificant jobs they have, packing and pouring and stuffing pills into plastic vials, are going to be over before they realize. Someone else will let them know soon enough; maybe Sherry in Thousand Oaks will leave her air-conditioned office and make the long trek down here to lower the boom. Or maybe not. On second thought, why would she bother? He probably didn't pay her much more than these two. Amazing how one man's death leaves so many loose strings behind, I think. Even if you know in advance, even if you plan ahead, there are always confused people out there on the right side of the grave, innocent souls like these two who just do their job, who didn't get the message, who need instruction.

The day is heating up. I head for my car. I'm not their teacher, I think. Let someone else take that on.

*   *   *

There's an In-N-Out Burger on Century Boulevard. I'm not yet ready for the trek back to Hollywood on the freeway—and okay, it isn't lunch time exactly—but I need a private space where I can clear my head; the minute I saw their big red arrow, I knew that's where I was going. To say that I grew up with In-N-Out is an understatement. It's another one of those quiet miracles that nobody pays attention to; it makes life in Southern California worth living. When I came back from the war in Vietnam, the first place Shelly and I went to after I landed was In-N-Out. It tasted like home.

I pull around to the window and order a Double-Double, fries, and a large iced tea with extra lemon wedges. That's the best meal they serve here. Hell, it's practically the only meal. I sit in my Honda with the windows down and eat. Jet planes lumber overhead en route to LAX, or leaving, I can't tell. A half dozen pigeons waddle amiably between the parked vehicles, dining on fries and bits of onion and lettuce tossed out. They're such regulars that even a car engine roaring to life a foot away doesn't faze them anymore—it's part of the ambiance.

I'm almost done with my burger, my blood sugar has hit that sweet spot, and there's only a few cold fries left in the cardboard tray, when I remember the booklet still in my jacket pocket. I start flipping the pages. Crocker did everything alphabetically, more or less. Just a series of names and numbers, most of which mean nothing to me. Until I get to the Gs, that is. That's when all at once my eyes fall on *Juan Guerrero*. A phone number is beside it, but since he won't be answering his phone anymore, I keep rifling through. H, I, J, K. Out of nowhere, a curious scene comes tumbling back at me—a sunlit afternoon in Miss Rubalcava's eighth-grade music class. I'm sitting in the rear, as far away from her as I can get, watching the clock on the wall, waiting for the final bell to ring. I'm desperate to go home and forget about school; I want to shoot hoops out by the garage. But Miss Rubalcava is so wound up, so excited, she's waving her arms and telling us about this glorious music she's playing on the phonograph, what Ferde Grofé intended—how, if we just closed our eyes and put ourselves in the picture, we'd feel in our bones what's going on. She's so enthusiastic, she lifts me up like an angel with her words, and she transports me to that hardscrabble place. And I can't explain it, but I know I'm there—I'm one with those thirsty mules in the Grand Canyon Suite. I'm running and sweating right alongside them, desperate for a drink, my heart beating in rhythm, faster and faster as they get closer to the cool, fresh water at the bottom. I reach the Ps and I halt. Now I'm staring at *B. Pereira*, along with his cell phone number. Jackpot.

CHAPTER 15

Lieutenant Malloy isn't the happiest man on earth, which is a shame, because right about now he should be, I tell him.

"And why's that, Mr. Parisman?"

"Because I have in my hand the cell phone number for Bartholomew Pereira."

"Really?"

"Really. Which means you folks can track his location."

"Give it to me," he says. His voice is flat. Ungrateful would be a stretch maybe, but not by much.

I read him off the number and there's a pause. Then I hear a thunk, like he slammed the receiver on the desk, followed by a muffled sound of someone shouting. The LAPD is swinging into action.

"We'll get on it," he says laconically, when he returns. "It may be useful, I mean, if he still has the phone on him. How'd you come by this little morsel, anyway?"

I tell him all about how I went back to the warehouse and chatted with the ladies. How they graciously let me poke around. How the book was just sitting there in front of Frank Crocker's desk, plain as day. How I'm surprised the police hadn't discovered it by now.

"The Inglewood PD doesn't have the same level of interest we do," he explains. "The man died in Hollywood. As far as they're concerned, that's another country."

"You're not suggesting they don't care."

"Frank Crocker paid taxes, that's what they cared about. The city of Inglewood lost a business."

"Okay, but businesses come and go."

"Exactly. And we lost a human being. That's the difference."

We talk about related things—how, since I found those names in his notebook, it looks pretty certain that Frank Crocker was involved in stealing the Torah, as well as other far more lethal things from the United States Navy. Malloy, understandably, is more interested in the latter. The Torah's just a roll of paper, he says. They can always print another one. I don't take offense at this. It's just how he is.

I ask him how Costello's discussions with Sykes are going.

"Sykes admitted taking a few devices and passing them on to Crocker. But as for murder, well, he's denying it, left, right, and sideways. Claims he never knew where Crocker lived. Said whenever he had a delivery, he'd call him up and Crocker would arrange a drop-off. He also claims—and here's where it really gets strange—he'd usually try to remove some tiny vital part of whatever he was selling him. He didn't want the Russians to use it."

"What a patriot."

Malloy tries, without success, to hide his contempt. "That's what he says he is, yeah. He was out to make a bundle, and still sell them shoddy merchandise. It's the best of both worlds."

"No kidding! Now that takes chutzpah. But is that true? I mean, the things the Mounties found at Sokolov's apartment—were they defective?"

"Costello didn't tell me, number one. And number two, you'll forgive me, I didn't ask."

"What about Crocker? Think he was in on it, too?"

"Maybe," Malloy says. "He didn't have much in common with Moscow. We've been looking into his background. He was raised in Arkansas, dirt-poor. His father never went past the eighth grade. He kept chickens. They sold eggs. That's no way to make a living, you ask me."

"No, not if you want to pay the rent."

"Exactly. They could barely make ends meet, which didn't matter

as long as his mom had her job with the utility company. Then she
got breast cancer. They were always taking her to doctors and alter-
native healers, visiting her in hospitals—that's what his big sister
told me on the phone. Frank was nine when his mother died. After
that, the old man fell apart. Started disappearing into bars at night,
drinking himself to death. You know how it goes."

"I've heard, yeah."

"Anyway, the boy grew up desperate. He wanted to make money.
He wanted to get out of Arkansas, see the world. That was his whole
political agenda, his sister said, just get the hell out."

Then Malloy says he's sorry, he has another call to take, and he'll
have to get back to me about the cell phone. He still doesn't thank
me for the tip, not in so many words, but I'm an intuitive guy, I can
hear in his voice that he's grateful. That's okay, I think, I just figured
you might be interested.

Another plane flies low overhead. Southwest Airlines. I'm done
eating, so I toss the remaining batch of fries out the window to
the pigeons, who make short work of them. We're all in this
together, right?

*   *   *

Carmen is gathering her sweater and purse, getting ready to head
out the door for the bus ride home, when the phone rings. It's Omar.

"Hey, man," he says, "I know you told me to let you handle it,
but I've been sitting here across the street from Mrs. Liebowitz's for
three hours. Guess who just walked in the door?"

I tell him to hang on a minute. I turn to Carmen. "Do you absolutely have to leave now?"

"If I want to catch the bus, yes."

"Yeah, but do you have to go home? If I drove you home later,
can you stay till ten or so? If I gave you an extra hundred dollars?"

She hesitates. "Antonio is in his truck, on the road from Sacra-
mento. He won't be home till tomorrow, so that's okay. And mi hijo,
Ricardo, he is playing now at Miguel's next door. I'll call there, ask

his mother if he can stay for supper."

I give her a hug. "I love you, Carmen." Then I'm back on the phone. "I'll be there in fifteen minutes, Omar. You stay put. Don't let him out of your sight."

The sun is low in the sky by the time I pull up just ahead of Omar's Camaro on Bonnie Brae. He's got his usual T-shirt on, but it's gotten cooler out and he's added a windbreaker that he keeps in the trunk. He's leaning against the hood. Behind the curtains, the lights are twinkling in Dorothy's house.

"Okay," I say. "I'm going in there. I'm hoping he'll let me talk with him. If he runs out on me, you'll be here to track him further."

"What? You don't want me to come in with you? The guy's a killer, Amos. Look what he did to Guerrero. Look at what happened to Crocker."

"He didn't kill Guerrero," I declare. "The cops are convinced of that. And there's no proof he did Crocker, either. He helped steal the Torah, I'll give you that. But that just makes him a *gonif*."

Omar frowns. "And why would he talk with you?"

I consider this briefly. For a lot of reasons, I wanna say. Because I'm a wrinkled old *alte katchke*, and if he's as virile as Zaslow made him out to be, he'll write me off as harmless. Because I'm not a cop. Because Dorothy will also be there in the room, and for her own purposes she wants this to end peacefully. For all of those things. That's not what I tell Omar, though. "Because I'm a Jew," I say to him, "and so is he. And we have a lot in common."

Now he shrugs. Omar has come of age on the streets of East LA, which might be good for some things, but for the most part it leaves you with a pretty jaded view of humanity. The dark look on his face now says he thinks I'm about to die. "I don't know about you, man."

"Just stay where you are," I tell him. "Trust me." I cross the street then and go up the steps to the front door.

"Funny," Dorothy Liebowitz says as she unlocks it, "I had a feeling you'd show up again, Mr. Detective." She's wearing a short white summer dress and sandals. Her hair is tied back, and a simple necklace of green Berber beads hangs from her neck. Every time I see her, she seems different, better.

"I hope I didn't disappoint."

"No."

"So is your friend here?"

"In the living room," she says. She's almost relieved to see me, like I am the perfect person to pump up the conversation. Or maybe I just solved a problem she didn't know she had. "We were having a drink before dinner." She leads me down the hall.

Bartholomew Pereira is sitting on the couch with his legs crossed. He's got a black sport coat on, with a lavender shirt underneath. No tie, and it looks like he intentionally forgot to shave. A dark-haired, scruffy, tanned, and reasonably attractive man in his mid-forties. High cheekbones, moody brown eyes. Something chiseled and classic in his demeanor. You could imagine him on a movie set. He might not be the star, but maybe the star's best friend. He's just swallowed a mouthful of whatever he's drinking, and if I've surprised him he doesn't show it. In fact, he doesn't show me anything.

"Bart, this is Amos Parisman, the investigator I told you about."

I come forward and he stands up stiffly, brushes back his mop of hair and shakes my hand. He's nearly a foot taller than me, and he's got a good tight grip. That's when I get a whiff of tobacco coming from him and I remember what the rabbi's wife said. "I didn't mean to interrupt," I say.

"Oh, yes, you did," Dorothy counters. She seems mildly amused at my mannered behavior. "Now, sit down and let's talk. We have a lot to talk about, right? Would you care for a drink, Mr. Parisman? It's gin-and-tonic weather."

I settle into a stuffed leather chair opposite them. "No, no thanks. I just need some information from you, Mr. Pereira, if you don't mind. Then I'll get out of your way."

"Call me Bart." He's looking at me steadily. I can't tell if he's armed, not that it would matter. I don't feel threatened, but we're only separated by a coffee table. Before I could ever get to the gun in my holster, he'd be all over me.

"Okay, Bart. First of all, I have to tell you, you're a hard man to find."

A thin smile. "I like to keep a low profile."

"Yeah, well, I guess it depends on what business you're in, right? My cousin, Shelly, for instance, he's in cars. He spreads his name all over town. Has to. It's all about name recognition, he says. But maybe the kind of investigative stuff you do, I don't know, maybe it's more circumspect. You're a private eye like me, I assume."

"I've done some work, yes."

"Here? Or in Israel? You're Israeli, right?"

"No. In Israel I worked for the government."

"Oh yeah? What kind of work?"

"I'm sorry," he says, "that's really none of your business. Dorothy told me you're looking for me. Well, mazel tov, you found me. Here I am. But I don't know why I should speak with you at all." He's still looking at me, and if he's blinked more than once I haven't noticed. He's not angry, not yet, but he's laying down a quiet predicate for anger. Stoking the fire.

"I'll tell you why," I reply. "Because the truth is, Bart, you're all alone and you're in serious trouble. And Dorothy here is a wonderful lady, and I'm sure she's fond of you, but she can't help you. I can."

He gives me a deeply skeptical look. Maybe those years of toiling in the shadows for Shin Bet and Mossad have left a well-formed callus on his mind. Take a wrong turn down an alley and it's fatal. Caution becomes a way of life. "And how's that?"

"Let's stop kidding around, shall we? I'm telling you the truth: Right now, the whole LAPD is hunting for you. They have your name; they know your friend, Juan Guerrero; and they know you two were involved in that heist of a Torah."

"Juan Guerrero? Who's Juan Guerrero?" Dorothy asks, setting down her drink. Maybe they discussed the Torah, but this is brand-new to her. "You never mentioned him, honey."

"Just somebody I know," Bart says.

"Somebody you *knew*," I correct him. "Actually, they found him the other day slumped over in a parked car on Fountain. Someone went at him with a switchblade."

"I didn't do that," Bart says adamantly. "I wouldn't do that."

"Somebody did."

"Yeah, well, it wasn't me."

"No," I say, "no, I don't think so, either. But the cops? Well, you know how they operate. They're not convinced. Believe you me, we've had many conversations about this."

He leans back on the couch, clasps his hands together. It's plain to him now that I've upped the ante. "Okay," he says tentatively, "you win. I've got nothing to hide. So what's your angle? What do you want from me, Parisman?"

"Simple," I tell him. "It's like this: I was hired by a very rich lady, Harriet Reines. Her husband was, well, I never met him, but judging from what she said, he was an immoral man. He made a boatload of money destroying other people's businesses. He died, and now she feels guilty for what he did. She's on a mission, she's doing the best she can sprinkling his money around town for good causes. She paid me to find the Torah you stole. More than I usually charge, in fact. She even wants it restored to that dilapidated temple on Beverly. Go figure."

"And if I help you locate this missing Torah, tell me, just how will that benefit me?"

I shake my head in disappointment. Here I thought he was coming clean. "It's not just about the Torah, Bart. You know that. It's about the dead security guard. It's about Juan. It's about Francis Crocker."

"What about Francis Crocker?" He seems stunned that I'd pull that name out of the hat.

"Who the hell is Francis Crocker?" Dorothy asks. Now she's genuinely upset. She hasn't touched her drink. The man she's sitting beside, the man she thought she knew, is morphing, bit by bit, into someone dark, someone unrecognizable. "Is he dead too? Is he another friend of yours?" When Bart is silent, she turns to me. "Well?"

Bart cocks his head, crosses his arms in front of him, then rubs them together as if he's feeling chilled. "Frank Crocker hired me and Juan to . . . to collect the Torah," he tells Dorothy. "I went along with it because Juan was going to go to the rabbi's house all alone, and if I didn't, well, I was sure it would get out of hand. You have to realize something about Juan. I knew him—he would have killed that couple. Juan—" he looks at me, and I can see he means it—"Juan was an outlaw. Crazy. Meshuga. You don't give a crazy man a gun. Crocker should have known better."

"So then it was Juan who killed the security guard?"

"I wasn't there," he says. "I joined the team afterwards. But yeah, that's what I heard."

"Tell me something, Bart. How'd you get involved in this caper in the first place? I mean, how'd you even cross paths with Frank Crocker?"

He takes a long, thoughtful swallow of his gin and tonic, jiggles the ice around in the glass, and sets it back on the coffee table. It takes him a while to form an answer. "I met someone at a mutual friend's wedding in Jerusalem," he begins. "Her name's Ronit. She was working in a different section than me."

"What were you doing?"

He rolls his eyes. "It was a government job," is all he says. "Anyway, she'd been drinking, she let me dance with her. And over several hours and several more drinks she told me a story about this ancient Torah. How it was smuggled out of her grandfather's temple in Algeria during the war. That was a long time ago, of course. The Jewish community there was gone, scattered. And the little temple had been burned to the ground by the Arabs or the Vichy, I dunno. Only, the Torah was still out there. Her grandfather could never stop talking about it, it was the last link he had to his childhood, and—"

"And what?"

"And she was naïve, and one night she promised him she'd find it and bring it back to Israel before he died."

"That didn't happen, obviously."

"No," Bart says. "He passed away the month after I met her."

"So?"

He turns briefly toward Dorothy, then me. "So I fell in love with her, Mr. Parisman. Or at least I was lonely enough after my divorce to think I was in love. I *wanted* to be in love. Maybe you can relate."

"Sure. Why not?"

Every few seconds, he glances awkwardly over at Dorothy as if to reassure her of his affection. I can tell he's in a bind; he hopes she understands. "She had other men interested in her," he says. "Rivals. But no one like me. I heard her story. And I guess I was the only one who bought it. I suppose I was a little drunk, but I was also sure of myself. I told her if she could be patient, a few months, a year, well, I'd make good on that promise of hers. That's what won her over."

Dorothy is staring down at the old threadbare carpet on the floor. She seems stiff, wooden—like she's aged ten years in the last five minutes. What can she say to this? Is she bitter? Resigned? Ready to move on? Still in love? How could she hope to compete with this girl in Jerusalem? On the other hand, if not for Ronit, Bart wouldn't be here now. It strikes me that they had probably just been getting into all this, that he had been on the edge of explaining things, when I rang the doorbell.

"It sounds like a fairytale," I say.

"It does, doesn't it? But right now I don't feel much like a knight in shining armor. Just a delivery boy with a Torah."

"Okay. So how'd you know it was here in Los Angeles?"

"Oh, that took some doing," he says. "I have a couple of colleagues in Lisbon; we traced it to where it landed in Rio. The person there who inherited it, Rodolfo Mendes, was a prominent Jewish lawyer at the time. For some reason, he decided the Torah was perfectly safe in Brazil, he thought it didn't need to be kept under wraps. In fact, he wanted to use it. It wasn't just a tree of life, he said, it was the perfect symbol to show our resistance against the Nazi war machine. How we could never be defeated, how much we value our traditions, that kind of thing."

"A poet, that guy."

"You think so? I'd call him a fool. Or not a fool, but he sure didn't know how to keep a secret; eventually there was a big article in a Jewish gazette about it, which nearly got him killed. After that, he shipped it off to a family in Buenos Aires. It became, how do you say? A hot potato. People passed it around. One by one I found them, and once I told them who I was, they gave me the next address in the chain. I traced it down to Aaron Kahn in San Gabriel. His mother had been storing it in her bedroom for years. When she knew she was dying, she asked him to drive it over to the temple on Beverly."

"Okay," I say, "great. You found it. Mazel tov. But then you go get yourself mixed up with Frank Crocker? Why the hell would you do that?"

"My friend Ronit works in another section, remember? They have many jobs, but one thing they do is track large-scale criminal activity—suspicious money transfers, stock, real estate, drugs, art theft. We have people in high places who hear things."

My eyes light up. "I'll bet some of your people speak Russian."

"Some. Ronit's friends told me about Crocker. What he said he did for a living. What he really did for a living."

"And what was that?"

"Frank Crocker? He's what you might call a personal shopper. He provides things to certain well-heeled customers. For our own reasons, we've been watching the man he often shops for."

"You're not going to tell me any more than that, are you?"

He looks wistful, like he wishes he didn't know so much; if he could, he'd love to find a way out of this labyrinth, "Sorry," he smiles now, shrugging his shoulders. "It's a secret. They'd shoot me."

"Funny," I say, "that's what happened to Frank Crocker. They shot him."

When he hears that, he blinks and his face goes numb. "Really," he mumbles. The atmosphere in the living room changes then; Dorothy puts her hand to her mouth, all this talk of people dying has overwhelmed her. It was an accident that she ever ran into anyone like Bart Pereira, an accident that she fell for him; but now she's an accomplice in his shadowy world, and she doesn't know where to turn.

"The man who shot him," Bart says, "I don't know who he is, but he's the same guy who killed Juan. I can guarantee you. Something must have gone wrong, don't you see? It's a pipeline they were running. It's not about the Torah. The Torah's worthless as far as they're concerned. They've got bigger fish to worry about. Someone was intercepted, someone informed the police. That's the only explanation. And now they've sent a fixer out to cover their tracks."

"A fixer?"

He tilts his head. It doesn't matter that I'm a fellow *landsman* and don't pose a threat. By his lights, I'm still a stranger. I can practically read his mind: he's sitting there privately debating whether to let me in on the whole story, whether I deserve to know who the sharks are back in Moscow, just how deep and treacherous the water is. "Frank Crocker was nobody, a zero. But the final address, the people he was shipping merchandise to," he says, hesitantly, "the one who had him rubbed out—now, he's what you'd call a perfectionist. He's willing to pay big bucks for what he wants, but in exchange, everything has to come off without a hitch."

"And that didn't happen."

He shakes his head. "Clearly not. Now it's up to the fixer. That's how it's done. My guess is, I'm next in line." He stands then, straightens his coat. "I have to leave," he says suddenly. Dorothy stands up as well. He puts his arms around her. "It isn't safe for you as long as I'm here. He probably knows where I lived. Do you see what I'm saying? These people are thorough. They don't leave witnesses."

"Where will you go?" she asks.

"Back to Israel for the time being, if I'm lucky enough to reach the airport."

"The airport? You can't do that. What about the police?" she says. "They'll be watching for you. Especially at the airport."

"That's true. They'll try to get one step ahead of me. They'll check the passenger lists of El Al—anything, really, that's flying to Tel Aviv. But I don't have to go direct; I can stop first in Paris, or Madrid, or Mexico City, and go on from there. Besides, they're after someone named Bartholomew Pereira. They might not know what I look like. And the good news is, I came here on another passport, courtesy of my government—Michael Lomax. He pauses for a moment, then turns to me and pulls something shiny out of his front pocket. He's talking rapidly now; he's used to taking charge, he's got a clear picture of what needs to be done, but he needs help. "The Torah's in a storage facility. A place called 24/7 on Sepulveda. Not far from the International Terminal. Here's the key. If you can deliver it to the temple, well, I'd be grateful."

"What about Ronit? When you show up empty-handed, won't she be disappointed?"

"I've disappointed a lot of people," he admits, "myself included. I called Ronit yesterday. First time we've spoken in months. And guess what? She's getting married in August. A captain in the air force, no less. She's pregnant; they're looking forward to the baby."

"Really! But I thought you were in love. I thought she was waiting for—"

"Yeah, I was, I was. Past tense. Things change. Time goes by, and women, well, they can't help it that their clock is always ticking away, can they? Biology, right? And besides, there's nothing to be done. We had no formal agreement. I didn't ask her to stop living while I was gone."

"Did you tell her you had the Torah?"

"I thought about it, yeah."

"And you didn't?"

"She was so excited about her brand-new life, her husband, the baby. That's all she talked about. How could I spoil her parade? Anyway, the Torah was my obsession, really, not hers." He kisses Dorothy tenderly. "I'll be back when things calm down," he promises her. "Don't forget me, okay? I love you."

"Like you love Ronit?" Her face has brightened considerably from a minute ago. She presses herself into his chest.

"That's over with," he says. "I loved the idea of Ronit. But it was *my* idea, and it was all in my head, all wrapped up in that Torah. She's not who I thought she was. A dream. I'm wide awake now."

"When are you leaving?" she says.

He taps the breast pocket in his coat. "I don't know when the next flight is. This evening? Tomorrow morning? But you know me: I travel light. I've got my passport right here. A couple of credit cards in my wallet. An overnight bag in the car. What more do I need?"

We walk out together. "I'll do you one more favor," I say. "You see my buddy Omar standing over there across the street? The tall guy with the shaved head? Since we're heading to the airport anyway, how about we both escort you? I'd like to see you get home in one piece."

CHAPTER 16

Night is falling fast, and we're barreling down the Harbor Freeway in Omar's Camaro, following two cars behind Pereira, when Malloy calls me on my cell.

"We found Pereira's phone," he says.

"Wonderful."

"No, not exactly. It was in a mailbox on Gower, a couple of blocks south of Franklin. So wherever he is, he's not hooked up."

I see Pereira's lights up ahead. He's driving an old white Volkswagen van with Arizona plates. It's been repainted recently and looks like something he bought for cash off a used-car lot. Either that, or he stole it. We're gaining on him, and I have put my hand on Omar's shoulder, cautioning him to slow down.

"I wouldn't worry about Pereira, Lieutenant."

"What do you mean, don't worry? We wanna talk to him. He's in hot water. He knows something about this case."

"He might know a little something, sure. He might know Guerrero. He might know Crocker. But tell the truth, Bill, you don't actually think he killed them, do you?"

There's a brief pause. "We don't have any hard proof, if that's what you mean, no. But he's certainly a person of interest. And besides, there's the little matter of the Torah."

"You don't have any hard proof of that, either. The rabbi and his wife couldn't identify whoever did it."

"She said the man smelled like a cigar."

"Lots of men smell like cigars. We call them smokers."

"I don't understand you, Amos. Not too long ago, you were champing at the bit to find Pereira. You brought me that switchblade from his house on Bonnie Brae, you thought you'd found the murder weapon. Now, all of a sudden, he can do no wrong. What's going on?"

We're right behind him now. He's pushing the Volkswagen as fast as he can, which isn't saying much.

"I dunno. I had another conversation with Zaslow, though, and—"

"You're wasting your time with him," Malloy says. Every time Pete's name comes up, he gets defensive and pissy, and I can't figure why. Maybe it's because Zaslow's world is built on rumor, gossip, and innuendo, and Malloy is just too honest, too square—he can't handle that sort of ambiguity.

"I don't think so, Bill. Your friend Costello wouldn't be spending so much time grilling Sykes if it were just a local heist. Frank Crocker ran a pipeline to Moscow, I think we both agree on that; and they were shipping military blueprints and hardware, okay, but other things, too. Whatever they could get their hands on. If you knew the right people, if you could pay the freight, well, it was probably open to anyone who wanted in, even civilians."

"You mean oligarchs?"

"That's how it works in Russia, right? The rich get rich, and the poor go to hell."

"I've never been to Russia," Malloy says soberly. "I'm sure I wouldn't know." He tells me they're going to stick with Pereira; that, so far, Sykes isn't panning out as the killer. Costello has already gotten him to cop to lifting pistols and other gear from the Navy, so he's looking at two to six years in a federal hotel. "Maybe that'll get him to tell us more."

"Maybe he doesn't have any more to tell."

"That could be, yeah. Which is all the more reason to double down on Pereira."

I think about spilling the beans and telling him about the Volkswagen just ahead of us, how we're about to glide onto the Santa Monica Freeway, how, if he wanted to, he could meet us at the El Al ticket counter at LAX and I'd introduce him to Bart Pereira in person. I expect that, if he didn't get too high and mighty, if he were willing to listen, the two of them would have a lot to talk about. I imagine Pereira could introduce Bill to a whole new level of chicanery if he wanted. I'd like to be at the table when that conversation took place. It could still happen someday.

*　*　*

We follow him into the brightly lit international terminal and watch as he approaches the El Al counter. It's not so crowded, only two middle-aged couples in front. They each have a pair of suitcases with wheels. The suitcases are all tagged with bright red ribbons on the handles and it's clear these people know each other from a previous life. Maybe they're distant relatives, or it's some kind of travel club they belong to. Whatever. One of the guys is telling a loud, mindless joke about which airline has the best cuisine. They smile knowingly, because they've heard it before. It's funny, Mitch, they tell him, but not again. Please. Even his wife begs him to stop.

When it's Pereira's turn, the uniformed young woman there regards him carefully. She looks like she has standards. Or maybe she's seen his kind before, I think—maybe she pegs him for one of those footloose Israeli movie types, an actor or a director. Doesn't bother to shave before he gets on a plane. She goes through his documents, his passport, his credit card. Then she points to his black leather overnight bag, and though I'm too far away to hear the exact words, she seems to be asking, with barely veiled incredulity, if that's all the luggage he has. Then they engage in an animated chat in Hebrew. Lots of gesticulating on his part. She shakes her head, then moves off and picks up a nearby telephone. There is another long, muffled discussion. Satisfied, the woman comes back to Bart and things seem to proceed apace.

Omar meanwhile has taken up a post by the sliding glass doors. His eyes scan back and forth. His hand rests behind his back and close to the gun he's carrying. We don't think we were followed here; which is to say there were no cars obviously tailing us into the big concrete parking facility. But if an assassin was going to put an end to Bartholomew Pereira, this would be his last best chance before he vanished forever up the escalator and boarded a plane for Tel Aviv.

After a few minutes he wanders over, ticket in hand. "The flight's not till eight thirty, but I'm going to make myself scarce, if you don't mind. This place makes me nervous. Too wide open for me." Then he fishes inside the front of his pants and hands me a car key. "I almost forgot. I bought that van from a guy I met yesterday near Trader Joe's on Vermont. He didn't say it was stolen exactly, but from what I paid in cash, it had to be. If you could drive it back to your car and leave it there, I'd appreciate it. My prints are all over it, and I'd rather the police didn't find it here and realize I'd left the country."

"Sure," I say. "Not a problem. I'm going to head over to that storage place on Sepulveda and collect the Torah now. You have a safe flight. I assume you'll be back, right?"

"Are you kidding? As soon as things calm down we'll meet again. Hey, I love LA. Besides, I have a date someday with Dorothy." He smiles, shakes my hand, grabs his satchel, and heads for the escalator.

We drive separately then, a mile or two away from the crucible of noise which is LAX. Omar accompanies me to the storage locker. As he did before with Pereira, he stands by, watching for trouble. I bend down and fumble with the key, but after a couple of tries it goes in neatly and twists to the right. The Torah is inside, hidden in a white plastic garbage bag, tilted at a jaunty angle. Two hundred years. And after all the pain and *tsuris* it's caused, here it is, just sitting by itself in a numbered, airless, tin box. At thirteen, I remember, I felt so differently. It was my honor as a bar mitzvah boy to carry the Torah up and down the aisle of the temple. Everyone was singing and grinning—my parents, my aunts and uncles and cousins. The whole congregation beamed at me, and a few old men reached out from their seats and touched the dark velvet cover as I shambled by. Then they all kissed the tips of their fingers, because that's what you did, because the words of the Torah, as the rabbi had explained in his sermon that morning, were naturally sweet; the Torah was made of honey.

Now I hoist it up against my shoulder, and Omar and I saunter casually out the sliding doors and into the unrelenting whoosh of jets and the thick summer night air.

* * *

I tuck the Torah in the back of Bart's van, cover it with an old blanket that's lying there, and slam the door shut. Omar says he wants to follow me. I tell him not to bother. It's not necessary, I say; Pereira was the target, not me, they wanted him eliminated. Soon he'll be thirty thousand feet up in the air, the captain will turn off the seatbelt sign, and he'll be free to move about the cabin.

I drive down the concrete ramp and merge with the steady silent stream of traffic flowing onto Century Boulevard. From all the take-out detritus left behind on the floor—paper cups and napkins and plastic forks—it looks as though he's been camping out in this Volkswagen the past few days. There's a lingering scent of tobacco everywhere, which doesn't dissipate much, even when you crank down the window. Also, it's stiff to drive. I don't know what kind of deal he got, or maybe I've just grown accustomed to more responsive, less mulish vehicles, but shifting gears is tricky—maybe that explains why Pereira was so slow on the freeway. I get off at Third, and take it nice and easy until I reach Dorothy's house on Bonnie Brae. The lights upstairs are still burning bright. I consider crossing the street and letting her know her friend Bart is on board a jet to Tel Aviv; he's gonna be fine, so she can relax. She's already had a difficult afternoon—hell, her whole life has been flipped sideways—but in the end I figure it's really not my job to sand down all the rough edges of their relationship, that's not what Mrs. Reines hired me for.

I take out my handkerchief and wipe off all the likely places in the car where my fingerprints might reside—steering wheel, door handles, gearshift, hand brake. I leave the door unlocked, both windows open, and, most importantly, Bart's key still in the ignition—on the off chance that someone will come along who needs a free set of wheels. The more strangers who get inside, the better, in my opinion. Then I pop the back hatch, grab the Torah, and sling it onto my shoulder. With my free hand, I grab the handle and lower the hatch. Then I wipe that down too. Bye-bye, bug. My car is halfway down the block.

I take five steps. I'm just passing out of the glare of a streetlamp when a shot rings out. A lone bullet sings past my ear and ricochets off a nearby metal fence. My heart goes into overdrive; I drop to the pavement, still cradling the Torah, and crawl forward into the shadows. I pull my Glock out of its shoulder holster; I release the trigger safety. But even in the dark, it's not okay to be where I am, I'm too exposed, so I crouch down behind the rear wheel of a used Toyota pickup that's parked right in front of the van. I prop the Torah up against it and make myself small. I'm listening, waiting. Waiting for what? Maybe the faint click of a door to open? For footsteps to come toward me? I peek my head around the side of the pickup. There's no one out walking. Four parked cars along the length of the street—he could be in any one of those. Or in one of the dark, ramshackle houses behind them, maybe—Dorothy's neighbors—but that doesn't make sense. Why would a local try to kill me? No, chances are, the shooter's in a car. Maybe he's been here a while, too, biding his time. And it's Pereira he wants. But does he know what he looks like? What kind of car he had? Doubtful. Bart said he just bought that piece of junk off a nameless guy. A fellow gonif. Paid cash. And there are a billion cars in LA. The address, then. Or Dorothy. Does the shooter know about Dorothy? That's a better bet. Pereira wasn't perfect. Did this meticulous Israeli professional slip up somewhere along the line, mention his girlfriend? Where he was sleeping? Did Marquez or Guerrero, or whoever he was, give him a ride home once upon a time and tell Crocker? Did Crocker write it down in a notebook for safekeeping? Could be. The cops traced him here, how hard could it be for this guy? He knows Pereira's running scared; he comes here, pulls the parking brake, waits. Then, just as his bones are aching and he's about to call it quits, he sees me climbing out of a van with something heavy on my shoulder; it looks like a Torah. Bingo, here's his chance. Why wouldn't he open fire?

The third car in line—it's an Audi or a Nissan—some kind of midsize sedan, pulls out sharply from the curb then, its headlights off. It lurches forward in my direction and stops when it's perfectly parallel with the van. I squat down. It's dark and I'm close, but not close enough to see who it is. The window by the driver's side glides down in silence, a hand reaches out and flings something into the front seat of the VW, and, just like that, the car speeds away.

I start to rise up slowly from my crouch. A second later, a thunderous boom knocks me flat on the pavement. It sets off car alarms everywhere. You can hear it downtown. My ears are ringing; I haven't felt something like that since Vietnam. Smoke billows up. The van mushrooms into a liquid ball of orange flame.

I grab the Torah, make a dash for my car. Up and down the block, windows are opening; lights are flicking on. People are streaming out of their houses now, too. They're gathering on the sidewalk at a safe distance, pointing, shouting, talking to one another in little clusters, phoning their children, phoning 911, phoning the police. One old bald Asian fellow in jeans and bedroom slippers rushes past me. He has a large fire extinguisher. He's standing as close as he dares to the burning hulk of the van, spraying away. A man whose car was parked directly across the street, behind the bomber's, runs out in his underwear, gets in, and drives off in a panic. The police arrive five minutes later, red and blue lights and sirens, one squad car, followed by two more, then the fire department. The fire is mostly out by the time they get there, thanks in part to the quick work of the Asian gentleman, but now I'm guessing also because Bart's gas tank was sitting on empty.

I watch the bedlam from inside my Honda. The Torah's safe in the back seat; it's still all swaddled up in plastic. If you didn't know better, you might mistake it for an infant fast asleep. Dorothy Liebowitz makes an appearance. She comes out briefly and stands on the wooden porch in her nightgown, leaning against a post, her arms folded. Does she realize what's just taken place? Maybe cars get torched all the time in this neighborhood. I turn away. When I look back again, she's gone.

After things calm down, I climb out, walk over, and tell the young man in charge—a Sergeant Peralta—that he really ought to call Lieutenant Malloy and tell him what happened.

"And why's that?"

"Because he'll want to know. He's been trailing a suspect who, until a week ago, was thought to reside in that house across the street. It's complicated, but whoever was just here threw a grenade or some kind of bomb into that van. I saw it happen."

"And you are?"

I hand him my blue business card. "I'm also looking for the same man. Apparently, a lot of people are."

He asks me if I got a look at the assailant. I tell him no, but that he was driving an Audi or a Nissan or one of those nice, middle-class family cars, and he drove off in the direction of Wilshire. I leave out the part about how he took a shot at me. I figure that will just scramble the issue further.

More police arrive, and I ask Sergeant Peralta if he needs me for anything more. When he tells me probably not, I get back in my Honda and drive off.

*   *   *

When I get back to Park La Brea, the kitchen counter is spotless, and Loretta has been in bed for over an hour. All the living-room lights are on. Carmen is sitting primly on the couch with her purse and her sweater beside her, eating a bowl of coffee ice cream and watching a Spanish-language show on television. Better her than me, I think, about the ice cream; I need to stay off that stuff. She's relieved that I'm home, but confused. I can't say I blame her; I guess it's not every day you see your boss walk in with a Torah wrapped in a garbage bag.

"Ah, señor. You're here. ¡Gracias a Dios! I was starting to worry. What is that thing in your arms?"

I set it down gently in the chair opposite and pull off the plastic. "This is what I was hired to find, Carmen. It's a Torah, the five books of Moses. You know it. *La Biblia?*"

Her eyes widen and she marvels at the silver casing, the little bells, the filigree. "This is the Bible? I don't . . . no, I don't understand."

There's a small part of my brain that's set to launch into a lecture about now, I could give her the whole spiel—where we Jews came from and all the crap that's happened in the intervening three thousand years. But hey, it's after ten o'clock. Somebody just tried to kill me. I'm tired and she's tired. So okay, in a nutshell, then: just the minimum. "The Old Testament. Adam and Eve? Abraham and Isaac? Moses and the pharaoh? You never read about them? What happened before Jesus? That's what's here."

"Oh sí, sí, I read about them. That was long ago."

I pull out a hundred-dollar bill from my wallet and hand it to her. "Thanks for staying so late, Carmen. You were a big help; you have no idea. Come on, I'll give you a lift home now."

"But what about the señora? Who will stay with her?"

"Loretta's not helpless. And besides, once she's out, everything's fine—she can sleep through an earthquake. Actually, she did sleep through an earthquake once. Don't worry, I won't be gone long."

Carmen weighs this information against her maternal instincts. She doesn't understand the many twists and turns of Loretta's illness, but she has spent a lot of time with her. She loves her, and she's seen for herself that Loretta can rise to the occasion, that she's surprisingly capable sometimes, when she wants to be. "Okay," she says finally.

It's a short drive to her home in El Sereno; traffic is light, especially this time of night. Carmen doesn't say much; I think she may not feel entirely comfortable with my driving her home, that my small act of kindness crosses some invisible line in her culture.

Maybe in Cuba, where she came from, this is frowned upon. On the other hand, things being what they are, it's too late to get a bus to her tree-lined neighborhood in Los Angeles. I ask her if she will be back again tomorrow, and she says yes, *por supuesto*. Eight o'clock, the usual time. I tell her she doesn't have to, she should get some rest; I'll take charge of Loretta until she arrives. And she nods, even though she doesn't fully appreciate what I'm saying. She and her husband, Antonio, have made a reasonable life for themselves out of hard work. Work is their saving grace, their mantra, that's all there is, really. All they know.

The lights are still on in the living room and the Torah is still nestled on the chair when I get home. I'm planning on taking it back to the rabbi tomorrow, but there's no rush. For now, it's safe where it is. Before I go to bed, though, I take a few simple precautions. I make sure the front door is bolted with both deadlocks. I prop a chair behind it. I balance a wine glass on the very edge of the chair. Now, in the unlikely event a determined intruder knows where I live, talks his way past the guard at the gate, makes it up nine flights in the elevator, and shoots his way in—well, I'm hoping when the glass shatters on the tile it will come as a big fat surprise. He'll know that I'm ready for him. But also, for tonight only, I keep the Glock loaded under my pillow. Just in case.

CHAPTER 17

A t some point in life, you wake up and realize you're not getting any younger and you probably can't do this anymore. Or you can, sure, you can go on and on, but you shouldn't—you're pushing your luck and it's not smart. The truth is, plenty of people have died doing what you do. Talented people. I can name three close friends. And maybe, you think—if you still have all your marbles—now's a good time to start looking around for an off-ramp. You could take a class somewhere, learn how to push watercolors on a plate. Or tai chi. Or bird watching. That's not out of the realm of possibility, is it? Find a bucolic hobby, doesn't matter what, really, just something that won't inevitably get you killed. That's the thought that lands on me the next morning as I'm sitting in my Honda letting the engine warm up. The sun is streaming down. Carmen is puttering about, doling out Loretta's oatmeal and orange juice nine floors above me. I told her she didn't need to come in, but since when has Carmen ever listened to me? I can't remember. The Torah survived the night unharmed in my living room and now it's sitting flat in the back seat. All's right with the world.

While the motor is idling, I call Omar and fill him in on my adventures of last night.

He's not very receptive. "I was right, goddamn it. If you'd let me follow you, we could have taken out that *pendejo* then and there. That would have been the end of it."

Omar is such a zealot sometimes: he thinks highly of himself; but, more than that, his heart yearns for solutions that are neat and clean. Even when it comes to an international spy ring. He wants his crime to look like . . . I dunno, like a birthday cake—something you can put in a box and tie a ribbon around. "Forget about it," I tell him. "Life doesn't work that way. The guy was a pro."

"He couldn't be that good. He missed you."

"Yeah, he missed me. By half an inch. I was lucky. But he didn't miss with Marquez and Crocker, did he? And yeah, if you'd been there, who knows?—you might have been able to drop him, but there's also a good chance you'd be lying in the morgue yourself right now. I'm not sure I could live with myself if that happened, Omar."

He goes silent then; he's weighing the dire implications. What would it mean if I was right? What would it mean if he were suddenly to die before Lourdes—the woman he thinks he loves—gives birth someday to their child? Can he imagine that? How her whole universe would go up in smoke? He doesn't know how to handle such large, sentimental questions. "So what happens now?" he says uneasily, after a bit.

"Now? Now I'm heading over to the temple on Beverly to deliver the Torah to its rightful owner. I'm going to make Rabbi Josef's day. Then, I probably should report in to our benefactor, Mrs. Reines, tally up my final bill to her. If she pays me on the spot, I'll come by and give you your share in a day or two."

That cheers him up immeasurably. He can resonate with that idea. After all, it's money in the bank for the baby. His unborn baby. He asks me if he should accompany me to the temple, just in case, and I say, no, no, it's only a few blocks. "You're fired, Omar."

*   *   *

The temple has undergone a sweeping transformation since I was last there. Apparently, even though she paid good money to turn the place into a fortress, in the end it was never Harriet Reines's intention for it to *look* like a fortress. That would never do. A land-scape designer has been thrown into the mix, and maybe a decorator, too. All I know is, it's different. In addition to the somber new set of steel-reinforced doors and the double-paned windows, there is a fresh coat of pale blue paint on the walls and a dark, fire-resistant tile on the roof. Behind the tasteful wrought-iron fence, the lawn has been restored in its entirety: the boxwood hedges around the front of the building have all been neatly trimmed and watered, and the path to the front doors is no longer a dismal patch of gray, caked dirt. Now it's paved and lined on either side with brand-new flowering agapanthus—lily of the Nile. A tall, thin, free-standing copper sign to the right of the door reads "Anshe Amunim" in an artsy kind of Hebraic script.

There's almost nobody out on the street at this hour. I notice a beefy guy from Oldies but Goodies. This must be the notorious Leo Schmidt, I guess. He's standing outside his store in a red-and-white-striped polo shirt with his hands in his pockets, silently staring at the temple. Hard to tell how he views all this renovation. As a business owner, there must be part of him that genuinely approves of it; after all, he can't lose—it's bound to drive more foot traffic his way, maybe raise his property values. On the other hand, if Omar's right and he really hates Jews and Jewish money—if he thinks we're all a bunch of scheming vermin out to rule the universe—well, this just confirms it, doesn't it?

I give him a nod hello, adjust the Torah on my shoulder, and saunter down the garden path into the temple. The foyer is no longer chaotic; it's well lit and doesn't look at all like a second-grade cloakroom anymore. There's a round oak table with neatly stacked prayer books and two wicker baskets containing yarmulkes and prayer shawls. It's silent and calm; instantly relaxing. Brand-new maroon carpet covers the floor leading into the sanctuary. Here is where Mrs. Reines's beneficence has really paid off. The sanctuary has been lined with rich, dark wood paneling. The jumble of metal folding chairs is gone, replaced by semicircles of cushioned pews, and everything focuses attention on the little raised stage with the ark and the eternal light hanging above it.

"So, what do you think?" a voice asks. It's Rabbi Josef.

I was so amazed at the new decor, I hadn't noticed him leaning in the doorway of his office at the rear, watching me. Now I wheel in his direction. I'm still toting the Torah in its white garbage bag. "What do I think, Rabbi? Well, it's a big surprise, isn't it? I mean, it looks like you won the lottery. What do *you* think? What does your congregation think?"

He walks down the aisle. He's trimmed his beard, and he's in more formal dress this morning, gray suit and pants, a white dress shirt open at the neck. Still an old man, but spritely.

He shakes my free hand. "We're grateful, Mr. Parisman. All of us. Grateful." He bites his lower lip then, tilts his head, and takes a deep contemplative breath. There's clearly something on his mind, something he needs to get off his chest. An announcement? A confession? "My wife tells me I'm a stubborn man," he begins. "Calls me an old dog. She's right, of course. I was resistant at first to your ideas. Not all, but many of them anyway. The security cameras, the special locks—I thought, I'm a man of God. What I know is God. If God won't protect me, if God lets me fall into a pit with snakes and thieves, well, perhaps that's what He intended from the beginning. You see my point? This was not entirely irrational."

"No. But now I take it you don't feel like that anymore."

He shakes his head. "Now? Now, it's different. I think God would very much like us to help ourselves. To participate. This new temple from Mrs. Reines, this would never have been. I'm . . . I'm grateful, that's all."

I lower the weight on my shoulder into one of the pews. "Well, Rabbi, here's something else you'll be grateful for." I slip off the garbage bag.

"Where did you find this? Where?" He is ecstatic. His face is flushed and he's practically jumping up and down, which, let me tell you, is not a great idea for someone his age.

"Don't ask," I say. "It's a long story."

"So tell me," he demands.

"Why do you want to know?"

He gives me a look like I'm crazy. "To explain it to the congregation, of course. Everyone will have questions. A hundred questions! What'll I say?"

"Tell them a good Samaritan brought it back, that's all. Didn't say where he got it, didn't leave his name. End of story."

"But that's a lie!"

"It's a small lie. Sometimes you have to do that."

"But why won't you tell me what happened?"

"I can't. Well, I can. But I'd rather not. For one thing, it wouldn't do you any good to know where it's been. And more importantly, Rabbi, the people who took this the first time? You remember them?"

"Certainly." He touches the back of his head.

"Well, they're still out there. We won this time around—but if there's too much noise about it, they may be tempted to try again."

"I see."

"I'm glad. Now you can do me a favor: put the Torah back in that ark and make sure all those sensors and security cameras are rolling. I went through a lot of *tsuris* to deliver this. It's all yours. But if you want to make me happy, you'll take care of it."

*　　*　　*

As I wend my way through the foyer and head for the heavy front doors, I'm feeling pretty damn happy about how I handled things. Rabbi Josef isn't a natural-born diplomat, but he's over the moon at having the Torah back in his possession; it wasn't that hard to swear him to secrecy about my role in this. He also hasn't forgotten what happened to Chandler, the security guard, and he doesn't ever want that kind of violence visited on anyone again.

"I thought I'd find you here." Lieutenant Malloy is leaning against the fender of his unmarked car. He's wearing a pale green tie and a tan sports coat made from some silky material, which he probably chose deliberately this morning to keep him nice and cool in the summer heat. He drops the cigarette he was smoking onto the pavement, stubs it out carefully with the toe of his shoe. "Actually, when you weren't at your apartment, I got back in the elevator and took the liberty of calling Omar. I might have woken him up. He told me you were going to see the rabbi about something or other. He didn't say what it was, though."

"Did you press him?"

"A little bit. I decided he wasn't going to tell me. Not unless I beat it out of him."

"He could have. But you know how Omar is, Bill. He's skittish sometimes, he still gets shy around authority figures. They're always doing him wrong."

"Yeah, well. Anyway, I came here and spotted your car. You should move it soon, you don't wanna get a ticket."

"I'll do that. Right away."

He's got his cop face on this morning. I'm trying to be light and breezy, but I can tell just looking at his eyes, he's all business. "So, what's so important about the rabbi, huh? Why don't we start with that."

"I was going to phone you, Lieutenant, let you know. Omar and I picked up the missing Torah last night. That's great, huh? Case closed. But I wanted to bring it back to Rabbi Josef myself. I mean, Mrs. Reines hired me to find it. That's where this *mishigas* began."

"Where'd you find it?"

"A storage locker near LAX. Bart Pereira left me the key."

"Left you the key? You spoke with Pereira?" His brow furrows. This is too much information all at once. He's suspicious, and maybe I'm crossing the line with him, I know that. On the other hand, I have to tell him something; it can't be helped.

"Yeah, but forget about him, Bill. He didn't kill anybody; and besides, he's not who you think."

"He stole the Torah."

"He took the Torah, yeah, he helped with that, but I wouldn't say he stole it. There's a difference. What I mean is, he wasn't like Marquez."

"What in God's name are you talking about?"

"Marquez was just a plain thug, you know what I'm saying? He was working for Crocker. He was the one who killed that security guard, not Pereira. Pereira hadn't even been hired at the time."

Malloy takes a deep breath. He's clearly having trouble with my Talmudic distinctions—if that's what they are. Hell, I never studied Talmud. "Maybe you'd care to expound a little more on Mr. Pereira. Sounds like you two know each other."

"I don't know him well," I shake my head. "Except that he's a passionate guy, a dreamer. He's also some kind of spook. Used to work for Mossad in Israel. Whatever he did for them over there, he was good at it. Anyway, he met a girl at a party in Jerusalem. They got drunk together. Her grandfather, she said, came from Algeria, from a village just outside of Oran."

"Wait, let me guess," Malloy says. He's starting to catch on. "Was this the same town with the famous Torah?"

"Right. Anyway, she grew up hearing all about it, how it was wrapped in a blanket and shipped overseas in the middle of the night. How it vanished. And how her grandfather wanted to see it again once more before he died. It was his hope. Anyway, I'll make a long story short: Pereira fell in love with the girl. I don't think she felt quite the same. She was an attractive woman. A number of eligible men were also in the picture, there was competition. But he didn't give up. He did some research; eventually he figured out when and where the Torah landed in LA. Then he got this big bright idea: he'd come here, spend some effort. He'd find it, take it back to Israel. The girl would be overjoyed; she'd marry him. Well, come on. It's a fairy tale, right?"

"It's crazy, yeah."

"But love makes you do crazy things sometimes."

"I guess," he says. "So you're telling me he got involved in this plot, but his plan was always to divert it back to Israel?"

"Exactly."

He puts his hand to his forehead. Already this is more than he'd bargained for. I don't know whether he believes me. In fact, it sounds a little pat, and I'm not altogether sure I believe it myself.

"But somehow, you ended up with the Torah. What went wrong?"

"I'm telling you, it's a love story, Bill. They always end badly. The girl he was hoping to marry? She got tired of waiting, took up with a pilot in the Israeli air force. Now she and her fiancé are expecting a baby in September. What can you do?"

Malloy extracts a second cigarette from the pack, thinks better of it, and taps it back down with the others. "Okay," he says, "okay, maybe that explains the theft. But what about Marquez and Crocker? You say he had nothing to do with those murders. So who did? And who threw that bomb or whatever it was into the VW van last night? The sergeant on duty gave me your card. You were there. What the hell happened?"

"The van belonged to Pereira. Don't bother looking for any paperwork on it. It's probably stolen, in any case."

"But who blew it up?"

This is where everything turns into speculation, I think. I tell him the little bit else I know—that when Pereira heard about Marquez and Crocker he got visibly scared; he started talking about a fixer, someone brought in from the outside to clean up the evidence: in this case, witnesses. He said he was probably next in line. That's when he gave me the key to the storage locker near LAX. We followed him down there in Omar's Camaro. He bought a ticket on El Al; but just before he left, he handed me the keys to the van.

"And you drove it back to Westlake?"

"That was the arrangement. That's where I'd left my car. And besides, he gave me the Torah, didn't he? I figured—what the hell—driving it back was a small favor in the big scheme of things. He was worried that if they found the van at the airport, they'd realize he'd left the country. They might even guess where he went to. These guys are determined. He wanted them in the dark as long as possible.

"So you drove it back, and then?"

"Then I turned off the engine, took out a handkerchief and wiped my prints off it."

"Why?"

"Because I didn't want to be associated with it either, Bill. I assumed it was stolen. Anyway, I took the Torah out of the back of the van, and was walking toward my Honda, when somebody took a shot at my head. They must have mistaken me for Pereira. Or maybe this fixer fellow doesn't know what Pereira looks like at all—that's my guess. Maybe they were staking out the house where he used to live."

"And how would they know that?"

"You're asking me? Maybe Marquez knew, maybe they extracted that information from him before they let him bleed to death. That's just a hunch. Who knows? But this guy was there, waiting. He saw the van pull up, saw someone get out carrying a package on his shoulder that's shaped like a Torah. Maybe that was enough for him. Whatever. He fired a shot. I dropped to the ground not far from the van, and the next thing I know he tosses something into the front seat—a grenade, a Molotov cocktail. Blows the roof halfway to Little Tokyo; it was fucking scary, let me tell you. I'm lucky to be alive."

* * *

There's just one other person I still need to talk to. On Sunday morning, after Carmen shows up, I take a spin out to Pasadena. The freeway is virtually empty at this hour; everyone's fast asleep, and even though we're in the trough of summer, I've never seen a sky so blue or as pristine. It almost makes me want to believe in God—if I were looking for that kind of thing, that is; and I'm not. LA's not the best town to find religion. There's too much repetition, too much concrete and stucco, too many dowdy little apartments with views of streets that go nowhere, streets with mellifluous Spanish names, broken dreams everywhere you turn. My late Uncle Meyer, who visited us from the Bronx for a week every January, used to call it paradise. He was wrong. Long ago it stopped being the most beautiful place in the world, if it ever was—but when you've lived here all your life like me, you learn to overlook inequities; you're grateful for small pleasures. The unexpected miracle. It's a miracle this morning that I'm the only car on the road; miraculous that there's no smog or haze, that the sky is flat and blue, and if you squint, you can see the top of Mount Baldy.

Zaslow has a regular tennis game every Sunday, but he promised he'd be back by the time I got there. "It shouldn't take too long to beat this guy," he said on the phone. "He's just getting over gout."

Now we're lounging in his back yard, on a bench beneath the giant spreading oak. The heat is already starting to build, but it won't be unpleasant for another hour. Zaslow's still in his white shorts and tennis shoes. He's clearly had himself a workout. Whether he won or not is beside the point. His polo shirt is damp around his chest, and his cheeks and forehead are red, but now at last he can relax. Between us there's an iced pitcher of orange juice and a plate of raspberry scones hot out of Muriel's oven.

"Tell me about Pereira," I begin.

"What's there to tell?" he replies. "I gave you what my friends in Israel had on him." He's not defensive. No, more like puzzled by the question. In all the years we've known each other, Pete's never deliberately withheld anything from me. That's just a feeling, of course; I have no way of verifying his facts, how he comes by them, who his sources are. Pete has friends all over. They're well read, and they have friends and cousins who work in embassies and listening posts. People are always telling him things; he never stops sifting through their words.

I finish my orange juice, jiggle the ice at the bottom of the glass. "Maybe I should bring you up to date, then," I offer. I outline the past couple of days: the meeting at the house on Bonnie Brae, Bart's revelations about the girl he fell for in Jerusalem, his sudden decision to turn over the Torah and get on a plane to Israel, the bullet that barely missed my head, the bomb in the van. "To me," I say, "that puts this case in a whole different light."

"Meaning what?"

"Pereira's a take-charge kind of guy, Pete. He may be impulsive; he may have come here to reclaim a Torah once upon a time. But now there's more going on. He's still working for Mossad, it feels like. My gut tells me something else is at play."

"You said you followed him down to LAX. Why?"

"Yeah. He was in a hurry to leave after he heard about Marquez and Crocker, and we thought it'd be a good idea to make sure he got to the airport in one piece. Also, it made sense: that's where the Torah was, near the airport. In a storage locker."

Zaslow takes a gulp of juice, and a small corner of a scone. "The people I spoke to in Tel Aviv," he admits, "they weren't nearly as forthcoming about him as I would have liked. Now, I don't know whether that's because their information was limited, or because whatever he was doing was under the radar. Either way, I just got the bare bones. I apologize for that."

"Understood. I'm just happy he got on a plane to Israel."

"You don't know that. Not for sure."

"I watched him go up the escalator with a ticket in his hand. Watched him disappear. Sure seemed like he was heading for the gate."

"He was heading somewhere, yeah, that much is certain. But he wanted you to deliver the Torah, and he wanted you to drive his van back to town. You. Not him. Think about it."

"You make it sound so sinister, Pete. He wasn't out to kill me."

"No, you're right. I don't think he was. I'd label him pragmatic, however, not impulsive," Zaslow says. "He's a survivor. He also didn't want to be a target when those contract guys came after him."

"At least they missed."

What he says next surprises me. "They didn't miss," he says. "They could have killed you if they'd chosen to. What you got was a message, my friend."

I pour a second glass of orange juice, let the late-morning heat wash over me. It's not quite July in Pasadena, and here we are under a majestic oak tree. Simplicity reigns. I'm alive. The scones are sweet, but not too sweet. The Torah is back where it belongs. And I marvel at the strange world Pete Zaslow inhabits, his peculiar take on things, the secrets he has stored up and can't disclose—thievery in high places, art being liberated from palaces and museums, the greed of some people—the greed of *everyone*, really.

"Tell me more about his girlfriend in Israel," he says now.

"I wish I could," I say. "Apparently it was never meant to be. That's how he described it."

"And yet," Zaslow says, raising his index finger in the air, "and yet he dropped everything to fly over here and track down this Torah." He's starting to cool down, I see; the color is slowly fading from his cheeks and he's becoming more even-keeled, more philosophical with each passing minute.

"He's only in his forties, Pete. His hormones are still hard at work."

"He gave you a cover story. I'll bet you a nickel there is no girl he's in love with. Not in Israel, anyway."

"The Torah's real. He went to some trouble to steal it. Why come over here and take that kind of risk?"

Zaslow unties his tennis shoes, pulls off his socks, and slowly rubs his swollen feet. "The Torah was just how he wormed his way into Frank Crocker's operation," he says. "If you ask me, he was here to monitor the flow of goods into Moscow. The Israelis were as concerned with that as we were."

"Well, Crocker's officially out of business. So why do you think he's still around?"

"The Russians are purists, they always like to start fresh. You can't blame them, really. For all they knew, Crocker was an informant. And the pipeline was tainted in any case. After they picked up Sokolov—and who knows what he told the Canadians—it couldn't be trusted. But demand doesn't end just because the supplier dies. I'm speculating here, of course."

*   *   *

After I say goodbye, I take Oak Knoll toward the mountains. I mull on the notion of going into downtown Pasadena and rummaging around in the used bookstore where Zaslow and I first met years ago. It's tempting: they have a good history section. The problem is, I have plenty I still haven't read at home. I turn left on Del Mar, then left again on Arroyo, which feeds straight into the freeway. On my drive back to Hollywood I listen to classic rock on the radio for a while until the commercials for sleeping aids and hemorrhoid ointments and laxatives start getting me depressed, then I flick it off and crank down the window. This blue Honda of mine is old and dented; the engine makes a tiny, high-pitched rattling noise once you pass fifty on the speedometer. Nobody's ever been able to track it down to the source, and every time it kicks in I think *okay, the time has come, Parisman, trade it in*. But somehow I never do. The rattle and the breeze and the hum from the other more efficient cars slipping by me on the freeway are refreshing, music—if you can call it that—to my ears.

Carmen will be fixing Loretta her lunch about now. She'll put together a grilled cheese sandwich on sourdough bread or a salad, or maybe both. They'll sit at the kitchen table and talk about Carmen's son, Julio, how he is doing in school, which is not so good. Julio is the cross that Carmen carries, day and night. She worries about Julio's spelling and math abilities, she says he needs to do better if he wants to go to college someday. Loretta will ask, does he want to? And Carmen will say no, he doesn't care; but it's not up to him. She wants him to go. He *has* to go. Loretta will also ask about Antonio, her husband, and Carmen will say he left early this morning before the sun came up. Antonio is always going somewhere. He was driving a load of onions. Or garlic. Or tomatoes. Sometimes she knows where he's going, but often she does not. She is not so worried about him, except that he drinks. Loretta does all the questioning, it's a one-way street, because whenever Carmen tries to ask Loretta, she has little to say in answer. I've heard this conversation many times; it never changes.

Like any private investigator, I'm always wanting things neat and tidy when it's over. The murderer found and put away forever behind bars. The balance of nature restored to some preexisting order. That'd be nice, but in my experience it's rare. Human beings go their own way, no matter what. You may find the thug, you may even get him busted. But then it all falls apart on the way to the trial. The cops forget to read him his rights, they lose the evidence, or, for a little cash, they flush it down the toilet. Even worse, for enough money they fabricate the evidence. A million things can go wrong. Or say you get to trial, and something crops up: the thug turns out to be crazy. Or the judge says something stupid and illegal from the bench. Or the one witness to the murder mysteriously vanishes the day he has to show up in court. Or the defendant hires an experienced, white-shoe lawyer, while the prosecutor is new, still wet behind the ears. You never know what the matchup will be.

Bartholomew Pereira stole the Torah, no question. But if you believe him, whatever Zaslow says, he did it out of love—love pure and simple—for that girl in Jerusalem he could never have. And to keep it out of the hands of a rotten first-class *gonif* in Moscow. And even then, in the end he gave it back. On top of that, as a practical matter, it would never go to trial. The rabbi and his wife wouldn't be able to pick him out of a lineup. He smelled like tobacco. Big deal, what's that mean? The LAPD still wants to talk with him about Crocker and Marquez maybe; but just to fill in the blanks, he's not a suspect. And if Costello from the FBI has checked with his counterpart in Mossad, which he no doubt has, I'm sure he'd rather let the whole thing drop.

My phone rings then. It's Malloy. "Just thought you'd like to know," he says. "We checked the flight manifest on that El Al flight to Tel Aviv. Your boy Pereira never got on. Not under that name, anyway."

"Why do you want him, Bill? He's not the one who blew up the van. He didn't try to kill me."

"Obviously," he says. "And the guys who did that? They're long gone too. We'll never find them. Not a prayer."

"You know, the last time I saw Bart, he was going up the escalator. Said he didn't want to hang around where people were gunning for him. But maybe you're right. Maybe he didn't get on that plane. Changed his mind. So where does that leave us? Think he pulled a fast one? That he's still around?"

"He's somewhere, yeah. But probably far away. Rio or Stockholm or Amsterdam. Someplace we'd never think of. LAX has lots of planes to choose from."

All at once it comes to me. I could point him to Pereira. I know exactly where he is. Or where he's headed, at least as soon as the sun goes down. Into the arms of Dorothy Liebowitz. "Gee, Lieutenant, I'll keep my eyes peeled. But you know what? LA's such a big goddamn town, what can you do?"

"Not much," Malloy says. For once in his life he agrees with me. "Forget about it."

ACKNOWLEDGMENTS

This book was not written in isolation. None of them are. But I have to thank a few people in particular for their advice, criticism, and honest, unflinching input. Ron Raley. Cheryl Howard. Richard Conn. The editorial folks at Turner Publishing. My brother Jonathan, who is always coming up with crazy plot lines. Lastly, the staff at Readers' Books—especially Jude and Rosie and Thea, who left me alone in the back office so I could write while they did the real work of selling books. In gratitude.

ABOUT THE AUTHOR

ANDY WEINBERGER is the author of *An Old Man's Game*, *Reason to Kill*, *The Kindness of Strangers*, and *Die Laughing*. He is a longtime bookseller and the founder/owner of Readers' Books in Sonoma, California. Born in New York, he grew up in the Los Angeles area and studied poetry and Chinese history at the University of New Mexico. He lives in Sonoma, where Readers' Books continues to thrive.